HIGH PRAISE FOR
CRIME WRITER PHILIP CARLO
AND *PREDATORS & PRAYERS*!

"Carlo posits a disturbing and believable theory on how pedophiles have managed to enter the Catholic church in such astounding numbers."

—*Publishers Weekly*

"This read is one of pain, love, hate, forgiveness and frank honesty that you will never forget. This is a must-read that you will not be able to put down."

—*The Midwest Book Review*

"*Predators & Prayers* is one of those rare books that is so well crafted and seemingly true to life that it is extremely difficult to remember that the events and characters of the story are fictional. Not only are the characters fully and realistically developed but the story is action filled with thought-provoking themes. These aspects make this book mesmerizing, virtually impossible to put down, and absolutely memorable."

—*TCM Reviews*

"Philip Carlo's *Predators & Prayers* is a must-read and I highly recommend it to anyone who wishes to understand the current crisis in the Catholic Church. Carlo's novel is a worthy companion to Malachi Martin's *Windswept House* and his writing wizardry puts him in the same category as historical fiction masters Robert Graves and Gore Vidal."

—*Radio Host William Kennedy*

"A few pages into a Philip Carlo novel and you're spellbound! His edgy and provocative writing transports you to the center of the st⬚⬚⬚⬚⬚ PLENTY of action!"

"Readers will finish this in one ⬚⬚⬚⬚⬚

D0391895

MORE PRAISE FOR PHILIP CARLO!

GETTING TOO CLOSE

I knocked on Dracol's office door. The door was opened by Oliver, the giant black dude with the snake-like dreadlocks. He didn't like me banging on the door. I told him I needed to talk with Belladonna; that it was an emergency. He, too, said she wasn't there, that she had phoned and said a relative was sick and she had to go to San Francisco. The two bouncers I knocked out came hurrying down the stairs. One lunged for me. I stepped back and drew my piece in two movements. "If anyone," I said in a calm voice, "lays a hand on me, I'm going to get upset." I had no patience for any of this anymore; far as I was concerned, I was in a war and they were a clear and present danger.

"Okay," dreadlocks said, "chill, man."

"I want to talk with Santos."

"He's not here."

"Aren't you his personal bodyguard?"

"He doesn't need a bodyguard," he said. "As I think you'll soon find out."

Other *Leisure* books by Philip Carlo:
PREDATORS & PRAYERS

SMILING WOLF

PHILIP CARLO

LEISURE BOOKS NEW YORK CITY

A LEISURE BOOK®

March 2006

Published by

Dorchester Publishing Co., Inc.
200 Madison Avenue
New York, NY 10016

Some names have been changed to protect the privacy of certain individuals connected with the story.

ISBN 0-8439-5678-X

Printed in the United States of America.

Visit us on the web at www.dorchesterpub.com.

*In loving memory of my grandparents,
Giovanni and Gaetana Bernardo Carlo,
Alberto and Filomina Mandato.*

SMILING
WOLF

"The law, cold and aloof, by its very nature, has no access to the emotions that might justify murder."
—The Marquis de Sade

PART ONE

THE CLUB BLOOD

CHAPTER ONE

It was one of those frigid New York mornings when just getting out of bed was a big deal.

I had been up late the night before watching an old movie on Turner Classic Movies—*Moby Dick* with the late great Gregory Peck. Half awake, I lay in bed listening to the wind howl like a lonely wolf in need of a mate, thinking they sure the hell don't make actors the way they used to. I was just dozing off again when the phone rang. I let the answering machine pick up and listened:

"Mr. De Nardo, my name is John Fitzgerald," a man with a deep voice said. "I was given your name by a detective in Missing Persons. My daughter has been gone for a month now and the police aren't doing much of anything about it. I was wondering if I—"

I reached over, picked up the phone, and said hello.

"I hope I'm not calling too early," he said.

"You aren't, that's okay—what can I do for you?"

"As I was saying, Mr. De Nardo, my daughter, Anne, vanished without a trace and the cops aren't doing diddly-squat. I need someone like you. Can you help me? Can I come see you? I have your card here, I'm just nearby."

"You want to come over now?"

"Yeah, if it's okay, sir?"

"Who gave you my card?"

"Detective Flynn in Missing Persons. He says you're the best there is."

"He's exaggerating. Okay, sure, you can come by," I said.

"I'm on my way," he said, and hung up.

I climbed out of bed, made coffee, and had some toast and a slice of cantaloupe as I stared out the kitchen window, hoping my two fig trees made it through the winter. It had been unseasonably cold and fig trees were dying all over the place, according to an article I read in the Metro section of the *Times*. As I was cleaning up, the doorbell rang. I checked the security monitor. A lone man stood in the vestibule. I buzzed him in, opened my door, and watched him slowly lumber toward me, our eyes meeting. He was a large man with wide shoulders and the ruddy complexion of someone who spent a lot of time near the sea— or a bottle of whisky . . . or maybe both. He had a slight limp.

"Thank you for seeing me on such short notice," he said, offering me a weak smile as he ex-

4

tended his hand, which was thick with calluses, though loose and lifeless, like a tough all-terrain tire suddenly gone flat. In his other hand he carried a scuffed black attaché case. I offered him one of the two chairs in front of my desk. He took off his worn leather overcoat and sat down with a heavy sigh. The look on his large, round face told me that he had come to me as a very last resort; the downward set of his thin-lipped mouth, the eggplant-colored, swollen circles under his eyes, spoke volumes. Over the years I had come to see it many times. He was hurting badly deep inside and it was written all over his face. I asked him if he'd like some coffee. He said he didn't want anything. He had, I noticed, a swollen lip and a golf-ball-size black-and-blue bruise over his right eyebrow.

"Tell me how can I help," I said, sitting behind my desk and giving him my undivided attention, wondering who beat up on his face.

He took a long, pained breath and said, "To the cops my daughter's just another missing person. A piece of meat. But to me she's the world. She's all I have. If it's okay, if you don't mind, Mr. De Nardo, I'd like to tell you a little bit about her. It's important you know who we're talking about here."

"Please, go ahead."

"So you can understand everything, I have to begin at the beginning, if that's okay."

"I'm all ears."

"Since my daughter was a child, she loved to

5

read," he told me. "She'd read anything she could get her hands on. And she began talking about writing when she was just a little peanut—what seven, eight years old. 'Daddy, I want to be a writer. Daddy, I want to be a writer.' If I heard it once, I heard it a thousand times. Of course, I did whatever I could to encourage her; gladly bought her all the books she wanted, let her stay up late to read. When other kids on the block were out playing, my daughter was reading, always reading. Mind you, Anne was a beautiful child. I mean, it's not as though she was staying in the house reading because she couldn't make friends or anything like that. In fact, she was very popular in school. She was voted class president in both grade and high school. But she went and dropped out of college. She said you learn how to write by going out into the world, living life and writing, not in a classroom. I didn't want her quitting school. I kept telling her not to drop out, that if her writing didn't pan out for her she'd always have something else to fall back on. But she was bullheaded beyond reason just like her mother was, and she up and quit college two months into her freshman year. I lost my wife when Anne was three. She was killed in a car crash on the Long Island Expressway," he said, suddenly becoming quiet and withdrawn and staring at the edge of my desk. His eyes moved back up to my face. They were now filled with tears, two glistening orbs looking at me, silently asking me for help. I cleared my throat.

"Please continue," I said.

He said, "So we got to arguing about her leaving school, and one thing led to another, and she ended up moving out of the house and going to live in Manhattan. Down on Orchard Street, just off Houston."

He sat back and again became tight-lipped. We stared at each other some more. I silently watched the silvery tears roll down his weathered face, moving faster and faster as they went. He angrily wiped at them. He seemed to be somewhere else now. I waited for him to come back. The front door opened. I heard my assistant, Louise, come in and sit down at her desk.

"I'm sorry," he said.

"No need to apologize."

"So after a time we made up, and again I helped her all I could, with furniture, a computer—anything she needed. If she wanted to write, if that was her passion in life, I was going to do all I could to help her, to support her . . . to be there for her, you follow me?"

"I do."

"What interested my daughter most were true stories. She just loved talking to people and getting them to tell her things they'd not tell anyone else. She kind of had a gift for that—getting people to open up—and in no time she got herself a job at the *Voice* and began writing stories for them, and her articles were really good. The third piece she wrote, about runaway children who were being abused at Covent House, won her all kinds of awards. I was so proud of her. I get all choked up when I think of her," he said, and still more tears started streaming from his long-lashed blue eyes. He opened the black case.

"Here it is," he said, putting an aged, yellowed copy of the *Voice* on my desk. "Her story about Covent House. I brought it along because I'm thinking maybe if you read it, Mr. De Nardo, you'll be able to see how special my Anne is, how sensitive, how smart. She also published three books. And received very good reviews and all kinds of awards."

"Please, you can call me Frank," I said.

Vaguely, somewhere in the back of my mind, I remembered this article, that it had caused a scandal at the Covent House; that it forced the degenerate pervert running the joint to resign in disgrace, a bleary-eyed, horse-faced Catholic priest named Johnson. I picked up the paper. It was stiff with age. The story was titled "Swear on God You Won't Tell." There's not much I can't stomach, but pedophiles masquerading as pious priests with a crucifix in one hand and their dick in the other is definitely one of them.

"How long has she been missing exactly?" I asked.

"Five weeks come tomorrow," he said.

Not good, I thought. The longer people are gone, the less the chance of their coming back.

"You sure she didn't just maybe decide to go away for a while, work on a story in peace, something like that?"

"No. She'd have told me. We're very close," he said.

"Was she seeing anyone?"

"I don't think so. She had a boyfriend, an actor she met at a book party, but they broke up months ago."

"Any problems with him? Threats of any kind?"

"Nothing like that, no."

"You know what kind of story she was working on when she went missing?" I asked.

"I do," he said. "That's why I can't sleep, that's why I'm having nightmares. That's why I'm here. She was writing an article for *Tell It Like It Is* about vampires."

"Vampires?" I repeated, sitting back and giving him a jaundiced once over.

"Yeah, vampires," he said. "Right here in New York. I've got what she wrote with me." Again, he opened the case. "She wrote by hand—has the most beautiful handwriting," he said, holding up a yellow pad so I could see the neat script on the pages.

"After it was all written up, she'd input it into her computer and worked on it some more. I read it. It's just unbelievable," he said, and slowly put the pad in front of me—as if it held dark, mysterious secrets, as if some slimy creature might slither out of it any moment.

"Please read it. It's the beginning of her story. When you do, you'll understand why I'm so upset. The police, I gave it to them, but they haven't done anything. They haven't even talked to *him*."

"Him who?"

"The one I believe is responsible for Anne's disappearance. His name is Santos Dracol. He owns a nightclub downtown called Club Blood . . . have you heard of it?"

"I have. . . . Over on West Street, I think."

"Yeah, that's it. I went there. I tried to talk to him. I waited for him outside the club for hours. He finally came out and I went up to him, but he just ignored me, looked right through me like I was a glass of water or something and walked away. I grabbed him by the shoulder. His bouncers took hold of me and one of them sucker-punched me and knocked me down."

"That how you got that swollen lip and bruise on your forehead?"

"Yes," he said. That didn't sit well with me, hitting a father looking for his missing daughter.

"Why do you believe this Dracol guy has something to do with your daughter's disappearance?" I asked him, sitting back.

"Because Anne made the mistake of trusting this creep. My daughter's fearless; she'd do just about anything to find out the truth of a thing. Why? . . . I feel it. I feel it in my bones," he said. "Mr. De Nardo, I'm not a rich man, but I'll gladly pay you whatever your fee is. I know experienced men like you don't come cheap."

"If you don't mind my asking, what do you do for a living?"

"I'm a lobsterman out of Montauk."

"That where Anne grew up?"

"Born and raised."

"Nice town. I used to go fishing out there all the time. How's the fishing these days?"

"All things considered, pretty good. Long lines hurt us bad, though."

"You say she trusted him. How do you mean trusted him? How do you know?"

"She spent a lot of time with him. She even went to his house—alone."

"And you believe he's . . . a vampire?"

"Read what Anne wrote. It's all there. Here's a photograph of him. Anne had one of those spy cameras, and she used it to take this," he said, handing me a stiff eight-by-ten glossy, which had obviously been taken when Dracol didn't realize it. The photograph was somewhat out of focus. He was getting out of a black Mercedes limo parked somewhere in front of the Hudson River. He was a tall, slender man with long black hair combed straight back, which highlighted a ghostly pale face, large, mirthless dark eyes, a high broad forehead.

"Is there any reason in particular you feel he is responsible for Anne's disappearance? I mean, did she tell you he'd done something out of line, threaten her, anything like that?" I asked, opening and closing my right hand. It was stiff and hurt me because of arthritis.

"No, but I'm sure he's at the bottom of this."

"You know if she taped the individuals she interviewed?"

"She said that intimidated people."

"Have you been inside her apartment since she's missing?"

"I have. She gave me a set of keys when she first bought the place. It's a condominium right over here on West Ninety-fourth just off West End Avenue," he said, pointing in the wrong direction. "Everything looks normal enough."

"Would you mind if I had a look?"

"Not at all. I was going to ask you to check it out, you being a detective and all. I'm sure you'll see things I'm blind to. Least that's what I'm hoping."

I told him I would do all I could. I had him sign a standard contract form and he gave me a cash retainer. I gave him a receipt. We soon left my place and started over to Ninety-fourth Street. It was bitterly cold outside. The sky was low and gray and mean. It looked like it was going to snow any minute. He told me that he had parked his car on my block, but we left it there and walked to Anne's place. Funny, I had this nagging feeling that we were being followed, turned around a few times, saw nothing suspicious. I offered to hail a cab on Columbus Avenue, but he said he had a recent knee replacement and needed the exercise. As we moved west, a powerful wind off the nearby Hudson came barreling down the street. It nearly knocked my hat off. The cold hurt my right hand, even more damage from the days I boxed professionally, and I've grown to hate the cold. I often think about moving to a warmer climate. Maybe Florida. Out to the West Coast. But every time I seriously consider the move, a case comes along and I get involved and everything gets put on the back burner. Though the truth is I was born and raised in New York and love the place. Even with its cold and crime and mean streets. Problem with me is that no matter how long I do this, I still feel people's pain and end up making their troubles mine, getting personally involved. It's kind of a bad habit.

CHAPTER TWO

Anne Fitzgerald lived at 313 West Ninety-fourth, in a four-story limestone with colorful stained glass over the front door. A red sign that said *No Menus* was screwed to the door, though menus still littered the vestibule floor. I got into a fight with one of these menu guys a while back. Every day there were stacks of menus in the vestibule. Sometimes they blocked the door from closing. I put up a sign asking that they please not leave them anymore. That didn't help. One day I caught one putting them down. I gave them back to him. He gave me some lip, put them back down. I gave them back to him. He pushed me, acted like he was Bruce Lee. I punched him and knocked him. Turned out I broke his jaw. He had to be hospitalized for two weeks. He sued me. Thank goodness my insurance covered it. He ended up getting sixty grand. Go figure. (If it weren't for friends in the NYPD, I would've gotten arrested.)

Anne's apartment was a spacious floor-through on the second landing. It had all the original woodwork intact. Thick mahogany beams criss-crossed the ceiling. The floors were stained white. Her desk was set up in front of two huge windows in the living room, which opened onto stark, winter-bare backyards. Everything was neat and tidy. There was a DSL line, but no computer hooked up to it. Her father told me she had a laptop, but it was not in the apartment. On the desk there was also a file for computer disks and CDs, but it was empty. I thought that kind of odd. He said he didn't know where her files were. There were photographs of Anne in gold frames on the wall to the left of her desk. She had light blond hair, big blue-green eyes, flawless skin, and a half-moon smile that went from ear to ear—a beautiful woman. Also on the walls were framed copies of her newspaper stories and book jackets. She also had, I noticed, a degree from a cooking school in Tuscany, Italy. There were a lot of photographs with Anne and famous chefs I recognized from television cooking shows—Emeril, Molto Mario, and Lidia. I enjoy watching cooking shows to get my mind off my work, to get new ideas, and to relax myself.

"Anne a good cook?" I asked.

"Amazing cook, actually," he said. "Next to writing, that's what she liked to do most. At her house in Tuscany she has all these Italians over for dinner, and they could never get over how well she makes, you know, Italian food. De Nardo—I expect you are Italian?"

"I am," I said, suddenly liking Anne—this woman I'd never met who loved to write about bad guys and to cook Italian food. My kind of woman, I couldn't help thinking.

Her father told me Anne had bought a farm house in Tuscany a few years before, that she loved to write there. He pointed to a photograph of a smiling Anne standing in front of the place—a tobacco-colored stone house with a terra-cotta-tiled roof and an endless glistening sea in the background.

"I told you she's beautiful," he said proudly.

"She certainly is, very beautiful. Mind if I have a look around?"

"Not at all, please feel free. Do what you have to do," he said.

I would have preferred that he weren't there. After all, he was her father, and there was no telling what I might find. I took off my coat and began snooping, looking at the papers on her desk, in her desk drawers, and in her appointment book. On the week she went missing she had a lunch date with her agent and a doctor's appointment, and a notation in her neat Catholic-school script said that Santos Dracol was supposed to call. There was a thin coat of dust on everything. The room smelled slightly of lavender. I asked him if anyone from the NYPD had searched the apartment.

"No," he said. "I asked them if they'd like to, but no one ever did."

I found some expensive recording equipment in her bottom right desk drawer, but there were no tapes or discs anywhere. That got me to thinking she did record her interviews, and judging by her excellent equipment she was doing it surreptitiously. Finished at her desk, I began working every room, including the bathroom. I didn't find anything that helped until I reached her bedroom closet.

In the closet, I got on my hands and knees and carefully studied the glistening white floorboards, tapping, listening. Most people have their secret hiding places in their closets. When I began knocking the west wall, I found a hollow-sounding spot, took out my knife, and carefully pried a foot-wide section of the wall up. Behind this panel there was a jewelry box, and above the jewelry box were thin wooden shelves filled with audio tapes and yellow envelopes.

"I never knew that was there," he said.

I looked at the tapes. There were twelve regular-sized cassettes and a few of those mini ones. All the tapes had a name and date written on them: *Ralph S, on 4/22/99, Susan Grier, 2/4/2000,* like that. There were two mini cassettes of interest—one that said *Santos, 12/2,* and another with his name on it dated *12/7.* The mini case marked *12/7,* the week she disappeared, was empty. The other did have a cassette in it.

"It looks like she did tape him," I said. The

phone rang. He went to answer it. I opened one of the yellow envelopes. There were dozens of black-and-white glossies and negatives in it. All of them had been taken clandestinely, it was obvious. Some of them, I realized with another start, were of nude or leather-clad people doing very kinky things to one another. I quickly slipped the envelope into my jacket pocket; these photographs were not, I was sure, anything her father should be seeing.

"Hello," I heard him say into the phone. He hung up, said it was a recorded message for a casino in Atlantic City.

"I'd like to hear this tape," I told him, holding up the mini cassette with Santos's name on it. "That okay?"

"Of course."

He followed me back to her desk, and I slipped the matchbook-sized tape into the mini Sony recorder and pushed the play button. The wind howled and pushed against the windows, rattling them. There was a ten-second snakelike hiss, then a woman said: "It's the second of December. Two A.M. I am on Farrell Drive in the town of Hastings-on-Hudson, Westchester, on my way to see Santos Dracol. For documentation, I am taping my interview with him." She paused. "That's Anne," Mr. Fitzgerald said.

She parked, got out of her car, and kept the tape running. We listened to the car door open and close, footsteps on gravel, large dogs barking, her ringing a bell, quietly saying: "Okay,

19

here goes." The door opened. Another woman's voice, low and with an accent: "Hello, Ms. Fitzgerald. Please to coming this way." The door closed, footsteps on a bare wood floor, a long pause, another door opening and closing, a man saying: "Welcome to my home, Ms. Fitzgerald, so nice of you to come." He, too, had an accent. One that I could not immediately place, though I would soon learn that it was Romanian. She said, "Thank you so very much for agreeing to see me. I appreciate it."

"Your persistence paid off. Would you like tea? I was about to have some," he said in this silky, Bella Lugosi–like voice right out of central casting.

"Thank you, no."

"Please have a seat. So you are a night bird?"

"Ever since I'm a kid."

"I, too, love the night. So much more quiet and serene. Less static in the air."

"Yes. . . . I'm curious, Mr. Dracol."

"Please—Santos."

"Santos, please call me Anne. Why did you agree to talk with me?"

"Because I'm sick and tired of all the lies perpetuated about me and my lifestyle—and I want to set the record straight."

"What record would that be, sir?"

"About me . . . about my people."

"You mind if I take notes?"

"I do mind, yes. Just listen and you'll have all you need and more."

"I like to take notes for dates and the like."

"One of my assistants can provide you with any relevant details. I want to look you in the eyes while we talk. Yes, like that. So where do you want to begin?"

"Well . . . first off, are you really a vampire?"

"I am, and proud of it."

"So, like, you sleep during the day, drink blood, and all the rest?" she asked with a hint of skepticism.

"Let me first say that I know what I tell you is for publication so I will naturally be prudent about all that I say. Yes, I drink blood, but only from donors—"

"Donors?" she interrupted.

"People who willingly give themselves to me, people who want me to have their blood—their energy. It's not just about blood, you know, it's also the life force. Unlike in popular novels and movies, we do not kill the people whose treasured blood we consume. That would make no sense—why kill the goose that lays the golden egg?" he said. "I also eat solid food, mostly rare and raw meat. My favorite meals are beef carpaccio and steak tartar with a glass of fresh blood mixed with vintage red wine."

Hearing this guy say that like he was talking about a stroll in the park on a sunny day caught my attention, all right. My eyes moved to the photos of Anne, knowing she went missing shortly after this interview. . . . Not good.

"When you say a glass of blood, I presume you mean fresh *human* blood?" she asked.

"Naturally human blood. I'm no animal," he said.

Funny guy, I thought.

"How do you manage that?" she asked.

"Just before consumption, I bleed them," he said.

"May I ask who 'them' are?" she asked.

"My disciples . . . willing donors."

"I see. I notice your canine teeth are particularly long and pointed. How did they get that way?" she asked, a hint of sarcasm, I thought, in her voice.

"I had them tailored for my lifestyle."

"Do you use them to bite people?"

"On occasion, yes," he said, and laughed. It was an eerie laugh filled with arrogant malice, as if he was laughing at a joke only he heard.

"These donors you speak of, where do you find them—or should I say how do they find you? Who are they? And can I perhaps meet some of them?"

"They come to me from all over the world. They are people of the night. People who have the courage to reject the hypocritical dogma of society, the Church, and conventional religion groups, freethinking individuals who want to express themselves as they please—sexually and otherwise—and not be controlled by a bunch of hateful old men with dried-up balls. All the repression of natural sexual instincts makes people crave and need sex—in all its various forms—all the more. I show them the truth. I open the door for them so they can feel the real joys of their bodies. Pain, for many, is a turn-on, is pleasure. I provide it. I make them look in the mirror and love and crave and savor what they see."

"I see. Would it be possible for me to talk with a few of your disciples?"

"Certainly. I have nothing to hide. I'll bring them in whenever you wish."

"They're here—I mean, like they live with you?"

"Some of them do. Here in Westchester and other places, other countries."

"Were you born a vampire?"

"For the sake of this interview, let's say I was born with the predisposition. Ever since I was a child, I had the strongest urges and desires for all things macabre and dark—movies, books, art— couldn't get enough. It was kind of an obsession."

"Did someone make you a vampire?"

"Yes."

"Who?"

"A family member."

"Who?" she pressed.

"That's personal."

"I thought you were going to talk to me?"

"I am talking to you."

"I mean confide—tell—"

"I am confiding."

"Who made you a vampire, then?"

"That's personal, I said," he said, sternly now.

"Where were you born?" she asked.

"Romania . . . but brought up and schooled in Paris."

"Lovely city."

"My favorite. I love its history."

"I lived there in 1995, on Rue de Cambon," she said.

"We have a club nearby."

"I know. . . . So vampires don't kill their victims, you say?"

"There are those that do, but *I* do not."

"I see. Are you immortal?"

"Immortal is stretching it, but we most definitely live longer than mortals," he said.

"So how old are you, then?"

He laughed. "You never ask a vamp his age," he admonished.

"How old," she pressed.

"I'd rather not say."

"Do you sleep in a coffin?"

"If I want a proper night's rest, yes. I must."

"Are there vampires that do in fact kill for blood?"

"Yes . . . mindless psychopaths I have nothing to do with."

"I see. Can you put me in contact with any of them? I'd very much like—"

"I'm sorry, no."

"Do you know how I can reach any of them?" she pressed. I admired her nerve.

"No," he said with annoyed finality.

"Is it really true that you are related to Vlad Tepes? I heard you were. Did he perhaps have something to do with your becoming a vampire?"

"You heard correctly," he said. There was a long, heavy pause, and here the tape abruptly ended.

"Takes your breath away," Mr. Fitzgerald said in little more than a whisper. "The pervert." He had paled notably. Wanting to hear more, I fast-forwarded the rest of side A, wondering who Vlad Tepes was. The rest of side A was empty, and so was all of side B. Strange, I thought, curious as to why the tape suddenly stopped. The interview had seemed to be going well. Hmm.

"I'm sure this creep is responsible for my daughter's disappearance," he said. I wasn't about to disagree with him.

"I'd like to talk to some police friends of mine and see what else I can find out about Dracol before I do anything more, and I'd also like to speak with Anne's agent and the editor for this vampire story. That okay with you?" I asked.

"Mr. De Nardo, please, you do whatever you think is best. You're the professional. I have complete confidence in you."

I copied down her agent's name, Alice Watkins, and her number.

My curiosity piqued, the hunt for Anne Fitzgerald on, we soon left her apartment. I took a recent photo of her with me. The sky had gotten lower and darker and strong winds with icy fingers pushed us along. We started back to my place. I was thinking it might be a good idea if I returned to Anne's apartment by myself and went over it without his looking over my shoulder. I asked him if that would be okay. He thought a moment and gave me, somewhat reluctantly, I noted, a set of spare keys. When we reached his car, he said, "Please let me know as soon as you find out anything more— anything at all. You can call anytime. Day and night."

I promised him I would. We shook hands. His handshake was firmer now. That pleased me. He slowly got into his SUV, waved, and took off. There was a sticker on the back of his car that said *Montauk is the End*. I went inside and asked Louise to type up Anne's interview with Santos Dracol.

"Be prepared," I warned her.

"Frank, with you I'm always prepared," she said.

Louise has long natural-blond hair, a chiseled heart-shaped face, and dark brown eyes. She is a tall, full-figured woman with a lovely smile she readily gives with no strings attached. Before Louise worked for me, she was a detective for the Transit Authority. She specialized in decoy work to catch serial sex offenders who stalked the subway system. She had been shot in the arm by a fellow officer while on duty and was forced to retire with a full disability pension. Even now, three years later, she cannot properly move her arm. We were involved romantically when we first met, but all that stopped a long time ago. We are best friends now, and close. I think the world of her. She was recently divorced from her husband, a detective in the midtown robbery division with a drinking problem and a bad temper. He was stalking Louise, getting drunk and threatening her, and I was forced to explain the facts of life to him.

At my desk, I opened the yellow envelope with the kinky photographs in it. Using a magnifying glass, I studied the pictures. They were all black-and-white. People were engaged in some seriously debauched sex while sucking and drinking blood from different places on their bodies, some quite intimate. They gave me a bad taste in my mouth. The things people do to get off never cease to amaze me. He was hard to discern, but I could make out Santos Dracol in several of the pictures, thirteen of them in all. I wondered how Anne managed to get her hands on them. I used the magnifying glass to see if she was in any of the photographs, but it didn't appear that she was, though there was a shapely blonde with her back to the camera that could very well have been her. I took a long, deep breath and called the Twenty-fourth Precinct and asked for Captain Ken Roe, a good friend of mine in the NYPD.

Before I went into business for myself, I was a New York City homicide detective. Ken Roe and I met at the police academy. We graduated in the same class and became tight over the years. I got him on the line and asked him to find out whatever he could about Santos Dracol. Soon as I said Dracol's name, he cut me short. "I know who this creep is. He owns this freaky-deaky vampire bar downtown. We've had our eye on him for a couple of years. A few months back, we suspected he had something to do with the murder of a woman from New Orleans we found floating in the Hudson River up near the George Washington Bridge. She was completely naked and didn't have much blood in her. We published her photo in the papers—"

"I remember the case," I said.

"Well, the girl's mother saw the photograph on the news and contacted us. It was she who told us the victim was living with this Santos Dracol. Right off we went to talk with him, but he put a wall of high-priced lawyers around himself and refused to be interviewed. He's a tall, pale dude with pointed teeth like a fuckin' German shepherd. Try as we might, we couldn't link him to the girl's death. I understand he's got a half-dozen women living with him, and clubs all over the world. We tried to talk to some of the women, too, but none of them would so much as give us the time of day.

"I know the writer Anne Fitzgerald disappeared shortly after she met with this asshole. Her dad was here. He asked me about you. Apparently, one of our guys passed him your name. At this point, we've done what we could."

I told Ken about the tape. There was nothing on

it, we both knew, that incriminated Dracol in any way. He told me they had a file on Santos Dracol three inches thick, and when I had a mind to I was welcome to take a look at it. We made plans to meet later in the day. When I hung up, I sat there thinking Anne Fitzgerald had gotten herself into something over her head that very well might have cost her her life . . . or worse, left her a prisoner in a dungeon somewhere.

I phoned the magazine and found out who her editor on this vampire story was, got him on the line, and told him I'd been retained by John Fitzgerald and asked if I could see him. He said he was leaving for the airport in ten minutes to fly to Los Angeles. His name was George Lewis. I asked him what he thought. He said Anne had not given any indication to him or anyone else at the magazine that there was any kind of problem.

"In fact," he said, "she was very pleased with the progress she'd been making. Anne is a gifted journalist. She has an uncanny way of peeling back all the bullshit and getting to the meat of a thing. One of the hardest-working writers I've ever known. She was very popular here. Hell of a lady. We're all very upset about this."

"Do you think this vampire story has something to do with her disappearance?"

"I really . . . Truth is, I really don't know."

"What does your gut tell you?"

"My gut tells me it very well could," he said. "Some of the people involved in this underground vampire scene can be very dangerous."

"Dangerous?"

"Mr. De Nardo, there's a whole subculture of people from all over the globe, from all walks of life, who are heavily involved in the vamp scene. Into heavy S and M."

"I don't get this 'vamp scene.' You mean like dressing up on Halloween like Bela Lugosi and going around trying to scare people?" I asked innocently.

"No . . . well, yes—there are those, of course, but what I'm talking here is more malevolent . . . sinister than that. I'm referring to people who are truly obsessed with all the trappings of vampirism . . . people who are real blood drinkers, who sleep in coffins, who only come out at night, who are turned on—sexually—by the sight and smell and taste of blood," he said.

Quite a mouthful, I thought.

"You mean actually drinking it?" I asked.

"That and other things."

"Please explain."

"The drawing of blood, blood being an aphrodisiac . . . dominating people to the point of death—"

"Death?"

"Death."

"Killing for blood—is that what you're saying?"

"Well, yes, that and more: becoming part of a belief system where drinking blood, becoming a true blood drinker—a creature of the night, if you will—takes on supernatural connotations and meanings, a commitment to a lifestyle, a belief system. That's why we commissioned Anne to write this story. To get a handle on what's really going on—names, dates, places, faces. She's the best at getting to the heart and soul of a story. But now . . . now she's gone," he said.

"When was the last time you heard from her?" I asked.

"Five weeks ago Thursday," he said. "I feel . . . to tell you the truth, I feel responsible. This was all my idea—her doing this story," he said, strain tightening his voice.

"Why?"

"Why what?"

"Why this story. . . . I mean, who cares about these freaks?"

"A lot of people. Just look at how popular vampire movies and books are. One of the most popular writers of all time is Anne Rice."

"But that's all make-believe."

"There's much more to it. That's why we asked Anne to do this piece. Everyone here is—was—excited about it."

"What can you tell me," I asked, "about Santos Dracol?"

"He's a very wealthy European, has vamp clubs in Europe—one in Paris and one in Rome, another in New York, and one in New Orleans. There have been a lot of sinister rumors about him, though nothing substantiated. The focus of the story was him."

"Why?"

"Well, in a sense he's a superstar in the world

I'm talking about. He's exceedingly handsome and mega-rich, and is dedicated to the vamp way of life. He's the Mick Jagger, if you will, of vampirism. He is also, it is rumored, a very dangerous man, a sexual sadist—a real blood drinker."

"He's a vampire."

"Yes, he is."

He said he'd really like to talk some more but that he had to run to catch his flight. He gave me his cell phone number and said I was welcome to call him anytime, that he'd be in L.A. for the next eleven days. I thanked him, hung up, sat there, and thought about what he'd said. I then called Anne's agent and explained that I'd like to talk with her about Anne's disappearance. She said I could come see her anytime.

"How about right now?" I asked.

"Fine," she said, and gave me the address. I left, hailed a cab on Central Park West, and headed for the East Side, thinking about those photographs. They weren't easy to forget.

The Watkins Literary Agency was on East Seventy-ninth Street just off Park Avenue, in a fancy town house with tall white pillars on each side of the front door. I rang the bell, was buzzed in after I identified myself. The first door on the right as you walked in was opened by a tall, willowy woman with short brown hair, a long straight nose, high forehead, and big intelligent buglike eyes that regarded me curiously. She wore no makeup.

"A pleasure to meet you, Mr. De Nardo. Please come in," she said, firmly shaking my hand with one so thin it was like a skeleton's. I followed her to the rear office. All the walls in the foyer were covered from floor to ceiling with framed book jackets. Some were best sellers I knew well. The four walls in her office were lined with mahogany bookshelves brimming with neat rows of new books. The room smelled of books, of ink, like a library. She sat down at her desk. It was just to the left of large bay windows that opened onto a garden filled with ceramic statues of animals, people, flowers, birds. She saw me looking at the statues and told me her "partner" was a sculptor. She asked if I'd like some tea or coffee.

"Nothing, thank you. I appreciate your seeing me right away," I said. I was thinking her haircut, the way she sat, how she regarded me, were kind of overtly masculine.

"As well as representing Anne, she and I are very good friends," she said, became quiet, and stared at me curiously with her enormous eyes.

"Mind if I ask you a few questions?"

"Please, no—not at all."

"Well, first off, did she tell you there was any kind of problem? Anything at all?"

"No. Nothing. We were close. She called me a few times a week and let me know what was going on, and she never said there was any kind of problem."

"I assume you knew she was working on a story about vampires . . . about Santos Dracol."

"Yes. When she was finished with the article, she was planning to write a proposal for a book. I already have a few editors interested. Mr. De Nardo—"

"Please, Frank," I said.

"Frank, Anne comes from an old school of writing. She thoroughly researched every aspect of the story herself, personally—even her fiction. She had an uncanny knack of getting people to open up. But Anne was careful. She wrote about crime and criminals, and she didn't want to do anything to put herself in danger. For the most part, she was prudent."

"You know she went to Dracol's house to interview him more than once."

"Yes. She was the only journalist he agreed to talk to."

"Why?"

"Hard to say."

"You discuss that?"

"Not really. She was very charming and . . . she enticed him."

"With what?"

"Herself."

"How do you mean?"

"Anne is a very sexy, beautiful woman, and she knows how to use that—her looks; her sex appeal."

"She came on to him?"

"In a sense, yes, you could say."

"Was she intimate with him?"

"Not that I know of," she said. I had my doubts about that. The plot was thickening.

"Did you know that she surreptitiously taped him?"

"She told me. She was concerned about being able to document what he said. When she went to Romania, she found out a lot about him—"

"She went to Romania for this story?" I asked, impressed.

"Yes. And it was there that she first found out that Dracol was suspected of murdering people in Sighesoara."

"Murder? Really? You mean, by the consuming-their-blood kind of thing?"

"Yes, and when she told me that, I warned her that she was getting into something that could be dangerous . . . very dangerous."

"And?"

"And she said she was being 'careful.' "

"Careful?"

"Yes."

"What do you think happened to her? Please tell me what your instincts tell you."

"I think Santos Dracol is at the bottom of this," she said with measured certainty. "It kind of stands to reason that if he found out she'd gone to Romania and learned things about him which could compromise him here—and I think she did—he'd want to silence her. I warned her. . . . Truth is, I pleaded with her to walk away from this, but she wouldn't. Ann is a Taurus . . . a very stubborn lady. When she got her teeth into something, she wouldn't let go."

"Seems she was playing with fire here."

"Yes."

She became quiet. We looked at each other across the neat expanse of her big, shiny desk. She had a slight twitch in her left eye. The wind blew hard. The bare branches of trees in the yard just behind her shook violently, as if they were large arthritic fingers. I was reminded of my hand. It hurt.

"Could he have seduced her?" I asked.

"Highly unlikely. I told the police, soon as Mr. Fitzgerald went to them, I told a detective what I thought . . . but I understand Dracol refused to even speak with the police."

"That's what I hear. Did you tell her father this?"

"No. He's worried sick already, and I felt sure my telling him what I just told you would only make matters . . . worse. Though I did tell the police," she emphasized. She obviously had guilt about Anne's disappearance.

"But she never said that she felt threatened or in danger because of him?"

"No."

"And you spoke to her a few times a week?"

"I did."

"Please tell me more about her. What kind of person is she?"

"In a word, Anne is unique. Kind of a lone wolf. Very content with herself. Loves her work, made a lot of money, and she was truly happy.

'*Molto contenta*,' as she liked to say. She bought an old farmhouse in Tuscany a while back, and she adored the place. My partner and I spent three fabulous weeks with her there this past summer."

"She speaks Italian?"

"Fluently. Spanish and some French, too. Loves languages. Has a knack for them."

"Why no boyfriend . . . a husband—kids?"

"She was, well, she was very—how do I say this . . . she was very into her writing, the art of it, the craft of it, and I think it was hard for her to find a guy who understood what she was really about, how important her work was to her. That, no matter what, her work came first. She didn't need to have that . . . I mean, a relationship. A man. She was content being by herself."

"But she, you know, did she like men?"

"Yes. She had some drop-dead-gorgeous Italian boyfriends, but nothing serious. No kind of commitment."

"So she was into men?"

"Actually, both men and women," she said kind of reluctantly.

"I see. Were you lovers? . . . I hope I'm not being too personal here," I said.

She stared at me for a couple of long seconds, said, "We had a thing when we first met, but that stopped and we became friends . . . good friends."

"I see. Thank you for your candor. How'd you come to meet her?"

"I read the piece she wrote on Covent House, called her, and signed her on. I knew she'd be a star. She's won just about every literary prize there is." She took a long deep breath, sadness filling her large brown eyes.

"I can't sleep at night because of this. I kind of . . . Well, to be perfectly frank with you, I kind of blame myself."

"How's that?"

"I mean to say I should have warned her off more. I should have insisted she not do this project. But really . . . well, truth is I couldn't have discouraged her. Like I said, when Anne got her teeth into something, she wouldn't let go. I nicknamed her 'The Bulldog'; she was like that—very tenacious; very dedicated."

"Why crime? I mean, why did she like to write about crime?"

"The inherent drama and pathos. Anne's about shining light into dark places. She felt that's what books and films should be about. For instance, she loved Steinbeck's *Grapes of Wrath*, how he had written a novel, a gripping drama, that actually changed the way migrant workers were treated. She also loved Picasso's *Guernica*—how it so brilliantly showed the suffering of the Spanish people. You follow me, what I'm saying?"

"Of course."

"With her work, her words, her prose, Anne was intent on entertaining and making—this might sound a bit overused, but making the world a better place."

"I was wondering if you had any copies of her books I can have?"

"Certainly," she said. She stood and grabbed three books from a nearby shelf and handed them to me—two crime novels and the true story of Long Island serial murderer Joel Rifkin, titled *The Gardner*.

"Thank you. And how did this vampire story come about?"

"*Tell It Like It Is* asked her to do a piece on the whole underground vamp scene, and one thing led to another."

"I see," I said. "You haven't heard from her at all in all these weeks?"

"No."

"Would she have had sex with Dracol to get an interview?"

"I . . . No. She wouldn't; just kind of teased him with the possibility."

"I saw secreted photos in her place of people having sex, drinking blood. How do you think she got them?"

"She did attend some kind of scene at the club. She told me about it, but she didn't participate."

"You sure?"

"She would've told me. She did, though, get an eyeful. Real kinky stuff. She had one of those secreted mini cameras in her jacket. She loved those gadgets. She wanted to document what really is going down. I think . . . fact is, she was planning to film what goes on there."

"There where?"

"There is a sex dungeon at the club. That's where she took those shots."

"I see," I said.

We talked a while more. I thanked her for her time, gave her one of my cards, and told her it was okay to call anytime if she thought of something more. She walked me to the door. Looking me square in the eyes, she said, "Anne is a very special person. Please find out what happened to her," tears suddenly filling her eyes.

"I love Anne, she's a sister," she said.

"I'll do my best," I said, and was soon on my way back to the West Side, mulling over what Alice Watkins had told me, imaging her and Anne having sex. Hell of a thing.

CHAPTER THREE

A couple of times a week, I do easy laps around the Central Park reservoir to help keep my head clear and my body in shape. I used to run every day without fail, no matter what the weather, but my knees aren't as cooperative as they once were. I'll be fifty come April. Getting old sucks.

My head filled with this new case, I changed and walked over to the park, stretched on a bench, and began jogging around the reservoir. The sky was still dark and mean. A chilled wind tore through the park. As I reached Fifth Avenue, it began snowing. The flakes were big and soft and felt like icy kisses against my face. I couldn't get the image of John Fitzgerald's sad face out of my head—how his eyes pleaded for help as he listened to Anne's interview with Dracol. I wasn't sure what happened to Anne, but I was sure whatever it was it wasn't good. Just above the park, a lightning bolt tore open the thick, gray sky. Thunder boomed, echoing and rumbling across the exclusive canyons of Fifth Avenue and Central Park West.

When I arrived back at my place, I showered and dressed, had an espresso, took a cab to 100th Street, and had it drop me in front of the Twenty-fourth Precinct. I said hello to a few detectives I know as I made my way up to the second floor of the two-story blue-brick precinct house. I found Captain Roe in his office, on the phone. Roe is a soft-spoken, easygoing man with piercing blue eyes that can look right through a person. He is the most popular captain in all of the NYPD, often works in the field next to his detectives. He is one of those rare, courageous cops who have no fear of bad guys; he has been, the whole department knows, in numerous gun battles, was wounded four times, is highly decorated and truly respected. He's the kind of guy you'd want to be in a foxhole with.

He motioned for me to have a seat, pointing to the Dracol file on the corner of his busy desk. I picked up the blue manila folder, put on my glasses, and began reading chronologically dated police reports. I first read the file on the Carole Smith case. She was the bloodless woman who had been found in the Hudson River. There were seven black-and-white morgue photographs of her. In the photographs she was a deep purple in color and her body was swollen to obscene proportions because she had been a "floater," as cops refer to dead people pulled from the water. There were close-up shots of her head. Before I realized I was doing it, I was looking for puncture wounds on her neck, but her hair was in the way. There were rings through both her nipples and her labia. According to the autopsy report there were two deep wounds on her neck. When I read that, I felt cold chills slowly move up and down my spine. I knew the doctor who had done the autopsy, Bob Ash, and made a mental note to talk with him.

A photograph of Dracol's Westchester home, a sprawling castle-like Tudor with black shutters on all the windows, was also in the file. A tall, pointed metal fence surrounded the place. There were guard dogs on the grounds, two large Dobermans who looked like they took their work seriously. These no doubt were the dogs I heard barking on the tape in Anne's closet. The captain hung up. We shook hands and hugged. I played Anne's interview with Dracol for him, as he sat there slowly shaking his head.

"Goddamn ghoul," he said when it ended. "What people in this town are capable of these days never ceases to amaze me. This creep should be kept in a cage, but here he's living the life of Riley, being driven around in a limo, and he has his own harem. I had a couple of teams following him around for a week, but we couldn't get anything on him. I even had the Feds look into his tax returns and he's all on the up and up—least on paper, anyway. Personally, I think he's a retooled Charles Manson with pointed teeth and a lot of money. Where'd you find this tape?"

"She had a stash in her closet," I told him, and showed him the photos. His eyes got wide as he looked at them.

"I'm glad I haven't had my lunch yet," he said.

He allowed me to make copies of everything I wanted in the file and we walked over to Amsterdam Avenue, had a couple of sandwiches, and caught up. When we finished, I walked him back to the precinct.

"Frank," he said. "Be careful with this creep. You need any kind of help at any time, day or night, don't hesitate to call, you hear—I mean it."

"I hear," I said, thanked him for everything, asked him to do a check on John Fitzgerald to see if he had any kind of police record. He said he would and hurried inside. I used my cell phone and called the Medical Examiner's Office and got Dr. Ash on the line. He told me he remembered the Smith case well and he confirmed that her body had very little blood in it, said the corpse was still at the morgue because there was an ongoing murder investigation. I asked him if I could see the body, knowing from many years of hands-on experience that you cannot, when it comes to murder, discount any possibility, and I knew, too, that I might very well find things that no one else had yet discovered on the corpse. I'm good at what I do. He said I could come right over. I hailed a cab and had it take me to First Avenue and Twenty-eighth Street. It kept snowing harder as we made our way to the East Side.

CHAPTER FOUR

The New York City morgue is in a squat brick building. Over the entrance a sign says: *Let Conversation Cease. Let Laughter Flee. This Is The Place That Death Delights to Help the Living.*

I paid my respects to the NYPD detectives assigned to the morgue, went downstairs, and found Dr. Ash just finishing the autopsy of a three-year-old boy who had been beaten to death by his mother's boyfriend, he told me, because the child had wet his bed.

We walked to the cadaver room. The smell was horrific. Carole Smith was in drawer number 213. I pulled the heavy drawer open and there she was . . . all swollen and blue-black, her upper and lower lips peeled back in a silent perpetual scream, monstrous to look at.

Dr. Ash, a tall, broad-shouldered man with gold aviator glasses, showed me the puncture wounds on the left side of her neck.

"They are directly on the carotid artery," he

said. "It's obvious someone purposely punctured the flesh for the express purpose of drawing blood." I pulled out my magnifying glass—my eyes aren't as good as they once were—and took a close look at the wounds. Under the glass I could clearly discern serrated tears in the flesh; and there were hematomas—hickey-like discolorations, around the wounds. We measured the space between the two wounds and they were two and a half inches apart, the distance, he said, between the canine teeth in a human mouth. I took color photographs of the wounds, and when I asked him what he thought, he said, "I think some loony bit into her neck and sucked blood from her body," his words having an ominous, eerie ring in this frigid house of death with the terrible smell that never leaves you once you experience it.

Still using the magnifying glass, I carefully scrutinized the rest of Smith's body. She had small contusions and whip marks all over the place, particularly on the buttocks. She also had been brutally raped, he pointed out—torn in the most intimate of places. There were, I noticed, concentrated black-and-blues on her wrists and ankles. It was obvious she had been bound by binding with padding. Had she been tied by rope or leather, the marks would be more raw, with strawberry-like abrasions. On the left ankle, however, there were the kind of marks a chain would make, and Dr. Ash said her left ankle had been broken. I wanted to take a long, deep breath but didn't. This was not the place to be taking long, deep breaths. The metal rings were still attached to her because, he said, they were part of the crime; someone had used them, he explained, to lead her around, fasten her to a wall in some underground chamber, no doubt, I was thinking, wondering what the hell had happened to her as a kid to drive her to do such things. There was a tattoo of a red-eyed bat, seeming to fly out of her pubic mound up toward her navel. I thanked the doctor, slowly closed the heavy drawer, and turned away.

Again, I thanked Ash and soon left, my nose filled with the rancid-sickening smell of human death. Hoping the strong winds off the nearby East River would get the odor off me, I began walking up First Avenue. It was snowing harder now and the streets were covered with a delicate, pearly-white blanket.

As I reached Forty-second Street, I called the office and asked Louise to see what information she could get off the Internet about this Club Blood, and to see if Interpol had a dossier on Santos Dracol.

I ended up walking all the way back to my place, through Central Park, thinking this thing out. The park had become a sprawling winter wonderland, all white and clean and innocent, much in contrast to the dark thoughts of murder, sexual sadism, mayhem, and blood in my head.

I own the building I live in. It's a four-story brownstone on West Eighty-seventh just off Central Park West. I bought the place for next to nothing back in the eighties before the prices around there became ridiculous. I live and work on the first two floors and have a large yard with a southern exposure. In the summer I grow all kinds of vegetables, and I've got my two large fig trees, given to me by my uncle Sal as seedlings, in the east and west corners of the yard. Every summer I've got more figs than I know what to do with. I rent out the other two floors. It's a nice setup, all things considered.

Back inside, I went straight to my desk and called Downtown Harold. Harold knows the whole New York night scene inside and out. He used to be a gossip columnist for page six, but freebase made him crazy and unreliable and as skinny as a train rail—and got him fired. Harold supplies most of the downtown scene with ecstasy and other assorted exotic drugs, and there's not much he doesn't know about what's going on. Recently, he opened an S & M club called Bottoms Up. Some rich Arab with too much time on his hands put up a lot of money and the place, I hear, is a big success. There is a stiff membership fee, and only people with money belong. They come from all over the world. A few weeks ago, a certain very famous actress was there—a blonde who won an Academy Award—having her ass whipped by her lover, the head of a big L.A. production company. They both had on masks, but someone made them and it was in the papers. A while ago, while he was still a reporter, I got Harold out of a jam with the Hell's Angels, and he owes me. I told him I needed to come over and talk to him. He told me he wasn't feeling too well, was getting over a bad flu. He said it was all George Bush's fault that he was sick, because he couldn't get a flu shot. I asked him if he knew or heard of Santos Dracol. He said, his voice a bit weak and strained, "Frank, listen to me: I know you're a tough guy and all, but I'm telling you this as a friend. Stay away from this dude. He's bad news, man, and very dangerous."

"Dangerous how?"

"He's a fucking vampire. He drinks blood, sleeps during the day in a coffin, the whole enchilada. He's a nasty piece of work—white like a corpse and mean like a rattlesnake. Frank, I saw this prick myself bite into a girl's neck—she couldn't have been more than eighteen, nineteen, a runaway that came to him—and he drank so much of her blood she passed out cold and fell to the floor like a broken rag doll. Frank, if you look up evil in the dictionary, you'll see his photo," he said.

"He kill the girl?"

"No. She was moving after a while, but she looked terrible. Gives me the creeps thinking about it even now, you know . . . bad news."

"How did you get to see something like that, Harold?"

"I used to sell him ecstasy and angel dust. He

feeds ecstasy to his groupies like jelly beans. He's not ashamed of any of this. . . . I mean, he doesn't try to hide it at all. In fact, he's proud of it, flaunts it like crazy—bad karma. I couldn't deal with being around him, I swear—and bro, you know it takes a lot to freak me out. But he comes to the club. He was here, what . . . two nights ago."

"What's with this Club Blood he has?"

"It's hot; all kinds of weirdos—vampire freaks, heavy-metal stars, Satanists, tops, and bottoms—hang out there." (Tops are sexual sadists and masochists are known as bottoms.)

"*Very* decadent scene," he said. "We're their competition."

"Is it a private club?"

"No. But you've got to look like you belong to get in."

"I want to come down and talk with you, see your new club."

"Sure. I've been trying to get you here for a while. I'll leave your name at the door. Dracol is involved with one of the girls who works here, Amy, I think . . . I'm pretty sure she'll talk to you. She's a submissive."

"Okay. . . . I'll be there. Thanks, Harold," I said.

"Okay, see you."

"See you," I said. Hmm.

Louise came back to my office. Her eyes somewhat incredulous, she said, "Frank, there are thousands of Web sites about vampires and hundreds of vampire chat rooms. There's, like, this whole underground society of them—from all over the world, all walks of life. I had no idea."

"Neither did I," I said, and she told me that she had contacted Interpol and that they did, in fact, have a file on Dracol and she already had them e-mail it over. I have a very good contact, Fred Reynolds, who runs the Interpol office in The Hague. She put it on my desk. I thanked her and read the report. It seemed Santos Dracol was a suspect in the disappearances of women in three different countries—in the cities of Berlin, Paris, and Madrid. Though he'd never been arrested, he had been questioned numerous times in missing-person inquires. *Mamma mia.* This, I was realizing, was a bad dude.

I picked up the phone and called Fred Reynolds. I first met Fred when he was an assistant district attorney out of Manhattan. We used to go see fights together. As a teenager, he had been the Golden Glove Middleweight Champion for four years running. I managed to get him on the line and asked him to find any of the details of the missing-person cases that Dracol was suspected of having something to do with. He promised he'd find out whatever he could ASAP and get back to me. I hung up and began looking at some of the Web sites Louise had found. They were bizarre, talking about where to get coffins, pointed teeth, willing donors of blood, books to read, places to visit, films to watch, how to meet one another—and they even offered junkets to

Romania for colorful tours of Prince Dracol's castle.

The Count Dracula, I soon learned, was actually a prince. His real name was Vlad Tepes. I remembered that Anne had asked Santos Dracol if he was really related to Vlad Tepes. Interesting . . .

This, I knew, was something that had to be checked out. I read that Vlad Tepes had terrorized Eastern Europe in the fourteenth century; that he had a fondness for torturing and impaling people on sharpened wooden posts for entertainment as he ate his dinner. He became known as "Vlad the Impaler," and some said he was responsible for killing over one hundred thousand people. Some claim he drank blood, was a cannibal and an extreme sexual sadist. Centuries later, I read, he was the inspiration for Bram Stoker's *Dracula*. Hmm. Who knew?

There were vampire message centers, chat rooms, clubs and groups and societies in every state of the union, in every country of the world. Club Blood was often mentioned as a "good meeting place" in New York. There were Club Bloods in six different countries, and they had an elaborate, very-well-put-together Web site from which they sold all things related to sadism and vampirism—dolls and clocks and baroque furniture, capes and coffins and photographs of Prince Dracula's castle in Romania. Whips and dildos of all kinds, contraptions to torture people with, a wide variety of tit and clit clips. They also had a message board where "vampires" posted mundane messages for one another and a nationwide list of dentists willing to "sculpt" canine teeth into "fangs." Funny.

I next turned to Anne Fitzgerald's writing pad and read what she'd written so far about Dracol. It started like this: *Santos Dracol is a tall, good-looking man, a professed "vampire," who can charm the stripes off a zebra.*

According to people in the know, he is a direct descendant of Vlad Tepes, the model Bram Stoker used for his immortal "Dracula." Santos is a very hot-looking man, tall and thin with cheekbones to die for. He has the presence of a bona fide rock star, lips as big as Angelina Jolie's. He is the prince of the Goth and S & M scene all around the world. Women, beautiful women, from all over the globe throw themselves at his feet. He is a true blood drinker and a sexual sadist as infamous as the Marquis De Sade. He is rich and charming and seems to have it all, made in the shade; if he has any problems, it is how to deal with all the submissive women who want to—need to—be abused and subjugated by him.

Though there is a dark, very dangerous side to Santos Dracol, few know about it. He is, in fact, suspected of being involved with missing women both in the States and abroad. He has been questioned in the disappearance of numerous women, though no charges have ever been brought against him, he is the first to quickly point out. When one looks at Santos Dracol, you can't help thinking of a wolf, a beautiful, dangerously feral wolf . . . and she went on to describe the clubs he owns, where they were located, and the many devoted people he surrounded himself with. It seemed to abruptly end with these lines: *If you go to www.ClubBlood.com, you can see for yourself how Santos Dracol has turned the macabre world of vampirism and sexual deviance, with all its dark trappings and accoutrements, into his own personal gold mine; a moneymaking machine . . .*

I stood up slowly and stretched, thinking about the best way to meet this Santos Dracol, stiff from all the sitting. I downloaded the photographs of Carole Smith into the computer. I have two hobbies; one is gardening and the other photography. I carefully studied the shots I'd taken of Carole, wondering what had happened to her— who she was, where she came from; how she ended up in the Hudson River as a bloodless, blue-black monster.

Before I worked homicides for the NYPD, I took photographs of murder scenes in all of Manhattan. If it weren't for the man I accidentally killed, I'd probably still be with the New York Police Department. Before I was a cop, I was a professional boxer, had eighteen fights and won all of them by KOs. My hands, therefore, are considered lethal weapons, and I'm not supposed to be getting into fistfights outside of the ring. It's illegal.

His name was Darnel Williams. He had slowly killed six prostitutes—that we knew of—by evisceration, and he was gleefully leaving their corpses in abandoned buildings throughout Brooklyn's Brownsville section. We knew, too, that he was a necromanic—that is, he was copulating with the corpses. I became separated from my partner the morning we found Darnel and caught up with Darnel on the roof of 111 Clinton Street. Rather than surrender after a ten-minute chase, he bushwhacked me and tried to throw me off the roof. Guy was as strong as a bull. We fought furiously. I knocked him down, and he hit his head on a vent pipe and never got up again. Far as I was concerned, I did the world a big favor, but the NYPD didn't see it that way and I was forced to retire. Because Darnel was an African American without a police record, there were protests in front of my house by racially motivated opportunists—one was particularly vocal, was overweight, had a strange hairdo and ridiculous aspirations to be president. I had to fight the city in court to get my pension. Like I said, I enjoyed being a cop and wound up getting a P.I. license to stay in the mix. I have been hiring myself out now for fifteen years.

I stood, stretched, and walked to the window, feeling a heavy, oppressive weight on my shoulders, my right knee hurting, thinking about this Santos Dracol. The backyard was covered with an unmarred blanket of snow. The wind blew hard against the windowpanes. Ghost like shapes of snow danced madly. Worried about my fig trees, I went down to the basement to make sure we had plenty of oil. They were saying on the news, over and over again, that there was a storm coming and we were going to have a few feet of snow. Snow in New York during the winter months is not the incredible, miraculous phenomenon the news media likes to make it out to be.

I spent the next couple of hours reading about vampires, more and more surprised at how many people out there seemed obsessed with this jive nonsense. The phone rang a few times. I let the answering machine screen my calls. When Fred Reynolds phoned from The Hague, I answered. Fred told me Santos Dracol was Romanian; that he had inherited a large sum of money when he turned twenty-one; that the police in a half-dozen countries believed he had something to do with the disappearance of "many individuals," which Anne had written.

It seemed, he said, that disillusioned people— both men and women, but mostly females—were drawn to Dracol from all over the globe and he gladly used these young people in the most debauched sexual perversions imaginable, involving esoteric bondage and blood drinking, extreme sadism, dungeons, black leather masks, torture and unspeakable degradation, which included animals and even the dead. But no one was ever willing to testify against him. His victims believed, Fred told me, that Dracol had "preternatural vampire powers," whatever the hell that was, and that he had threatened them all and they adamantly refused to testify against him. Witnesses even disappeared. He also owned, Fred explained, a film production company in Amsterdam that produced extreme S & M films for distribution all over the world. It was called

Blood Red Productions. There were rumors, too, that he also was responsible for the making of snuff movies, films in which someone was actually murdered in front of a camera—"suicide while being fucked," Fred called it. He said these women signed contracts, were paid handsomely before they were killed. "They gave the money," he said, "to family and friends."

"Charges brought against him regarding this?"

"No," he said. "He insulates himself very well."

When I asked him how old Dracol was, he told me there was no record of his date of birth, but that there were numerous police reports about missing women involving him that had been written in the 1980s in a Romanian town called Sighesoara.

I thanked Fred for the quick response. He told me he still had feelers out for me and that he'd call if anything more came his way. He said he would be in New York in April and we made plans to have dinner.

I was thinking it was time I saw for myself this Club Blood and meet Santos Dracol. I called the club, told the woman who answered the phone who I was, and asked if I could speak with him. She put me on hold for a couple of minutes, came back, and said I could meet with Dracol in three hours at the club. I told her I'd be there, walked to my closet, and strapped a custom-cut Beretta to my left side and slipped a .38 derringer loaded with dum-dums into a hard-to-find crotch holster. The derringer is no larger than a cigarette pack, but at close range it can knock down a healthy horse. I also strapped a particularly thin German fighting knife to the back of my right calf; one side of it is razor sharp, the other side serrated, and it is perfectly balanced for throwing. I hoped I wouldn't need any kind of weapons, but on the street there are no rules or regulations, no referee to jump in and make sure everyone plays fair. I went back outside, got into my SUV and pointed it downtown, put on a mellow jazz station, and listened to Stan Getz's "Slaughter on 10th Avenue." The wind blew harder than ever and the snow came down in swirling lace curtains so thick it was difficult to see more than a block. Sanitation trucks were out spreading salt.

I went through the Battery Tunnel and headed for Brooklyn. I come from a large, tight-knit Italian family and my mother's brother, Sal, was having his seventy-fifth birthday party and I had to be there. I was very close to this uncle. My mother had seven brothers, but I was always the closest to uncle Sal. He stood for me at my christening and is my godfather. My father had been killed in a really stupid accident at the Long Island Railroad, just outside the Jamaica station. Shortly after his death, my mother and I moved in with my uncle Sal and his wife Luchia, better known as Aunt Lu Lu. She is the best cook in the family and I loved living in Uncle Sal's house. He never had any children of his own, and I kind of became the son he always wanted. Unlike my mother, who was born in Brooklyn, my uncle Sal had been born in Sicily, and he still speaks with a slight Italian accent.

I had no idea what Uncle Sal did for a living until my late teens. I'd been working with him in his much-beloved garden in the back of the house when half a dozen men in black suits with the same haircut walked into the yard, purposely trampling our vegetables, put handcuffs on him, and took him away. When I saw the news later that night, they said that my uncle was the second in command of the Genovese crime family; that he was a ruthless killer suspected of masterminding numerous murders. This bowled me over. I always knew him to be a kind, gentle man; I never even heard him raise his voice. He took me fishing, to ball games, to boxing matches, and always made sure I wanted for nothing

When my mother came home from work that night, she told me not to believe what I saw on television, that the FBI had it in for my uncle because he was Italian, but I started asking questions around the neighborhood and soon learned who my uncle Sal really was. Though all that never had any kind of effect on our relationship until I told him I wanted to be a cop; that didn't go over too big with him, but he reluctantly learned to live with it. It was my uncle Sal who was there for me at all my birthdays, with the greatest presents at my first communion, when I graduated from high school; and when I got in trouble with the law for fighting, he hired a lawyer for me and all the charges suddenly disappeared. It was this Uncle Sal who gave me my fig trees when they were seedlings, and who taught me how to grow fruits and vegetables under the most dire of circumstances. "You have food growing in the yard, you'll never go hungry" was a much-repeated mantra of his.

Uncle Sal and Aunt Lu Lu lived in a simple two-story house on Ocean Parkway and Avenue M. I parked out front and started inside. As usual, there were a few FBI agents sitting in a van parked across the street. I waved to them and they waved back. They knew who I was and didn't hold against me the fact that my mother was Sal Russo's sister. The living room was filled with my relatives, aunts and uncles and cousins, and I hugged and kissed every one of them. I found my mother in the kitchen cutting up a giant tray of pesto lasagna. My mother is tall for a Sicilian, nearly six feet. She has large round, knowing brown eyes, high cheekbones, and a perfectly heart-shaped mouth. She and Aunt Lu Lu walk several miles every day to keep in shape in nearby Prospect Park. My mother lives in the lower level of Uncle Sal's house. He had it completely renovated for her, put gorgeous marble floors in the kitchen and bathroom. They are very close. She is his only sister and he is extremely protective of her, and me, though in all the years I've been in law enforcement I only turned to him once, and that was to help me find an American child who had been kidnapped at the Pompeii ruins just outside of Naples, Italy. I kissed and hugged my mother hello, and she stuck a plate filled with steaming pesto lasagna with meatballs in my hand.

"I was afraid you'd have trouble coming because of the snow," she said.

"How's the roads? How are you? You look too thin. Here, eat that and I'll make another dish for you. You want some salad? Take some meatballs. Why you so thin?"

"That's okay, this is fine, I'm on a diet," I said.

"A diet," she said, as if it were a dirty word. "Why, you're so skinny already. I'm your mother. I'm telling you you're too thin. As you get older, it's not good to get thin, Frank. Makes you look drawn and tired. You need a good woman. Stop playing the field."

"I'm not playing any field, just been busy."

"Join Match.com. I hear there are all these lovely ladies on it. Your cousin Joe met a girl, a doctor, and they're going to get married."

"I'm not joining an online dating service—forget it."

"Why?"

"I'm not going to."

"Why?"

"I'm not desperate. Mom, I'm happy . . . okay? Let up with this," I said, getting a little heated, and she knew why—and became quiet.

"Where's Uncle Sal?" I asked.

"Inside somewhere."

I finished my lasagna and some salad, had to fight with my mother not to have a second helping and more meatballs, and went looking for my uncle. There were maybe fifty people there, but they had prepared enough food to feed twice that many for a week. Italians, my family, always eat like it's their last meal. I figure it's because they had such a hard time when they first immigrated to this country and wanted to make up for all the food they might have missed back then.

I found my uncle in the den playing with my cousin's children. He is crazy about kids. He has an incredible knack of getting children to trust him, to open up to him . . . to treat him like one of their own. He was doing magic tricks with cards and wearing a large red clown's nose. He stood when he saw me, kissed and hugged me and told me I don't visit my mother enough, which isn't true. I see her, religiously, every Sunday unless I'm out of town. My uncle Sal has bright blue eyes and a dark complexion, a thick head of silver hair, which he combs straight back. He is a handsome man with a strong jawline and a striking profile. He looks like what you'd expect a distinguished senator of ancient Rome to look like. He always dressed in casual clothes around the house, old jeans and sweatshirts, but he has an amazing wardrobe—fifty Armani suits. He promised my cousin's children, ten of them, he'd be right back and he put his arm around me and said he wanted some fresh air, which I knew meant he wanted a cigar. Uncle Sal has a penchant for Cuban cigars. We went out back and he lit up a mini Cohiba. We began walking the neat lanes, which he had cleared of snow, of the different things he grew.

"It's no good to get old alone," he began. Here we go again. "When're you going to find yourself a good woman? Your mother is concerned; I'm concerned; your aunt is concerned. It's been a long time now, Frank."

"Don't be concerned," I said. "I'm very happy the way things are."

"Nephew . . . I'm talking about down the road, you know, in years to come, a man should not be alone. It's not natural."

"I'll find someone. Don't worry, I'm searching the Internet all the time," I joked, but did not laugh. This was a tiring conversation I had many times with my uncle. "I'm joining Match.com," I said.

"I'm serious, Frank. We aren't going to be around forever, you know."

"I've been busy."

"Don't be too busy to find yourself a good woman. The years, they go by fast. Before you know it, you'll be old and by yourself." We both knew it had been nearly six years since my wife had been murdered in Central Park for the bike she was riding and the ten bucks in her shorts. That was something none of us ever talked about directly, though that is what he meant when he said "it's been a long time." For me it sometimes seems like a hundred years ago. Sometimes like it was an hour ago . . .

We had been childhood sweethearts, separated when I went into the service, met again in the police academy, and soon married. She was a good-natured woman with a heart of gold, was always giving needy people money from her own pocket. Her name was Barbara Perrali and she was the only woman I ever loved, trusted, put ahead of myself, and she was beat over the head with a brick—her brain smashed—for her bike. A bike I just bought her. It was the first time she was riding it. A mountain bike she wanted. When she was murdered, I found out after she was autopsied, she was two months pregnant.

I promised my uncle I'd look harder for a good woman. He offered to introduce me to some of my female cousin's friends, of which I had twelve. I told him not to bother himself, that I was just waiting for the right woman to come along.

"And that's the problem. Stop waiting and start lookin'," he said. "Make your mother happy. She would love to have a grandchild. You're an Italian; you need a woman, capice?"

"I know. I'm on the case," I said. "Let's talk about something else, okay?" This was becoming tiring.

He finally dropped the subject, could see in my eyes the searing anger I still felt about what had happened to Barbara. We discussed our fig trees and soon headed back inside. I caught up with all my cousins, we sang a loud, boisterous happy birthday to uncle, I had some of his birthday cake and two cups of espresso, said so long to everyone, which took a half an hour, and headed back to the city, thoughts of Barbara filling my head, her laughter, her beautiful smile, her giving heart, her in a coffin at Campell's Funeral Home on Amsterdam Avenue . . .

I forced myself to think of other things—this new case—turned on the radio, and listened to the news. By now, six inches of snow had fallen and I had to drive slowly.

CHAPTER FIVE

I first headed to the Bottoms Up Club. It was in a fancy two-story warehouse on Thirteenth Street, between West Street and Eleventh Avenue. Even with the snow, they seemed to be doing well. A few limos and town cars were lined up outside. There were two pretty women manning the door, wearing fur coats, letting people in. I parked and made my way over to the two doorgirls. They were both model-beautiful, two very tall blondes—Viking-like.

"Evening, sir," one said respectfully.

"I'm De Nardo. I believe Harold left my name at the door."

"Yes, sir; please, sir, come in, sir." In their world, "sir," I knew, was an anachronism for "master." She removed the rope. I smiled and winked at her and walked inside.

A Hell's Angel was sitting on a stool inside the door. We greeted each other. Another woman met me and asked me to follow her.

"This way, sir," she said.

A long corridor with red leather walls adorned with all kinds of whips led into a high-ceilinged room. A crowded bar was on the left. Electric music blared. People were dancing. There were many half-naked females ... a few completely naked ones. A lot of leather and spandex. Many of the women wore collars. A few had leashes attached to them. It would've been kind of funny if they weren't so attractive and alluring. On the left there was a stage. A full-figured woman with a black mask on her face and sexy underwear on her body was bound to a rack. Another woman, all dressed in skintight latex, was spanking her, while still another woman was on her knees eating her. The smell of raw sex hung strong in the perfumed air. I followed the woman who met me at the entrance to a rear door. She opened it and led me down stairs.

"Sir, Harold is waiting for you in his office," she said.

We moved along another red leather corridor, passing a door every ten feet or so. Harold's office was at the end. She knocked. He opened the door. "Hey, Frank," he said. "How're you?" Harold is a tall, skinny dude with a black patch over one eye, a red beret on his head.

"Come on in, Frank," he said.

"Thanks for seeing me on such short notice."

"You're the man. I owe you. Anything I can do, my pleasure. How about a drink?" he asked.

"I'm good, thanks."

He led me over to a couch next to a series of black-and-white drawings by Aubrey Beardsley—all with an extreme S & M theme.

"What's this about?" he asked, crossing his skinny stick legs.

"I've been retained to find a missing woman, a writer—"

"For *Tell It Like It Is?*" he asked.

"Yes."

"Anne . . . something?"

"That's her. You know her?"

"I met her. She was here asking questions about Santos. I didn't know that's what this is about. I'm kind of not surprised. Beautiful lady. Killer smile."

"You talk to her?"

"Yes."

"About him?"

"Yes, but I didn't tell her much. I mean, I knew whatever I said was for public consumption and so I gave her, you know, the pasteurized version of what I know. Dracol is not the kind of person you want as an enemy. Even the Angels stay clear of him.

"Really . . . How'd she find her way here?"

"Truth is I don't know. Just showed up one night with a member."

"Who?"

"A woman in the book business."

"An agent?"

"I think so."

"Wears glasses—kind of looks like a bug?"

71

"That's her."

"She did talk to Amy."

"Who's Amy?"

"The girl I told you about. She's a bartender here. She's at the bar now. She belongs to Santos."

"Belongs?" I repeated.

"Yes. He branded her. She's an extreme sub, loves to be abused, to be degraded; and she found the perfect man."

"What's this about?"

"What's that?"

"All these women who want to be abused?"

"For them it's not abuse, Frank. It's a turn-on. It's a form of . . . well, love. Pain, degradation, humiliation for a submissive is love—it's extreme undivided attention; it's intensity. Normal sex to a sub is, well—it's boring. They want more, and they get it through pain and humiliation. That's pretty much the sum of it."

"Go figure."

"Yeah."

"So business is good?"

"Booming, actually. A lot of people are into the S and M scene, Frank. You'd be amazed. We are opening clubs in Chicago and Houston in the next few months. You like the club?"

"Yeah, great; real classy. Some hot babes upstairs. I was watching the show. They . . . didn't seem to be acting."

"They aren't acting. They're real subs and a dom."

"But they're getting paid to do it?"

"No, actually. They do it because they like it, need it, crave it . . . are into it. Fact is, some of them actually pay us to be on stage to be abused."

"You're kidding."

"No."

"Beautiful women like them—those two?"

"Fucking A. Beauty is only skin deep, my man," he said.

"Hmm. What are all these doors down here?"

"Dungeons . . . they lead to our dungeon rooms."

"Really?"

"People love them. We have every one of them booked solid for the next two months."

"You're kidding."

"No way, straight up."

"Wow."

"Wanna see?"

"See what?"

"What's going on in the dungeon rooms?"

"I'm not sure," I said, and laughed.

"Don't be a prude," he said.

"Sure," I said. *What the hell*, I thought. *I'm here to learn.*

"We have camera hookups in every room. We want to make sure nothing goes too far."

"How so?"

"Someone gets killed."

"It's that intense?"

"Oh yeah. This is the real thing," he said, and turned on a television on a shelf behind him.

There was a black room. A naked guy with an erection was tied to a rack. A little Asian woman with ridiculously high stiletto heels was whipping him. She had a pushed-in dog face . . . like a pug. Each time she whipped him, he said, "Thank you, Mistress Tonya, may I please have another?" Harold pressed a remote. Another room; another rack, a woman bound to it, while a second female was putting tit clips on her. There was a clothespin on her tongue. Harold again pushed the remote—and another male/female couple were abusing each other. She was bound to a cross. He was sodomizing her. A big black guy was whipping him. Harold pushed the button eight more times—and one scene was more bizarre than the next, I swear, some involving . . . bathroom functions. I'd seen enough, thanked him for the show. I suddenly had a bad taste in my mouth.

"Are you recording them?" I asked.

"We have to, just in case someone goes too far and we get sued."

"Amazing, go figure. What happened to romance, wining and dining . . . kissing and making love?"

"Ha," he said. "Frank, don't you get it, these people—they're making love—making mad passionate love." *Mad indeed*, I thought.

I wanted to get back to the reason I was there. "What more can you tell me about Dracol?"

"The sum of it, Frank, is to be fucking careful.

He is very rich, very smart, a bona fide sadist and a blood freak. He has connections, too."

"What kind?"

"Political—his lawyers are all former federal prosecutors. Top-notch. I know his clubs are very successful, and I heard he's got some kind of kinky movie company in the Netherlands."

"I've heard that too . . . snuff films?"

"Yes—that's the rumor."

"True?"

"Yes, I'd say so."

"You see any?"

"No, but I've heard about them from people who have."

"Really, who?"

"Different people over the years, you know. Careful with him, I'm telling you, Frank," he said solemnly, still again. I was thinking he maybe knew something he wasn't telling me.

"Come on, Harold," I said, "I'm from Brooklyn."

"This is something different. This guy . . . Frank, I think he is a stone-cold killer, if you want to know the truth."

"Really?"

"Yes, straight up. And you know," he added conspiratorially, "he's got the biggest cock I ever seen. Fucking guy is hung like a racehorse, I swear."

"How'd you see that?" I said, not really giving a flying fuck.

"At one of his S and M orgies. There's a sex

room at his club. I saw a sub sucking his dick. It was kind of dark. At first I swear I thought it was his arm, but it was his cock. Humongous."

"That's why so many women have the hots for him?" I said, and laughed.

"Ha," he laughed. "Women fucking love him; he's the ultimate bad boy."

"Anything you can tell me? Does he use drugs?"

"Some . . . a little toot maybe. Not hung up at all."

"Can I speak to this Amy?"

"Sure. I'll go get her and leave you alone with her if you wish."

"Good. Thanks, Harold. You rock. I owe you."

"My pleasure. Be right back," he said, got up, and left. I mulled over what he said, thinking maybe I should get the hell into another line of work . . . rather than deal with a sadistic vampire with pointed teeth and a horselike cock. I got up and looked at the Beardsley sketches. They were bizarre, depicting all kinds of debaucheries. There was a soft knock. The door opened. A willowy redhead walked in, shy and timid.

"Sir," she said, "you want to talk with me?"

She was very pretty, had a demure attractiveness about her, but there was a cigarette-length scar on her right cheek. She was wearing a kind of old-fashioned black leather apron.

"My name's De Nardo. I'm looking for a friend. Please, sit down."

She sat on the couch next to me and regarded me curiously.

"Why do you want to talk with me—do I know your friend?"

"I'm not sure. Her name is Anne Fitzgerald."

"Sorry, I don't think I do," she said, I believed honestly, her brow lining with thought.

"She's a writer."

"No, sorry, sir, doesn't ring a bell. But I do meet a lot of people here—"

"She was writing a story about Santos Dracol," I said. Soon as I said his name, she stiffened notably. Paled a bit.

"You know him, correct?"

"Yes . . . you know I do, sir," she said.

"Well?"

"I'm his slave," she said proudly, though not defiantly.

"Did he ever mention Anne Fitzgerald to you?"

"No."

"I'd like to talk to you about your master, okay?"

She didn't answer me, just stared with her odd-colored eyes.

"Okay?" I repeated.

"Why?" she said.

"I believe he knows where my friend is," I said.

"Ask him—not me," she said.

"How did you meet him?"

"At a party."

"How long do you know him?"

". . . Two years," she said, and moved uncomfortably.

"Did he really brand you—"

"Look, I know you are Harold's friend and all, but I'm not comfortable talking about master, okay, sir?"

"I understand . . . Whatever you tell me won't leave this room, I promise."

"You a cop?"

"I'm a P.I."

"I see."

"Did he really brand you, Amy?"

"Yes—I wanted him to. I'm his slave. I'm his property."

"I see."

"Want to see?" she proudly asked. *Sick bitch*, I thought.

"Yes, please," I said.

She stood, pulled up the apron. She was naked underneath. She had a gold ring through her upper labia. Above the pubic hairline she was indeed branded. *Santos Dracol*, it said, in goth block letters about an inch high.

"I'm his property," she repeated.

She dropped the apron back down. *Mamma mia*, I thought.

"I see. What's he like?"

"The best master in the world," she said. "He keeps me in a cage to use me as he sees fit. I'll do anything for him."

"Was he your first master?"

"No . . . my father was," she said. "Listen, you seem like a nice man, but I'm afraid. If he finds out I spoke to you, I know he'll be angry. He's warned me to never talk about him. Sir . . . I've already said more than I should've." She stood up and made for the door.

"I understand," I said. "Thank you for talking with me." She left. Harold soon returned. I thanked him for all his help. He walked me upstairs, offered me another drink, which I declined. It was time for me to meet Santos Dracol.

Outside, the fresh air felt good. I got into my SUV and headed downtown.

CHAPTER SIX

I found Club Blood on West Street, just off Varick. Two huge bouncers stood at the door behind velvet ropes attached to fancy brass stands. They were probably the ones who had beat on Mr. Fitzgerald. Even on a night like this, people were waiting to get in and there was a line of limousines out front. I parked across the street, in front of the Hudson River, and sat there watching the place, listening to the howling wind, thinking about Amy—wondering how an attractive woman like her could end up so . . . fucked up. Most of the people entering the club were pale-serious, heavy-metal types wearing all black. I saw some extremely attractive women.

Soon a sleek black Mercedes limo slowly pulled up at the club. The windows were tinted and I couldn't see inside. One of the doormen hurried to open the rear door and Santos Dracol himself stepped out of the car, talking on a cell phone. I grabbed a small pair of Nikon binoculars I keep in the glove compartment to get a better look at him. He was taller and thinner than I had imagined, his face as white and cold as the snow. He stared directly at me with menacing coal-black eyes. Wearing a long black cape with a high collar, he was a strikingly good-looking man with a severe triangle-shaped face, high cheekbones, a broad forehead. He was so attractive, his features so refined, he could have been a woman. For a moment I thought he was a woman. Snowflakes covered the top of his black hair as if they were an icy crown.

The doorman closed the car door and Dracol started toward the club, his steps slow and deliberate, and went inside. I got out of the car, crossed the street, and walked to the front door. The stone-faced doormen saw me coming. I told them who I was and one of them moved the rope so I could enter. On the right as you walked in there was a woman behind a counter made out of plastic bones. She wore a black bodice, had long blond hair and bright red lipstick. White fangs hung over her lower lip. I told her I was there to see Dracol, and she said that I could go right in, that I was "expected."

I walked down a half-dozen steps. On both sides of the steps there were large black-and-white portraits on the walls of infamous killers—Ted Bundy and John Wayne Gacy, Ed Kemper, Gilles de Rais, Jeffrey Dahmer, Charles Manson, Richard Ramirez, aka The Night Stalker, Countess Erzsébet Báthory, the Marquis de Sade, and

Ed Gein, the inspiration for Alfred Hitchcock's
Psycho. There was also a large, ominous portrait
of Dracol. He was standing in front of a neatly
stacked, symmetrical pile of skulls.

At the bottom of the stairs, I found myself in a
large black room with black leather booths on one
side and a long black marble bar on the other.
Red-eyed stuffed bats hung from the ceiling. I
thought about Carole Smith's tattoo. More black-
and-white photographs, all having something to
do with vampirism, covered the walls. I slowly
moved to the bar. It was crowded with an odd as-
sortment of people—all pale, all wearing black or
red, talking in hushed tones, some necking, others exploring private parts. To the left of the bar
was a dance floor behind a smoked-glass wall.
People were dancing to strange Gothic music. I
took a seat and told the woman behind the bar
that I wanted a bottle of water. I was tempted to
order a Bloody Mary but didn't.

As my eyes adjusted to the dark, I could see
that some of the people at the bar were not only
necking but were actually sucking blood from
small cuts on one another's arms, legs, and
necks—a thing I'd never seen before. This place
made Bottoms Up seem tame. The thick, purple
smell of blood came to me. A huge portrait of
Vlad Tepes hung on the wall behind the bar. On
either side of Vlad's portrait there were large ter-
rariums, one housing foot-long, licorice-colored
leeches, the other a huge live bat. Its eyes were
wide open, and it seemed to be looking directly at

me. The bartender poured a small bottle of Pellegrino into a tall, thin glass.

"That a vampire bat?" I asked.

"Of course," she said

"Of course," I said. "Silly me."

I sensed her coming before I saw her, turned, and she was walking straight toward me, a tall, exquisite brunette with luminous white skin and long, stick-straight black hair. She wore a blood-red leather outfit that highlighted an outrageously curvaceous figure. I thought of Jessica Rabbit.

"My name is Belladonna," she said, giving me a long, tapered hand. "How do you do? I manage the club."

"Hello, Belladonna, it's a pleasure," I said, gladly taking her hand, and it really was a pleasure, because she was truly beautiful, had a heart-shaped face with huge dark eyes above full, bloodred lips. I couldn't resist: "What's a girl like you," I asked, "doing in a place like this?"

She smiled demurely, showing me her pointed canines. "Keeping out of trouble," she said.

"Did he send you over?"

"He asked me to welcome you. He'll be a few minutes," she said.

"Did you know Anne Fitzgerald?"

"I never had the pleasure."

"I'm here investigating her disappearance." I took out Anne's photo and showed it to her. "Ever see her?" I asked, carefully studying her eyes.

84

"So many people come in here—I see so many faces. He's on a conference call at the moment. When he's finished, I'll bring you down," she said.

"Okay. Thank you. I'm fascinated by all this. I never knew so many people were into this whole vampire thing," I said. "I never knew the club existed."

"Welcome," she said.

We stared at each other. She had intense, sultry dark eyes, black like onyx. I felt like she was undressing me with them . . . which I had no particular problem with. She smiled and showed me more of her pointed canines. Unlike Amy, this was a strong-willed woman, with a presence of strength and confidence. Kind of night and day.

"Your teeth really like that?" I asked. "I mean, they aren't plastic clip-ons?"

That made her laugh. Despite her teeth, she had a warm, gracious smile—not an easy thing with those teeth.

"They aren't plastic clip-ons," she said.

"Is this like a lifestyle thing with you, or are you really a vampire? . . . I mean, do you drink blood; do you sleep in a coffin and all?"

"Yes, I drink blood, though of course I eat food. And yes, I do sleep in a coffin," she said, proud of it.

"You seem so nice; nothing like you'd expect a vampire to be."

"Nice of you to say," she said, and smiled, exposing still more of those German shepherd teeth of hers.

"Hell of a smile," I said. "I assume you use the teeth to bite people?"

"Only when I'm hungry," she said, smiling coyly. A cell phone she was carrying meowed like a cat. She excused herself and slowly walked away, talking on the phone as she went. I drank some of my water, got up, and went to the john. The toilet bowl was black, in the shape of a bat. More stuffed bats hung from the ceiling. There was a full-length portrait of Bela Lugosi as Dracula in the 1922 Broadway play. I could hear a couple in the next stall speaking heated Russian and greedily snorting coke. They started fooling around; she moaned. It sounded like he bit her. They began having sex. I was tempted to look over the top of the stall but didn't. When I got back to the bar, Belladonna returned with her flawless skin and big red kissy lips.

"He can see you now," she said, and I gladly followed her down a fancy spiral staircase. Her hair glistened like black oil. The sweet smell of musk came from her. We passed a VIP room and she knocked on a tall silver door, which was soon opened by the biggest black man I'd ever seen. His shoulders filled the doorway. He had long gold canines and thick, snakelike dreadlocks halfway down his wall of a back. A sobering sight.

Santos Dracol was sitting behind a long black

marble desk in a black candlelit room. As I approached the desk, he stood and extended a hand that was as strong as an iron vise. There were large red-stone rings on all of his fingers. An odd smell came from him. Not a particularly pleasant one. Kind of like wet leather.

"How do you do, Mr. De Nardo. Your reputation precedes you," he said.

"And your reputation precedes you," I said, quickly letting go of his hand, wondering if he was wearing makeup to be so white. Courtly and gracious, he said, "Please have a seat." Both the giant black guy and Belladonna disappeared. I was sorry to see her go. The flickering candlelight glistened in his dark eyes. We both sat.

"What can I do for you?" he asked.

"I'm looking for Anne Fitzgerald; her father is very concerned. He's asked me to help find her. I understand she was writing an article about you . . . about the vampire scene."

"Yes, she was. I did meet with her several times. We had another appointment, but she never showed up," he said.

"Met with her here?"

"Here and at my home."

"When was the last time you saw her?"

"Sometime in December . . . early December. We were wondering why we hadn't heard back from her. Would you like something to drink?"

"No, thanks. I understand you refused to talk to the police. Why's that?"

"My attorneys advised me not to talk with them. Simple. Nothing more than that."

"Why, then, are you talking to me?"

"You aren't the police, and I don't think you have any preconceived agenda, as the police surely do. Yes I am a vampire, and yes I have an unconventional lifestyle, but I do nothing illegal. I pay taxes, stop for red lights, and would gladly help an older person cross the street. I am not the heartless monster the police constantly try to make me out to be. Someone's missing, blame Santos Dracol. I'm the perfect scapegoat. Don't you think I know I am under police scrutiny? Why would I do anything to lose all that I have? It makes no sense, Mr. De Nardo."

"I want for nothing," he added.

Nice speech, I thought.

"In my limited lifetime," I said, "I've seen a lot of people do things that don't make sense. That are outright stupid. We aren't a predictable people. All kinds of elements come into play—lust, greed, power, and sex are just a few of the things that drive people to do dangerous things that make no sense. Always have."

"Well, I don't. And I'm sorry, but I know nothing about Anne Fitzgerald's disappearance. I cannot help you."

"But you drink human blood and all, correct?"

"None of that has anything to do with why you are here. I am fond of Anne. She has a very keen mind, is very dedicated to her craft. A talented writer. But as you may know, she had a tendency to stick her nose where it didn't belong. I think that might have gotten her into some trouble."

"Maybe . . . but I have this kind of hinky itching at the back of my neck that tells me you do know what happened to her. I was at the morgue this morning, Mr. Dracol, and I saw the body of Carole Smith."

I carefully looked for any change in his face, his eyes; there was none. He was a cool piece of work.

"Are you calling me a liar?" he asked, his right eyebrow arching belligerently, like he was cocking a pistol and pointing it at me.

"I'm not calling you anything. But you knew Carole Smith, didn't you?"

"You apparently know I did," he said, sitting back.

"Well, don't you think it an odd coincidence that you have a thing for blood and she ends up in the Hudson River with blood sucked from her neck?"

"Carole Smith was a masochistic drug fiend. She freebased for days at a time. She savored being abused. She got herself mixed up with some satanic vampires, and that's what satanic vampires do. You lie down with dogs, don't be surprised if you get up with fleas," he said. "Same old story. I've heard this before. Someone's missing, blame Santos Dracol. Truth is, it's getting tiring."

"I hear you're a sexual sadist—that true?"

"That's my business, not yours."

"I hear you have a film company in Amsterdam—that true?"

"You obviously know it is."

"You produce snuff movies?"

"That's ridiculous. You've been a busy bee."

"Just doing my job."

"I understand you're a professional busybody, but you are sticking your nose where it doesn't belong."

"It's a bad habit of mine."

"Could be dangerous."

"You don't scare me, Dracol."

"I don't mean to."

"I'm not a lost woman you can dominate."

"Funny guy, you."

"I was the class clown in high school. So do you like abusing women?"

"I'm a dominator, yes," he said.

"Someone whipped Carole Smith."

"Not me."

"Why do you like to hurt women?"

"Look, De Nardo, you're becoming rude. What makes you think it's okay to come in my office and start making all these ridiculous accusations—it's not," he said. "I could have you thrown out on your ass." My intention was to get his goat.

"Try that," I said.

"You're armed, I'm sure."

"Fucking A I'm armed—and a very good shot."

We stared at each other. I didn't like this prick, and I know it was written all over my face plain as day.

"You kill Carole Smith, Dracol?" I said, pushing the envelope.

He laughed. "I told you she was an extreme bottom and *she* got herself killed."

"So she's to blame for what happened to her?"

"Let the truth fall where it may. Does the truth bother you, De Nardo?"

"That's what I'm doing here—looking for the truth. Would you know who these satanic vampires are? Can you give me any names, addresses, phone numbers? I'll be happy to check it out."

"There are thousands of satanic vampires across the country, around the world. Just go take a look at the Internet if you doubt me."

"Are *you* a Satanist?"

Again, he laughed. "Satan," he said, "is a Christian, man-made entity created to manipulate the masses and excuse bad behavior. 'The Devil made me do it. Beware, the power of the Devil is mine. The Devil is behind me.' All nonsense. Satanists are nothing more than psychopaths and sociopaths who haven't come to grips with their own empty lives. . . ."

"No, I'm not a Satanist. You want to find Satan, Mr. De Nardo, go look in the Vatican in Rome; that's where he lives, with all the child molesters." I couldn't argue with that.

"So then, to help clear the air, would you take a lie-detector test?"

"I have no particular adversity to that, but it

would ultimately be up to my attorneys," he said. *The slimy prick*, I thought.

"Would you ask them?"

"Certainly."

"I'd appreciate that. I'm curious . . . why all the portraits of famous killers on the walls?"

"A marketing theme," he said, and stared at me some more with his glistening black shark eyes in which the golden flames of the candles quivered. His eyes seemed to be all pupils; I wondered if he was on some kind of drug. I remembered what Captain Roe had said about him being "a Manson type with money and pointed teeth," and there truly was something in his eyes, about his face, a capacity for sudden, irrational violence that reminded me of Charles Manson; that reminded me of a hungry shark. I wanted to punch him in his pretty face.

"If you don't mind my asking, how old are you?" I said.

"Older than I look. Longevity runs in my family," he said. "I have some very pressing matters now that need my attention."

He stood up to dismiss me. I stayed put, said, "It seems to me not much goes on in the vampire community you wouldn't know about. Would you try to find out what happened to Carole Smith for me?"

"I thought you were looking for Anne Fitzgerald?" he said.

"I think the two cases are linked."

"I'll do what I can," he said. I gave him one of my cards and left.

Belladonna was waiting for me outside. I was glad to see her. It was hard not to be. She walked me back upstairs. There were even more people there now. We returned to the bar. She didn't seem in a hurry to leave . . . fine with me. I didn't want her to leave.

"It must be exciting to be a private detective," she said. "I've always fantasized about being one. When I was a child, I read all of Agatha Christie's books many times over. What do you have to do to become a P.I.?"

"Give the state a hundred bucks, get licensed, and put your number in the phone book."

"That's how people find you, in the phone book?"

"Some. Also referrals from other clients, lawyers, and cops I know."

"I see. You know you kind of look like Brando. People ever tell you that—a rugged Brando?"

"I've heard it a few times."

"De Nardo. So you're Italian, no doubt?"

"I am."

"It's in your face, especially your eyes. Lovely eyes you have . . . very intense."

"Nice of you to say. I was wondering, you ever see nonvampires—I mean, like socially?"

"Not often, but I do make exceptions."

"Would you make an exception for me?" I

asked, sure she could help me with the investigation, sure she could help me understand what the hell was really going on here. What Santos Dracol was really about.

"I might," she said.

"Just tell me when and where."

"How about tonight, later tonight—if it's not too late for you," she said.

"It's never too late for me. I don't sleep much."

"Me either. I don't leave here until two o'clock. Can you meet me outside, then, for a nightcap?"

"Absolutely. He won't mind? I wouldn't want to create any kind of problems for you."

"I have a life outside of the clubs," she said.

"You seeing me because he asked you to?" I asked—sure she was.

"Nobody tells me who to see," she said, looking me dead in the eyes.

"Okay. See you later, then," I said, and left, feeling her eyes follow me as I walked toward the stairs.

CHAPTER SEVEN

Outside, the snow was coming down even harder. The cold-clean flakes felt good after being in a room alone with Santos fucking Dracol. I started my SUV and headed uptown, sure that no matter what Dracol said, how polite or well-mannered he was, he was at the bottom of Anne's disappearance—and who knows what else.

He was, it was obvious, a very charming man who had a powerful aura about him. He'd been, I was thinking, hurting people and playing the police for fools for a long time, if what Fred Reynolds told me was true: that there were police reports about him going back to the eighties, which I was sure was true.

I parked in my garage at Eighty-seventh and Amsterdam and walked home. People were out shoveling the sidewalks. There were still tired Christmas decorations in some of the windows. I had time to kill, and I did it by thinking about all I had learned and reading Anne's story about the

Covent House. She wrote beautifully, had a precise, poetic kind of prose. I also read more Web sites about vampires and was more and more amazed at how many people were into this jive bullshit vampire nonsense. I could understand the whole S & M scene, more or less, but not this vamp thing. A little after 1:30, I made myself an espresso and left to go meet Belladonna.

By now the snow had stopped and the wind had died down to a polite whisper. The streets were quiet and still, the air clean and crisp. In the west the sky abruptly cleared and the light of a nearly full, bone-colored moon covered the snow like sweet cake frosting. There were few cars on the road and fewer people on the streets.

I reached Varick and parked. In a few minutes, I watched Dracol leave the club and get into his black Mercedes limousine. Belladonna came outside at 2:05. She was wearing a long, black fur coat and a large black fur hat, which highlighted the stark whiteness of her beautiful face. She kind of looked like the actress Catherine Zeta-Jones—she had those kind of huge, almond-shaped eyes and full lips. I got out of the car and opened the door for her.

"I was thinking," she said, "maybe you wouldn't come."

"Nothing could've kept me away."

"Lovely. I know a nice quiet place on Green Street where we can relax, have a drink."

"Let's go," I said, put the car in gear, and took a right on Canal, looking in the rearview as I went.

"You seem nervous," she said. "Don't be. There's no need. I won't bite you."

"I'm not nervous; it's just that I've never been out with a vampire. . . . Do you bite on the first date?" I asked.

"Not usually," she said, and laughed.

"I can't help wondering how you've gotten so wrapped up in all this."

"All what?"

"This whole vampire thing."

"It's just a lifestyle choice. Some people are Catholics, some agnostic, some Muslims. Some people eat meat, some don't. Some people are sadists, some not. And some people are vampires. It's really that simple."

She became quiet. The smell of her kept coming to me, a sweet, musklike fragrance that was appealing. We reached Green Street. I parked at a hydrant and put my NYPD parking permit on the dashboard. "I thought you were a private investigator?" she said.

"I'm a retired New York City detective," I told her.

"I see," she said. I opened the door for her, took her arm, and we walked toward the club. There was a lot of snow and ice on the sidewalk. She was wearing knee-high boots with tall heels.

The place was called Candlelight. It was a fancy after-hours club just off Spring Street. The doormen smiled and kissed Belladonna on both cheeks. It was surprisingly crowded inside, considering the weather. New York really is the city that never sleeps. We were shown to a cozy red velvet booth. I sat so I could look her in the eyes as we spoke, my back to the dance floor, which was in the rear of the club.

"Do you like champagne?" she asked.

"One of my few weaknesses."

She ordered a bottle of Cristal. The crowd here was upscale, uptown, chic, and elegant. The waitress carefully poured the champagne into tall frosted flutes and put a bowl of giant strawberries in front of us.

"To the night," Belladonna said. We touched glasses and drank. The Cristal was ice cold and delicious and made me want to smile.

"The only thing I like more than blood is champagne," she said with a straight face. For a moment I thought she was pulling my leg, but she wasn't.

"If you don't mind my asking, how often do you drink blood?" I asked.

"When I have the urge. I particularly like to feed during lovemaking," she added. "There's so much more energy in the blood then—when it's mixed with the endorphins that come with good sex," she said.

"Hmm, really . . . interesting," I said, "who knew," sitting back and looking at her, not sure if I should get up and quickly leave or move a bit closer. I opted to move closer. We finished the bottle, and I had a pleasant buzz. With a wave of her hand she ordered another one, put a big juicy strawberry in my mouth. I carefully put one in her mouth. The strangest thing was that I had this odd compunction to kiss her and told her so. She leaned forward and planted a soft kiss on my lips. It was the most wild sensation, being kissed by a beautiful woman who had long, pointed canines.

My left hand brushed against her exposed thigh. Her skin was soft and hot, like sun-warmed silk.

"You put a spell on me?" I asked.

"No, silly, relax," she said, coming closer to me.

"Don't you bite me," I said, drawing away from her.

"I never feed unless I'm invited," she said. "Don't worry yourself, De Nardo."

"Good," I said, and we toasted again.

"So you have no idea about what happened to Anne Fitzgerald?" I said.

"No."

"Did he ever mention her?"

"No."

"You're sure? You don't seem sure."

"I'm telling you the truth. I don't know anything about Anne Fitzgerald's disappearance . . . I swear on the treasured souls of my grandparents," she said.

"Yeah, well, the thing of it is, I have to find out what happened to her. . . . Can you swear on the souls of your grandparents that *he* had nothing to do with her disappearance?"

"No. That I cannot do, because I really don't

know. What Santos does in his private life outside the club is not my business—nor anything he shares with me. Ours is strictly a business relationship. Please understand that. It's always been that between us. I can tell you this: People, *donors*, come to Santos from all over the world, and they beg him to take them, to teach them, to feed from them, to have sex with them, to abuse them. He is the most sought-after dominant in vampire society. . . .

"We live in a confused world. Masochists just love him—his power, his dominance. He has obsessively devoted *bottoms* all over."

"Would you take a lie-detector test that you don't know anything about Anne's disappearance?" I asked.

"Absolutely I would, of course, because I don't," she said, and I . . . well, I believed her. I'm not an easy man to fool.

"How many clubs does he have?"

"Six worldwide—two in the States, one in New Orleans, the New York club, and the rest are in Europe. I'd rather not talk about him, if you don't mind." She poured us more champagne. "Okay?"

"Fine," I said. "When did you first realize that you were . . . this way?"

"I've always known, since I was a child, I was drawn to the vamp life."

"Your parents force you into it, something like that?"

"No. It was inside me. Something I wanted."

"What kind of childhood did you have, if you don't mind my asking?"

"Not very good," she said, a sudden sadness coming to her eyes.

"Where were you brought up?"

"San Francisco."

"Great town."

"I miss it very much."

"I'm sorry. . . . I know you don't want to talk about him and all, but how'd you come to meet Dracol?"

"We met at a party in Paris. He had all these gorgeous women around him, literally groveling at his feet and such. He's quite the celebrity in Europe. He is a blue blood. I didn't grovel. And that made him want me all the more. Same old story: You've got to have what you can't have."

"So you were lovers?"

"Never. And because I wouldn't give in to his entreaties, he came to respect me, and before I knew it I was running his Paris club, and from there one thing led to another."

"A vampire club?"

"Yes, of course."

"Is he straight?"

"He's all things."

"Bi?"

"Let's just say he's very *unusual*. You're persistent."

"Is he a sadist?" I asked, knowing the answer.

"Yes. . . . And he has a thing for the young . . . for innocence."

"Really. How young?"

"Young," she said. "Innocence, for Santos, is an aphrodisiac."

"Are you a sub?"

"Hell no," she said.

"Great."

"Have you been to the Bottoms Up?"

"Yes . . . it's fun. I like to see the show of it."

"I hear Dracol has a sex room at Club Blood— that true?"

"It's really just a VIP room, but people do get it on there."

"You too?"

"No way. I told you, my relationship with him is just business. I don't ever mix the two— business and pleasure. I just happened to be a vamp that works at his club. That's why he and I get along . . . I won't have anything to do with his whole scene." I was glad to hear that, but still wasn't sure she was being straight up.

"Let's stop talking about him, okay?"

"Okay. . . . How old are you, if you don't mind my asking?" She was in a hurry to change the subject; clearly, she didn't like talking about him. Curious.

"Older than I look. Never ask a lady her age," she said.

"Sorry—I was just wondering if you are, you know, immortal," I joked.

"You have beautiful eyes. . . . Let's talk about you. How long have you been a P.I.?"

"Too long," I said, and we drank some more of the fine champagne. I looked at my watch, wondering if she had an adversity to the sun. She seemed to read my mind: "I sleep during the day," she said. "I don't like the sun."

"Never go to the beach, I guess."

"Heavens no."

"Just kidding."

"Dance with me?"

"My pleasure," I said, and she took my hand and we walked to the back of the club. There was slow music playing. She came to me, and I held her close.

"You're armed," she said, feeling my Beretta, looking me in the eyes.

"Always," I said. It was the strangest sensation, holding her close. She might be a professed vampire, but she had hot blood in her veins. She provocatively pushed herself against me, grinding on me. Spurred on by the slippery slope of the champagne, I brought her closer—pushed back.

"Ooh-la-la, you excite me," she said. "You have such a strong body. Your muscles are like steel cables. I love men with strong bodies and big pistols. I meet so few of them these days. Is your pistol big, De Nardo?" she asked, smiling.

"I carry a nine-millimeter," I said.

"Hmm. It's in your face, you know, your eyes . . . even the way you walk."

"What's that?"

"That you have no fear; that you're very sure of yourself. I find that so attractive."

"I find you so attractive."

We stared at each other. This was going someplace I was not sure I wanted to visit, but I wasn't about to say no.

"Be careful with Santos. He's not a man to take lightly," she said.

"Careful is my middle name. Because I've got balls doesn't mean I want to lose them. Belladonna, do you know anything about Carole Smith?"

"Nothing," she said.

"Did he tell you to warn me off?"

"No. Stop being so paranoid."

"Are you sure?"

"I'm sure he doesn't like you sticking your nose into his business."

"Until this is resolved, his business is my business."

"What's your sign, De Nardo?"

"Aries with a Leo rising."

"Ahh, I should have known—all fiery determination." She took my hand and we went back to our booth. As we sat down, I saw the two bouncers who worked the door at Santos's place.

"The guys that work the door at the club are here," I told her, wondering if she was setting me up. They were both looking over at me, giving me the hairy eyeball. I don't like being stared at, and I gave them some hairy eyeball right back. The first thing any predator does before they eat you is stare at you. Size you up, imagine how you'll taste.

"A lot of people who work in clubs come here to unwind," she said, and put another strawberry in my mouth. Having these two guys there, though, was making me kind of uneasy, and I was about to get up and go say hello to them.

"I sense your discomfort," she said. "Would you, perhaps, like to come back to my place? Would you be more comfortable there? I live close by."

"Sure, I'd like that," I said, wanting to see where this would go, what I could learn from her, if she was trying to set me up in some way. I called for the check. She told me it was taken care of.

"How's that?"

"Don't concern yourself."

"I don't want you paying."

"I'm not—you can leave a tip."

I put a couple of tens on the table for the waitress and we got up to leave.

"I hope my home doesn't shock you," she said as we walked toward the door, passing the hostile, staring-at-me bouncers.

"I don't shock easily," I said.

We got back into my SUV and I drove the few blocks to her place on Houston Street. Dawn had broken by now and the sky above the city was a deep charcoal gray streaked with giant brushstrokes of black. In the east, giant spears of golden sunlight pierced the foreboding sky.

Just as we entered the loft building where she lived, I saw a tall white-faced dude wearing all black in a doorway halfway down the block.

Setup, I thought, the word ringing in my head like a fire alarm. I slowed, stopped. "What's wrong?" she asked.

"I saw someone hiding in a doorway."

"And you think I am trying to set you up?"

"The thought crossed my mind."

"Nonsense—what man?" she said, went back to the door, and looked down the block. I looked, too. He was gone. I saw only the wind and the indifferent gray of a frigid New York dawn.

"No setup, De Nardo," she said. "I know you are a dangerous man. I know you are armed. I'm not stupid. I wouldn't do anything to risk my own safety. I mean far too much to myself. Contrary to common belief, we are not impervious to bullets, and I'm sure you are a very good shot."

"I was the NYPD Pistol Champion for five years running," I said, taking off her sunglasses and looking her dead in the eyes. I saw no deceit at all. I am not an easy man to fool.

"Okay, let's go," I said, but I did open my coat for quick access to my guns. We went up to the third floor. She opened the elevator door with a key and we walked into her place, which was a large loft with black walls and floors. The windows were covered with thick, red velvet curtains. She had a strange altar set up against the far wall filled with large crystals and statues.

There were thick, black and red candles burning at each end of the altar.

"Chill," she said. "There's no one here but you and I." She took my coat, went and changed into a silky black caftan, opened a bottle of Cristal she had in the fridge. She poured, and we toasted, sat in large easy chairs. She asked me how I ended up a P.I., and I told her how I'd been fired from the NYPD for killing Darnel Williams and began working as a private investigator.

I was curious about her childhood, and when I asked her to tell me about it, she became quiet and withdrawn. I pressed her. And she slowly told me that both her parents were "sexual deviates," that they were members of a group that advocated sex with children—The Lewis Carroll Society—and that she had been used in child porn and her parents "loaned" her out to other couples who were interested in such things, and I suddenly knew why Belladonna had her lovely head screwed on slightly backward.

"I'm sorry," I said. "Must have been tough."

"Fucked me up good for a while."

"The police," she said, "busted them all when I was about ten and I was sent to live with my grandparents—two of the kindest people on the face of the earth. Thank God for them. If it weren't for them, I'd probably be in a nuthouse right now . . . or something worse."

She became quiet and still and suddenly looked very young and vulnerable. The winds blew hard and shook the oversized windows of the loft. She got up to pour us more champagne. I followed her to the kitchen.

"Can you hold me?" she asked. "Can you maybe just hold me?"

"My pleasure," I said, reached for her and took her in my arms, held her tight, and before I knew it we were kissing deeply and I could feel the points of her teeth on either side of her long, silky, strawberry-tasting tongue.

"I've never been kissed like that before," I told her, my voice suddenly hoarse, I realized.

"You haven't made love until you've been with a vamp," she told me, and led me over to her canopied bed. It was draped with glistening red silk curtains that seemed on fire. Next to the bed, there was a gilded coffin—a chilling thing to see in someone's home. She lit a red candle. It gave off a peculiar odor.

"What's in the candle?" I asked.

"I make my own candles. There's belladonna and *special* blood in it . . . it's for lovemaking," she said, and in one easy movement she slipped out of the caftan and she was suddenly completely naked. *Mamma mia*, she had the most beautiful figure, as finely formed as a Michelangelo sculpture. White like alabaster. I hadn't been planning any of this, but I wasn't about to stop it. I brought her close, kissed her again. The elevator started up. I tensed. "You're safe here," she said. "Just someone going to work . . . chill."

It stayed quiet.

"You are the most beautiful woman I've ever seen," I told her truthfully, caressing her, feeling that incredible white skin of hers.

"Bet you say that to all the girls," she said, and kissed me so passionately my big toes curled up in my shoes.

"Feed me," she whispered in my ear, and slowly went down, deftly taking me into her mouth. Thinking of those pointed teeth, I was *really* on edge now.

"I won't hurt you, I promise," she whispered, "I'll be ever so careful," laying me down, undressing me, her sultry jade-black eyes not leaving my face. I let her put my guns and knife on her night table next to the candle.

"Such a lovely, powerful body you have," she said. I felt intoxicated by her passion . . . was buzzed from the champagne, but was still wary. She put protection on me and straddled me as she kissed me deeply, desperately, with hunger.

"De Nardo, relax—just give yourself over to me," she whispered in my ear, leaning forward and sensuously moving her hips back and forth and up and down. She set me on fire. Because all the windows were covered, the room was completely dark except for the quivering candlelight, which caressed and moved about her beautiful face.

"De Nardo, I am hematophiliac," she said in a soft whisper, no louder than the sound of a turning page. "Please, will you feed me," she said, looking at me with those huge sultry eyes of hers.

"A what? What are you?" I asked, not quite sure I even wanted the answer.

"Blood excites me, erotically. It always has," she said. "It's something I have no control over," she said, shy about it.

I knew what she was asking me now and was about to say "*No way*! Get up and get the fuck out of there," but she said: "Only a little; that's all I need. I won't bite you. Just let me put a tiny nick on your finger. I'll be *ever* so careful. I'll use a sanitized scalpel.

"Please, how I crave your blood—please feed me," she begged, alarm bells ringing loudly in my head. I knew I should get dressed and leave, but I lay there staring at this gorgeous creature begging for my blood. Hell of a thing.

Catlike, she moved from the bed and opened the night-table drawer, withdrew a black velvet box, and opened it. In it was a pointed scalpel sealed in plastic and some alcohol swabs. "Please say yes," she whispered.

Fascinated and curious to see and understand this phenomenon, I said, "Go ahead," kind of even before I knew I said it. She went and got a beautifully engraved crystal shot glass, very carefully pricked my finger, and let my blood flow into the glass. She seemed to be on fire now. Hot blood colored her white cheeks crimson red. Her breath quickened. She moaned softly. I never saw anything like this. When she was satisfied, she carefully covered my finger with a Band-Aid, picked up the glass, and slowly, savoring every drop, she drank my blood. It seemed as if she was having an orgasm—*bizarre*. If my uncle Sal saw this, he'd disown me. When she finished, her breasts heaving, she put the empty glass down and again straddled me.

This is sick. Get the hell out of here, I was thinking. But I stayed put, and she took me to a place I'd never been.

Afterward, I fell asleep and dreamed about the New York City morgue. Carole Smith sat up in her drawer in the cadaver room and began talking to me out of her rotting mouth: *I didn't know; I had no idea they would kill me. Please, you must make them pay. The only reason I got involved with them was because I was mixed up, depressed, and lonely and he killed me. I'm no innocent in the woods, I'm the first to admit it, but I didn't deserve to die like that, to be dumped in the freezing river like some piece of garbage.*

Who killed you? I asked her.

Please, you must make them pay. There are so many people here that he's murdered. You must stop him— you must! Don't you see you are the only one who can? He knows how to use the system; he knows how to get away with murder—he's a serial killer.

Who, Santos? I begged.

Children too, she said. *He killed the children of those who came to them, and runaways—mixed-up, confused young girls, they are all here. You must stop him—*

Who!? I demanded of her, and that's when I

woke up. The candle was still burning, my guns and knife still on the night table. But Belladonna was nowhere to be seen. I got out of bed and found her in the coffin, sleeping peacefully, a slight smile playing on her full lips. What the hell did I get myself into? Shaking my head in disbelief, I quietly began to get dressed, my mind playing over the evening's events, having serious mixed feelings about what I'd done. I was kind of hoping I had dreamed it all, but then I saw the crystal glass on the night table and her little black box. I looked at my watch. It was already ten o'-clock. As I put my guns back on, she woke up and slowly sat up in her coffin; what a sight that was.

"Sorry I woke you," I said.

"Must you go?"

"I've got to."

"I'll let you out," she said, and stepped out of her coffin. The sight of her exquisite charms brought it all back in a rush of sights and sounds and smells.

"I've never known a woman like you," I said. "When can we see each other again? There's a lot I need to talk with you about."

"Tonight if you wish, but after work."

"You have any nights off?"

"Every other Sunday, but I do take the whole month of August and part of September off."

"I'll pick you up in front of the club, okay?"

"See you then. . . . Please, De Nardo, be careful with Santos."

"Of course," I told her—thinking he was the one who needed to be careful, not me.

One way or another I knew Belladonna could help me, that I needed to know all she could teach me, show me, tell me. I sensed that I could trust her, but still she was an intricate part of Dracol's world . . . a thing I'd be hard-pressed, indeed foolish, to forget. She walked me to the door.

"So I'll see you tonight, De Nardo," she said. We hugged, and she threw me a kiss as the elevator door slowly closed.

I took a long deep breath, was soon outside, shaking my head in disbelief over the evening's strange events.

CHAPTER EIGHT

It was again snowing heavily. I drove over to the FDR Drive, which runs parallel to the East River, and made my way uptown. The water in the river was a murky dark green, rough and moving swiftly. I repeatedly tried my office, but couldn't get a line until I reached Twenty-third Street. Louise told me that Fred Reynolds had called from Interpol, and that Larry Alter, Santos Dracol's attorney, had phoned and left a message that I should leave Dracol alone, that if I had any questions I should direct them to him. I knew Larry Alter well. He's a fast-talking criminal attorney, a weasel of a man who does a lot of work for the Gambino crime family. He is pushy and aggressive and knows his way around a courtroom the way a rat knows the way around the sewer system. He often appears on Fox News to comment on criminal matters. He's the type of man who loves to hear himself talk and has no compunction about interrupting people.

Again, my mind played over the strange night I had—my talk with Dracol in his office, his pointed teeth and condescending ways—and I kept seeing what Belladonna had done to me.

As I passed the Bellevue Hospital Complex, the place where the New York City morgue is located, where Carole Smith was waiting to be put in a grave, I remembered my dream of her, how she had begged for help. It was like no dream I ever had; it was as if she had somehow found a way to talk to me from the other side. The wind suddenly blew with terrific force.

Captain Roe phoned to tell me that John Fitzgerald had a criminal record; that, in fact, he did time for murder and he had been arrested twice for beating on his wife. I asked him for a copy of his record. He said he'd send it over to my office. I thanked him, hung up, thought this over, and called Anne's agent. She said Anne had never mentioned any problems with her dad. They seemed, she said, "very close." I got the number of Anne's attorney from Alice and called her, found her in her office. Her name was Suzanne Barnes. I explained who I was, that I'd been retained by Anne's father to help find Anne. She too told me nice things about Anne; that she was "very upset" about her sudden disappearance. I asked her if Anne had a will. She said she did, and that Anne's father was the sole beneficiary of the will. This I found of particular interest and somewhat troubling. I didn't know what Anne was worth, but I knew it was substantial. I remembered Fitzgerald crying in my office, his tears on my desk. If he was acting, it was an Oscar-worthy performance. I got off the drive at Sixty-second Street and headed to the West Side, mulling this over. If I learned anything in my business, it was that you could never judge a book by its cover; that people are capable of doing all kinds of terrible things for money, for all kinds of inexplicable reasons.

I reached my block, found a spot, and parked. The first thing I did when I got inside was take a long, hot shower. I then put a new Band-Aid on my hand, shaking my head in disbelief that Belladonna had actually got off drinking my blood. I looked up the word *hematophiliac* and it said such a person was "erotically aroused" by the sight and taste and smell of blood. . . .

I returned Larry Alter's call, left a message, then called Fred Reynolds.

"Frank, I've got a lot for you," he said. "I managed to locate a Romanian police inspector named Marco Vacaresco, who wrote up the nineteen eighty-six police report about Dracol. He gave me an earful—are you ready; are you sitting down, Frank?"

"I'm sitting down."

"Well, first off, Dracol is a genuine blue blood. His family is Romanian aristocracy. In fact, his great-grandfather on his mother's side going back seven, eight generations was the king of Romania. He says that's why he was able to do what he did and not be bothered by the police."

"What did he do?"

"I know this sounds bizarre, but this is what he said: It seems he has a penchant for sadistic sex with women and underage girls—and actually drinking their blood." He waited for me to react. I didn't say anything; this was already old news to me. He continued. "There were rumors that he was killing them, too, but never any solid evidence. Vacaresco tells me they searched his castle several times but didn't find any bodies. It was the parents and relatives of the missing who kept telling the police that Dracol was responsible, that he was a serial killer, but the police could never pin anything on him. Then, finally, the brothers, fathers, and uncles of the missing stormed Dracol's castle looking to kill him, but he escaped through a secret passageway within an inch of his life. They did kill, however, three of his servants, tore them apart. And it was the servants that said Dracol was murdering people in the basement of the castle. The police did locate an old well in the lower levels of the castle, above an underground lake that's miles deep, so deep that no one was ever able to reach the bottom of it. Vacaresco said they found pieces of human flesh and hair on the walls, but that's it. He says he'd bet his pension the missing women and girls were all dumped down the well.

"But then word came from the Romanian ministry to stay away from Dracol's castle. Years went by, and after a while it was kind of put on the back burner. Vacaresco says he's sure that Dracol's been murdering people for a long time and getting away with it. He told me he still regularly has nightmares about the well. He personally spoke to the fathers whose daughters and wives disappeared."

This sounded a little too familiar, because it was a woman's father who had come to me for help, and Carole Smith's body had been dumped in water. Serial murderers, I knew, had a tendency to stick to the same MO. I was thinking this whole vampire thing was just something Dracol had wrapped himself in to disguise who and what he really was—a serial killer boldly hiding in plain sight. A big masquerade.

John Wayne Gacy, I remembered, wore the face of a clown; Ted Bundy played the role of a conservative Republican, even worked at a suicide hot line. And this guy, Dracol, was boldly strutting around, taking on the outward guise of a vampire, when in truth he was a stone-cold serial killer.

"Vacaresco tells me," he said, "that Dracol comes back to the castle a few times a year, but he has not seen him because he moved in with his daughter who lives in Bucharest."

"I'm thinking it might be a good idea if I talk with him. Would that be a problem?"

"Not at all," Fred said, and gave me Marco Vacaresco's phone number in Bucharest. I again thanked him for all his help and hung up, thinking about what I had just heard. Sure was a mouthful.

As I was about to make myself an espresso, Dracol's lawyer, Larry Alter, phoned and, in his nasty, high-pitched way of talking, told me he didn't want me "bothering his client," that I should "stay away from him."

"I'll be happy to leave him alone when I know he has nothing to do with Anne Fitzgerald's disappearance. If he'll take a lie-detector test and it—"

"You don't seem to get it—he's not taking any lie-detector test."

"Why not?"

"They're inconclusive, can be biased. He's not taking one—period. That's why not," he told me.

"Well, then, Counselor, he's at the top of my shitlist and I'm not leaving him alone," I said.

"Sounds like you are looking for trouble, De Nardo," he said.

"I'm looking for the truth, and if I happen to run into trouble while I'm looking for it, so be it. What else is new?"

"De Nardo, for your own good, listen carefully: You bother him, I'll drag you into court for harassment and sue you for everything you're worth, including your license and your home. I assume you're licensed?"

"I'm licensed," I said, wondering how he knew I owned the building. I wanted to tell him where to shove it, but said: "Counselor, I know you've got a job to do, that Dracol is paying you well to try and scare me off, but I, too, have a job to do.

Anne Fitzgerald is missing for five weeks. Her father is brokenhearted. She's his only child. He cried all over my desk. Come hell or high water, I'm finding out what happened to her, you understand? And if your client had anything to do with her disappearance, with hurting her, I'm going to nail him to the nearest wall. It's really that simple."

"Apparently, you think you are a tough guy. You want to see what tough is, I'll show you what tough is," he said.

"I'm just telling you how it really is. Listen carefully, Alter. I suggest you ask around about me before you lock horns with me. Do yourself a favor," I told him, and hung up on him, knowing I would hear from him again soon, the little prick.

A lie-detector test would not, I knew, prove anything conclusively, and its results are not admissible in court in New York State. But still, when someone is willing to take one it usually means they have nothing to hide, and when they refuse to take one they do have something to hide.

Water. I kept thinking how Dracol was suspected of getting rid of bodies in this underground lake. Murder and water, I knew, have always been linked together—like peanut butter and jelly. There is a long list of killers who happily used rivers, lakes, and oceans to hide their dirty work. At the turn of the century, in New York, the five crime families—and the Irish mobs before them—gleefully dumped their victims in the East River. There were, at times, more bodies floating in the East River than boats. Then there was the Green River Killer in Seattle, who disposed of dozens of women in the Green River; and Wayne Williams, who dumped his victims, seventeen children he raped and murdered, into the Tallahassee River.

I brought up the photographs of Carole Smith's body, found the two I had taken of her right ankle, and magnified them, remembering how Dr. Ash had said her ankle had been broken. There clearly was excessive discoloration, and it was obvious that some strong pressure had torn the tissue, as if a heavy weight had been chained to her—a weight that apparently slipped off when she was thrown into the Hudson River, hence the reason she'd been found floating near the G.W. Bridge. I knew Dracol lived up in Hastings-on-Hudson, Westchester, and I would have bet my house that his place was only a stone's throw from the river. I tried to phone Inspector Vacaresco in Bucharest but couldn't get through. I knew, too, that if you wanted to keep a body submerged in water you had to cut open the stomach cavity so gases could not build up and give the body buoyancy. The fact that Carole Smith's body had not been eviscerated was further proof that she had been weighed down by something that had slipped off.

It was time for me to go up to Westchester and snoop around. I wasn't crazy about driving up there with all the snow, but there were things I needed to see, to know. As I was just walking out the door, Larry Alter called back. He said, "I'm sorry we got off on the wrong foot. Why didn't you tell me who you were? I understand you have a job to do and certainly respect that," all meek now.

Alter had obviously found who my uncle Sal was. I knew he would because of some of the clients, mob guys, he represented.

"So when will Dracol take a lie-detector test?" I asked him.

"As his lawyer, as I think you know, I can't allow that. I'm sorry."

"Okay. I understand. But I have to do what I have to do . . . you understand?"

"Of course," he said.

I hung up, had some coffee, left the house, and drove north on the Henry Hudson Parkway. The sky was the solemn gray color of cremated ashes, the winds were back with a vengeance, and the river was choppy and mean, the current hurrying south. Large solitary snowflakes fell from the angry sky. As I passed under the George Washington Bridge, where Carole Smith's body had been found, I remembered her in the cadaver room—the terrible smell of the morgue immediately coming back to me, giving me a bad taste in my mouth. Like old pennies handled by dirty hands that had been in dirty places.

I had gotten Santos Dracol's address from the file Captain Roe had shown me and had little trouble finding the place. It was a sprawling Tudor with at least ten acres of land surrounded by a tall metal fence with unfriendly barbed points. To the left of the house there was a fancy Tudor doghouse, and I was sure the Dobermans lived in it. Their tracks and droppings dotted the snow that covered the grounds. Two Mercedes-Benzes were parked in the cobblestone driveway, one of which was the limo I'd seen Dracol get out of in Manhattan.

I went looking for the Hudson River and, lo and behold, found it directly behind the house, at the end of a dirt road that led directly down to cliffs, which majestically rose five stories above the turbulent river. The cliffs were the color of wet leather, jagged and rough. Bare winter foliage surrounded the area and naked trees trembled in the powerful winds whipping off the Hudson. I parked in a small clearing above the cliffs and stepped out of the SUV. It was just getting dark, still snowing heavily. I walked to the edge of the cliffs. There was no guardrail or fence. A locked gate behind Dracol's residence opened onto a snow-cleared, flagstone path leading from the gate directly to the cliffs. It would be just a simple matter of opening this gate and walking fifty steps or so to get to the cliffs. . . .

None of this surprised me, and I was pretty sure Anne Fitzgerald was at the bottom of the river. I moved to the very edge of the cliffs. The drop went straight down, and there was no beach or rocky area where a body might get caught or hung up. I picked up a heavy boulder and dropped it into the water, and it disappeared into the river with a large splash. I went and got my camera and took a dozen photographs of the cliffs and the rear of the house from different angles, stood and stared at the water, the wind causing my eyes to tear.

I could just make out the George Washington Bridge, ghostlike off to the left, majestic and stately in the gathering gloom. It was the perfect place to get rid of a body. There were no other homes about. No one to see anything. Quiet like a country graveyard at midnight.

I thought of Dracol, tall and pale and arrogant with those pointed teeth, carrying a body to the edge and casting it into the secret-holding Hudson. I turned and slowly made my way back to my SUV, my mind reeling with the ghastly implications of all this. As I reached my wheels, I thought I saw movement in the thick foliage, a pale face for a brief moment. I stood still and strained to see. The wind blurred my vision. I had this uneasy feeling that I was being watched.

I slid into my SUV and slowly returned to Dracol's house, checking my rearview as I went. Now the shutters of some of the windows were open and butter-colored lights were on inside, which seemed to melt out onto the snow.

I parked right in the driveway at the front entrance, wanting him to know I was here if he didn't know already; that I was not going to go away; that I would be a thorn in his side. An oil truck pulled up and made a delivery. The front door soon opened and a tall, broad-shouldered woman as white as chalk walked down the three front steps and straight toward me. She reached the locked gates and opened them electronically. Her lips were purple. She had unblinking mean eyes. I rolled down the window.

"Evening," I said.

Speaking with a heavy accent, she said, "Master Santos would inviting you for ze tea."

"How nice. I'd be honored."

"Please to parking your car in the drive," she said, which I did, but before I got out of the SUV I called Louise and told her where I was going, then followed purple lips toward the front door. She was definitely the woman who had greeted Anne and whom we had heard on the cassette in Anne's closet.

"My name's Frank De Nardo," I said, trying to make conversation.

"I am Cassandra."

"It's a pleasure. I'm looking for Anne Fitzgerald, Cassandra. She's been missing for five weeks."

"Yes, I've heard, how sad. I met her. A very nice woman. I hope notzing bad happened to her," she said.

"So does her father."

"Ze world has become such ze dangerous place," she said, and I got a glimpse of her pointed canines.

"It's always been a dangerous place, since Adam and Eve," I said.

She led me into the living room. There was a roaring fire going in the fireplace. All the furnishings were Gothic antiques, dark and gloomy. Like a funeral home. Somewhere mixed in with the smell of burning wood, I was sure I could discern the distinct odor of blood. Images of Carole in the morgue came to me. "He'll be right with you. How would you liking your tea?" she asked.

"Just plain," I said. She went away. The walls were covered with paintings in glittering gold and red frames. All of them had something to do with the macabre—with vampires, werewolves, sexual sadism, and deviance. They were, I realized, by some of the greatest painters the world has ever known—by Goya and Degas, Titian, Renoir, Pissarro, Monet, and Giotto.

In one painting, a vampire chased a naked woman through a swamp lit by a frowning quarter moon; in another, a mustached vampire with bloodshot eyes stood at the battlements of a Venice castle; in still another, a painting by Goya, voluptuous female vampires fed on baby Jesus in the manger. There was also a perverted rendition of the Little Red Riding Hood fairy tale by Balthus, and a large canvas by Hieronymus Bosch that masterfully depicted all kinds of sexual debauchery, horrific mutilations. Amazing stuff. I never saw such art and stared at the painting, wondering where Bosch had gotten the inspiration for such monstrous thoughts and images. He had seen—and apparently knew well—a part of human nature few are privy to.

"Good evening, Mr. De Nardo," Dracol said as he entered the room through a doorway hidden behind a bookcase as silently as a puff of smoke, tall and thin and pale, dressed all in black, obviously not happy to see me.

"Nice of you to join me. What a pleasant surprise," he said, his voice like the hiss of a venomous snake, his large black eyes not leaving mine.

"Pleasure's mine."

"I admire your persistence," he said. "It's refreshing to meet someone so dedicated to what they do in this day and age where everyone is looking for shortcuts."

"Nice of you to say. I was admiring your art collection. Are they all real?"

"Don't be foolish. Of course."

"Must be worth a fortune."

"Actually, they are priceless."

"You must be very rich."

"I manage."

"I'm impressed."

"So you are an art lover, too . . . a real Renaissance man."

"Only from afar. I spoke with your lawyer earlier."

"I've heard. Seems you have an uncle who is a big shot in the Mafia. How interesting."

"Seems like you aren't willing to take a lie-detector test—I find that interesting."

"As I told you, such a decision would be up to my attorneys."

"I remember."

He gestured to large burgundy velvet lounges to either side of the stone fireplace. We both sat. The wood in the fire crackled. Its heat felt good. He silently stared at me. He didn't like anything about me, and it was all over his white face plain as day. He looked at me, and I looked right back at him.

"I'm wondering if you are wearing a wire," he said.

"In fact, I'm not. I had no idea we'd be having tea and a chat."

"Seems to me you are the kind of man who would be prepared for all possibilities."

"Perhaps, but I'm not wired."

"Mind if I check? I want to know if I'm being recorded."

"Not too trusting, are you? Sure, go ahead and check."

He rang a little golden bell on the table next to his chair. The huge black guy I had first seen in his office entered. I stood. He searched me well. He found my Beretta but not the derringer or my knife.

"He's armed," he told Dracol, "but not wired."

"Thank you, Oliver," Dracol said, and Oliver the giant left. I sat back down. He stared at me some more down his long, straight nose, like I was an annoying fly and he was about to swat me. Cassandra brought the tea on a large silver platter. I didn't want to drink the tea. The last thing I was going to do was allow these weirdos to slip me a Mickey.

"I see you are reticent to drink your tea," he said.

"Put yourself in my shoes," I said.

"Where I come from, it would be bad manners to poison an invited guest. I know the Mafia does such things, but I don't. I've been accused of many improprieties, but never bad manners." I drank the tea, though only a small sip, to shut him up.

"Bravo," he said. "You still apparently believe I had something to do with Ms. Fitzgerald's disappearance."

"You could say that."

"Why in God's name would I harm a journalist whose well-connected employers knew very well that she was in my company?"

"That's a good question. I'm thinking it's because you think you are above the law; or maybe Anne found out something about you that you didn't want to be made public. She was very good at finding out things, I'm told."

"Yes, that's obvious from her work, but she left here at about four A.M. on the morning of December 7, and we never saw her again. I suggest you see what other stories she was working on. You might very well find some clues that can help you. I *cannot* help you," he said like he was slamming a heavy door in my face.

"I'm sure you know I found out that you've

130

been questioned about the disappearances of women in Europe."

"I've never been convicted of anything. As I told you, I'm the ideal scapegoat . . . as evidenced by your very presence here this evening."

"Yeah, well, where there's smoke, there's usually fire."

Again, he stared at me long and hard with his buggy, Charles Manson shark eyes.

"I hear there were police reports about you as far back as nineteen eighty-six," I said.

"You've been a busy bee, haven't you?" he said, a slight smile filled with not-too-subtle malice playing on his lips, his canines suddenly visible. No matter how many times I saw those stupid teeth, I would never get used to them. I remembered Belladonna, her kisses, her canines . . . *uffa*.

"What happened to Anne, Dracol?"

"I have no idea."

"And so take a lie-detector test and prove it."

"If that will make you happy and get you out of my life, I will, okay?"

"It will make me happy. How about tomorrow? I can have an expert come out. What time would be convenient for you?"

"You really are pushy."

"That's the only way you get results in what I do."

"I'd expect so. If I ever need a private investigator, I'll surely contact you. I don't get up until five. Let's say at seven-thirty."

"Fine. I'd appreciate it. Thank you."

The doorbell rang. He stood up. "Some associates from Europe are here," he said. "I must tend to them."

"I'll be on my way. Thanks for the tea and your time.

"By the way, is there really an underground lake below your castle in Romania?" I asked, almost as an afterthought. He did not like that question. His cheeks actually reddened. He looked as if I'd slapped him.

"In fact, there is," he said.

"Why were you chased out of Sighisoara by the townspeople?" I said.

"I wasn't chased," he said. "I left because a mob of criminals came to the castle to rob and pillage."

"I understand this 'mob' were the relatives of missing women and young girls."

"Nonsense. That's a vicious lie perpetrated by my family's enemies; by the Communists—a bunch of mindless thugs."

"I'm curious—are you really related to Vlad Tepes?"

"I am a direct descendant of his brother Radu," he told me with a straight face, and I could feel the little hairs on my back stand at attention.

He went on. "My ancestor was a hero. He bravely fought against the Turks and tirelessly defended the honor of the people of Wallachia— of Romania."

"*Hello*—he was also the original Dracula," I said.

"That's all nonsense, only in fiction. In reality,

YES! ☐

Sign me up for the Leisure Horror Book Club and send my TWO FREE BOOKS! If I choose to stay in the club, I will pay only $8.50* each month, a savings of $5.48!

YES! ☐

Sign me up for the Leisure Thriller Book Club and send my TWO FREE BOOKS! If I choose to stay in the club, I will pay only $8.50* each month, a savings of $5.48!

NAME: _____

ADDRESS: _____

_____

TELEPHONE: _____

E-MAIL: _____

☐ **I WANT TO PAY BY CREDIT CARD.**

☐ VISA   ☐ MasterCard.   ☐ DISCOVER

ACCOUNT #: _____

EXPIRATION DATE: _____

SIGNATURE: _____

Send this card along with $2.00 shipping & handling for each club you wish to join, to:

Horror/Thriller Book Clubs
20 Academy Street
Norwalk, CT 06850-4032

Or fax (must include credit card information!) to: 610.995.9274. You can also sign up online at www.dorchesterpub.com.

*Plus $2.00 for shipping. Offer open to residents of the U.S. and Canada only. Canadian residents please call 1.800.481.9191 for pricing information.

If under 18, a parent or guardian must sign. Terms, prices and conditions subject to change. Subscription subject to acceptance. Dorchester Publishing reserves the right to reject any order or cancel any subscription.

JOIN NOW!

he was a brave, patriotic hero fighting against the hordes of bloodthirsty Turks who tortured, raped, and murdered our people. They left nothing alive in their wake. That's the real truth if you are truly interested."

For the first time, he was becoming emotional. I had apparently pushed a sensitive button. I planned to push it some more. "Did he really impale people while he had dinner and watched them suffer?"

"He impaled his enemies—the Turks and those who conspired against him. But that was a common way to get rid of your enemies back then in that part of Europe. Just look at what the Romans did, the brutality of the Coliseum—how they crucified their enemies, many thousands of them. They crucified Jesus Christ himself. Point is that that kind of brutality, over the ages, was not so unusual nor uncommon in Europe. See *The Passion of the Christ* if you doubt me," he said.

"I've already seen it. You mentioned that Carole Smith might have been murdered by satanic vampires. Can you give me a name, a place, a phone number—anything?"

"Like I said, there are many of them spread out all over the globe."

"You know who she was hanging out with?"

"I don't know. I was forced to ask her to leave and have no idea where she ended up."

"Why did you ask her to leave?"

"She broke the rules; she had no sense of proportion or propriety."

"What rules?"

"She prostituted herself for drugs, and she allowed herself to be fed on indiscriminately. I really must tend to my guests now."

"Thank you for your time. We'll see you tomorrow, then." We both walked toward the front door.

As I passed the living room, I caught a quick glimpse of a cluster of pale-faced people in black sitting and standing, and talking in hushed tones. They lit up like Christmas trees and bowed their heads when they saw Santos, as if he were the Pope himself. Cassandra showed me to the door. I thanked her for the tea and left. It was good to be back outside.

CHAPTER NINE

Thinking Dracol was a cunning psychopath the likes of which I had never even heard of, I carefully drove back to New York. The road was slippery and the driving treacherous. It was still snowing hard. Cars were sliding into one another, hitting lampposts. Wondering how deep the water in the river was behind Dracol's house, I kept trying to use my cell phone, but I couldn't get a line.

When I arrived at my place, I found three messages on my machine. One was from Belladonna. "De Nardo," she said. "I just wanted to tell you what a lovely evening I had. I look forward to our rendezvous tonight."

I look forward to it, too, I thought.

John Fitzgerald said: "Hello, Mr. De Nardo. I hope I'm not bothering you. . . . I was just wondering if you made any kind of headway. Thank you." The third call was from Larry Alter: "I understand," he said, "you went up to Westchester and had tea with my client. I called to let you know that he's changed his mind and will in fact not be available for a lie-detector test at this juncture— I'm sorry. I trust this doesn't inconvenience you at all. Please, in the future, if you have any questions regarding Santos Dracol, be kind enough to direct them to me, not him. Thank you."

This didn't surprise me. I was half expecting it. I downloaded the photographs of the cliffs along the Hudson near Dracol's house from my camera to the computer. Then I got on the Net and found all kinds of maps of the Hudson River, and that the current of the Hudson moved both south and north with the ebbs of the tide, and a body could have easily have floated downstream from Dracol's place and ended up near the G.W. Bridge. It was coming together. The water near Hastings-on-Hudson was 200 to 250 feet deep. I stood up and slowly paced back and forth.

Before I became a New York City cop, I was a sergeant in the Navy SEALs. As I said, I've always loved the ocean and I enlisted in the Navy and asked for placement in the SEALs because I knew I'd be near the sea and being a SEAL was challenging and involved stealth and cunning, which I found particularly appealing. It was in the Navy that I started boxing in the ring, and while I was in the service, I also became tight with Bobby Marino.

Bobby, like me, comes from Brooklyn and, like me, he'd gotten in some trouble with the law as a teen and joined the Navy to get out of Brooklyn and 'see the world,' as we used to say. These days, Bobby runs a diving school from a loft on Fourteenth Street. I called him on his cell phone and found him at his shop and told him that I had to check out the floor of the Hudson River, which ran parallel to Westchester.

"In this weather?"

"It's got to be done ASAP. I don't have a choice."

"What are you looking for?"

"Bodies."

"Somehow that doesn't surprise me. How deep are we talking about?"

"Between two hundred and two-fifty."

"Forget about diving in this weather. Use the Fish Cam. I got two of them."

"That's what I was thinking."

A Fish Cam is a torpedo-shaped camera that can be lowered to just about any depth. Bobby keeps his boat, a thirty-nine-foot Bertram, at the Seventy-ninth Street Boat Basin, and I asked him if we could use it to get to the waters behind Dracol's house. He said that wouldn't be a problem— weather permitting. We made plans to talk in the early A.M.

I didn't bother calling Alter back. I did, however, return John Fitzgerald's call and ran down for him all that had occurred since we last spoke, leaving out Belladonna. Nor did I mention that I was thinking Santos Dracol had his own under-water graveyard. I didn't ask him anything about his police file; I wanted to read it before I mentioned it. I promised I'd keep him posted and soon hung up, put my coat on, and walked back to Anne's apartment, wanting to search it without John Fitzgerald looking over my shoulder.

I carefully went over the whole place again. I didn't learn anything that could move this thing forward, though I kept having this gnawing sensation that I was missing something. I went back to the bookcase and started looking at every single book, opening them, shaking pages. I spent nearly two hours doing that but found nothing except some naked photographs of a very tan Anne on a white beach somewhere. On the back of the photo it said: *Agari Beach Mykonos*. I slowly put on my coat and hat and left, taking with me a book about Romania and a biography of Vlad Tepes. It was called *The Real Dracula*.

Next I knocked on the doors of all her neighbors, and the few I found home were polite and helpful and told me, after I showed them my ID, that none of them had seen or heard anything out of the ordinary. The building was a condo, and they all knew Anne well and had nice things to say about her—how sweet and helpful she was, what a "good neighbor" she was.

Outside, it was snowing harder than ever. An ice-cold wind off the nearby Hudson River came tearing down the block. I stopped at the Saigon Grill on Amsterdam Avenue and had some coconut-shrimp soup and slowly made my way home, looking over my shoulder as I went. I kept having this gnawing feeling that I was being tailed, but I didn't see anyone suspicious.

When I arrived at my place, the first thing I did was try to reach Marco Vacaresco in Bucharest. This time his daughter, Carolina, answered. She could barely speak English, but I managed to tell her who I was and that I would like to speak to her father. She said he was playing cards at a friend's house but should return within the hour. I thanked her, hung up, and turned on The Weather Channel to see what was predicted for tomorrow—not good: strong winds, a lot of snow. "A mother of a winter storm," they forecasted. I went and took a hot Epsom-salt bath. My arthritis was acting up, and the wet heat felt good. When I finished soaking and thinking this thing out, I took a few aspirins, went back to my desk, and again phoned Vacaresco. This time he answered and told me he was waiting for me to call. Speaking with a heavy accent, he said, "You know, I'm not surprised to hear a detective is calling all the way from the great city of New York because of Santos Dracol. In my heart, I know what kind of beast this man truly is. I try to forget; I try not to think about him—but that is impossible. I pray to Jesus. I light candles in church and ask that God will stop him. That God would send someone to finally put an end to his evil. He is a killer of the worst kind. Do you know, Mr. De Nardo, about the poisoned blood that runs in his veins?"

"You mean that he is related way back to Vlad Dracul?"

"Ha-ha, that's the least of it," he said. "He is a direct descendant of Vlad's younger brother, Radu the Handsome. Vlad was a choirboy next to Radu the Handsome."

"How do you mean? What did he do?"

"What Vlad was fond of doing was impaling people through the body in an upright position, you understand?"

"I've seen sketches of it on the Internet."

"Ah, yes, but listen, Mr. De Nardo—"

"Please, sir—Frank."

"Yes, okay, Frank, thank you. Please listen: Radu would impale people on top of one another, through the belly button—ten, fifteen people on top of each another, children too, whole families. He would make sure that their spines weren't damaged so the pain stayed sharp longer. He personally skinned people alive. For him this was lovemaking. This is the kind of beast whose blood courses in the veins of Santos Dracol. I tell you this is true. You must be so very careful with him. He has, you see, the preternatural abilities."

"You mean like he can change form and all the rest?" I said, thinking Vacaresco had seen too many horror movies.

"Yes, yes, exactly," he said with sober conviction. After hearing him say that, I suspected everything the man said.

He went on. "He is not a man, he is a monster—he only looks human. He is a demon from hell that took on the guise of a human being. He is of Satan. His family made a pact with Satan long ago, you see," he said.

Yeah, sure, I thought, *and I've got this great bridge I can sell you for next to nothing.*

"To kill him, you must cut out his heart and decapitate him, and you must make certain to then destroy the head. If you do not, the body will surely try to find it and reattach it. This is a creature created by the devil himself, I tell you—you understand?"

"Yes, I understand," I said, sitting back, the wind howling. He began to say something more about a spike, but the phone suddenly went dead, no dial tone—nothing. I tried calling him on my cell but couldn't get through.

My eyes moved to the windows overlooking the yard, and I swear I thought I saw a pale face out there in the dark; gave me goose bumps. I stood and walked to the window, peered out; whatever I thought I saw was gone. I stood there staring out the window.

I put on my coat and slowly walked out into the yard. There was no one, no tracks in the snow. Thinking I was beginning to see things, losing it, I started back inside and noticed the broken phone line. Apparently, a chunk of ice had fallen and snapped the line . . . *strange*. I went inside, grabbed my cell phone, and tried calling Vacaresco from the yard. This time I was able to get through, but the connection was filled with static. I managed to tell him that we were having a snowstorm and that my phone line had been broken, that I would call him back on a land phone as soon as possible.

"Come to Romania," he said, his voice fading in and out. "I will show you . . . will teach . . . the evidence . . . you need to know—" and the connection was lost.

I tried to reach him again but couldn't get through. I even went up on the roof and tried up there, without luck. Because the phone line was down, I couldn't get on the Web either. Remembering the urgency and dread in Vacaresco's voice, I began looking through the book on Vlad Tepes. As I was doing that, the doorbell rang. It was one of Captain Roe's guys with John Fitzgerald's police record. I thanked him for bringing it over, went back to my desk, and read the report. It said that Fitzgerald had a drinking problem, and that he had killed a man in a bar in Montauk called the Shagwon Inn. He had gotten into a fight and hit the guy in the head with a cue stick, was sentenced to seven to twenty years, did six years, and was released. It said, too, that he had been arrested for hitting his wife, presumably Anne's mother, on two occasions, and that he did another sixty days for these infractions. The crimes were committed a long time ago: The killing took place in 1968 and the domestics in 1979. Since then, he wasn't in any kind of trouble with the law. I thought about calling him up to discuss his record, but decided against it. At this juncture, none of this seemed linked in any way to Anne's disappearance, and a lot of people have trouble with the law early on in life. I myself did. People change. But still, I knew now that John Fitzgerald obviously had a bad temper; shouldn't drink.

I began reading the book on Vlad Tepes. I learned that *Dracul,* in Romanian, meant "dragon," and that Tepes had been called Dracula, or Son of The Dragon, because of his sadistic ferocity in war. In a letter to the Hungarian king for military help in 1466, Vlad Dracula had written: *I have killed men and women, old and young . . . 23,884 Turks and Bulgarians without counting those whom we burned alive in their homes.* With this letter Vlad had also sent sacks filled with human heads, noses, and ears to prove the accuracy of his body count. There was no mention, however, of his younger brother, Radu the Handsome.

If Santos Dracol really was related to these people—which I had my doubts about—he could very well, I was thinking, have a genetic propensity for irrational violence and severe sexual deviance; there are people born with loose screws and nuts. I wrote a note to Louise that she should call the phone company and have them send someone out to fix the phone line right away. Again I tried to reach Marco Vacaresco, but I still couldn't get through. By now it was nearly time to meet Belladonna, and I dressed and left the house and fought against frigid, muscle-bound winds as I made my back to my wheels. I turned around to see if I was being followed, but I couldn't see more than fifty feet with all the snow and wind in my face. I bought myself a double espresso on Broadway and headed downtown, drinking my coffee and remembering what Vacaresco had told me. I turned on the news. The weather report said we were in the middle of a snowstorm that would last for two more days; that three feet of snow and tornado-like winds were expected. I really wanted to see what was in the waters behind Dracol's place, but with this storm that wasn't possible.

When I arrived at the club, a long line of snow-covered limos was out front. One of the doormen told me there was a party going on for a heavy-metal band called Blood Red, and that Marilyn Manson was inside. Wearing a gorgeous black velvet dress, Belladonna came out a little after two o'clock and told me she would be at least a half hour longer, that someone had been hurt in a "catfight." I told her I'd wait, no problem. She kissed me and smiled, showing me those pointed teeth of hers, and hurried back inside.

I thought of what we'd done the night before, grainy black-and-white images of it slowly moving before my eyes. I didn't want to remember; I tried to push the memories away, but that proved easier said than done. I picked up the book about Vlad Tepes.

He's a real vampire. Come to Romania—I will show you, I remembered Vacaresco saying as I now watched Dracol walk out of the club surrounded by an entourage of pale-faced people in black, some of whom I had seen at his home earlier. He stared in my direction for a few moments. They got into one of the limos and disappeared into the storm-filled night, as a giant lightning bolt ripped open the sky above the nearby Hudson River and thunder rumbled across the water as though a huge cannon had been fired. I thought of following them, but I stayed put and waited for Belladonna, knowing she had answers to questions circling inside my head like buzzards over something dead.

I turned up the volume of the music and listened to Beethoven's Fifth Symphony, the snow and winds seeming to move with the dramatic highs and lows of the piece. An ambulance arrived and a couple of medics in orange jumpsuits leaped out of it and hurried into the club with a stretcher. In a few minutes, they came out with a girl strapped to the gurney, put her in the ambulance, and took off. Belladonna soon walked out of the club and made her way over. I opened the door for her.

"I'm sorry," she said as she got in. "These crazed groupies of one of the musicians got into a fight—stupid, mixed-up girls. You have no idea how lost some of these people are." That was funny coming from her. She hugged me and kissed me on the lips. She tasted sweet, like dark rum. "I'm hungry," she said.

"Don't look at me," I said.

145

"I want to thank you for giving me that trust. All day long, you've been inside me. You see how *intimate* it can be."

"Not quite," I said.

"You will," she said. "I really am hungry. Would you like to go for something to eat in Chinatown? I know a great place—nothing fancy, but the food is wonderful."

"Let's go," I said, and we started out.

"Did you think of me today?" she asked.

"That's all I've been thinking about. Let me ask you something—do you believe that there are *real vampires* . . . I mean, like the supernatural kind?"

She became serious. The smile that had been playing on her lips suddenly went away.

"I believe there were," she said, "but not in modern times . . ."

"Could Dracol be one?"

"No . . . as far as I know, anyway," she said.

"I can tell you this: He's pissed that I slept with you," she added.

"You told him? Why'd you tell him?"

"He asked, and I don't lie—that's why. He's just jealous, but he'll get over it. Truth is, he's got harems all over the place. You wouldn't believe how women literally line up for him; it's actually quite amazing."

"Is he really related to Vlad Tepes?"

"Far as I know he is."

"Have you personally ever seen him hurt anyone, Belladonna?"

"Not, really . . . no."

"What's not really?"

"I mean, I've seen him dominate bottoms, but they wanted to be abused—and he accommodated them."

"Abused how?"

"Degraded," she said. "Bottoms thrive on degradation. It's their sunrise and sunset."

"But not physically abused?"

"No, I've not seen that. Enough about him, okay?"

"Sure, no problem."

We arrived at the restaurant. It was called Huey Chow's, on Mulberry Street just off Canal. Inside it was packed with an eclectic group of people—punk rockers, slick uptowners, burly night workmen going off and on duty. We had to wait five minutes for a table. People kept coming over to Belladonna and giving her hugs and kisses. People lit up when they saw her. She was popular, all right. She and I made an odd couple, me with my hard face and suspicious cop-eyes, and her with that incredible white skin, beautiful face, and those pointed canines. Even the stoic Chinese guy who owned the place, Huey Chow, a little old man with a face as lined as a raisin, gave her a big snaggle-toothed smile and hug when he saw her.

"Hellooo, Ms. Belladonna. Hellooo, Ms. Belladonna. How are you?" he said, and he shook my hand. "So nice to see you.

"You are a so-very-lucky man. She most very beautiful woman in all New York."

"Yes, I know," I said. He said we'd get the next table and hurried away.

"You really are a vampire with personality," I said. "You should have your own reality television show."

"I'm in public relations," she said. Huey found us a small corner table in the back.

"This very nice quiet special table only for you," he said. She ordered vegetable noodle soup with ginger scallops, and I had the same.

"I'm curious," she said. "Why are you asking me if Santos is preternatural?"

"I have feelers out about him and I'm . . . hearing things."

"Let me give you some advice: There are all kinds of bizarre rumors and incredibly exaggerated stories about him and his family. Don't go believing everything you hear."

I took her hand and held it, leaned forward. "Belladonna, look me in the eyes and tell me what you really think. Could he be killing people for their blood? Because he enjoys killing?"

"I have never seen or heard anything to make me believe something like that," she said with conviction. Our soup came. It was served in huge white bowls brimming with colorful vegetables, buckwheat noodles, and grilled scallops. And it was delicious. We ate quietly. People kept coming in the front door. I asked Belladonna if she'd ever been to Romania.

"No—for the most part, it's a big tourist trap.

Thousands of people a week go to see where the *famous* Dracula lived. It all began with Bram Stoker's book. He loosely based his Count Dracula character on Vlad, but he never even set foot in Romania. It's all made up. As a piece of fiction, it's quite brilliant. I read it a half-dozen times before I was fifteen, but it can be a dangerous book for a young person—particularly an impressionable girl—can put strange thoughts in your head; certainly give you nightmares. But my grandparents explained what it really was—fiction, made up, and it never particularly troubled me . . . in fact, I loved it. I still read passages from it now and then. Have you read it?"

"I've not, but I'm thinking I should."

"Yes, you really should. You'd appreciate it. It's hard to put down. It kind of hypnotizes you. It's never been out of print; one of the most popular books of all time."

"You think maybe it's possible that Bram Stoker heard things . . . I mean, learned secrets about the Dracol family, about preternatural vampires, and wrote the truth *disguised* as fiction? You know, like what Shakespeare did with his *Romeo and Juliet.*"

"What do you mean?"

"This whole thing of rising from the dead. You remember how Juliet took a poison which simulated death and how she was supposed to be given the antidote so she could rise from the dead to be with Romeo and they could flee their warring families and live happily ever after?"

"Yes."

"Well, that's what actually happened with Jesus Christ."

"How do you mean?" she said, leaning forward, her high, wide brow creasing slightly.

"What happened was, before Jesus was crucified, one of his followers administered a dose of tetrodotoxin to him by rubbing it into his open wounds. It was all over the famous towel that Magdalene used when he was on the way to the cross. Tetrodotoxin simulates death. It stops the heart and breathing—the whole nine yards. And later, when the Romans took his lifeless body down, Jesus' followers administered the antidote, datura, which brought him back to life. And that's how he was able to rise from the dead. He was given a drug—datura."

"I never heard any of this."

"Well, Shakespeare definitely did, and he used it masterfully in his immortal story of lost love."

"I always felt all that rising from the dead was a bunch of hocus-pocus."

"Oh, he rose from the dead, but with the help of a drug. It's made from a mushroom. Tetrodotoxin comes from the West Indian puffer fish. That's how zombies—the living dead—are made in Haiti, you see."

"How'd you find all this out?"

"I'm a detective. My business is the business of crime and deceit in all its varied forms. So what I'm saying is that maybe Bram Stoker somehow learned the truth about preternatural vampires and wrote it like it truly was—*disguised* as fiction."

"Hmm. . . . Certainly possible.

"I spoke to a retired police inspector in Romania that told me Santos was suspected of killing women there."

"Like I told you, there are all kinds of exaggerated rumors about him," she said.

"You don't think that possible?" I asked.

She looked at me long and hard.

". . . No, I don't," she finally said.

"He invited me to come to Romania. He said he'd show me proof that Santos is a serial killer."

"A serial killer?"

"Yes."

"Really?"

"Yes."

"Well, if you go, I'd like to tag along, if you don't mind. I need to get away. The club is very wearing after a time. Truth is, I'm thinking of doing something else. Maybe start a Web site business to provide things for the vamp community."

"I'm not going to Romania anytime soon. I'm curious—where do your people come from?"

"On my mother's side, Russia, and on my father's side, Scotland."

"And where'd you get those cheekbones?"

"The Russian side. There were Tartars mixed in there way back. This case all you are working on?"

"It's got most of my attention right now. I've got a small agency, and I like it that way."

"It must be exciting. It's something I'd really like to do—I mean, be a P.I."

"A lot of detective work—in fact, most of it—is all about wearing down shoe leather and asking people questions—actually, not so exciting. Was Marilyn Manson really there tonight?"

"Yeah, musicians, rock stars, all the heavy-metal people just love the place. We make certain to protect their privacy, never allow any press in—any cameras. This Romanian policeman who told you Santos was suspected of killing women—did he say Santos had preternatural powers?"

"Yes, he did."

"I wouldn't give too much credence to any-thing he says," she said.

We finished our soup, had some green tea, ice cream. She told me she was in the mood for a ci-gar. "I know," she said, "a great little place nearby that sells real Havanas—would you like to go?"

"You're a bad influence on me," I said, and paid the check. Huey Chow gave her a big hug and we left and went to this place called the Viper Bar a block north of the restaurant. On the ground floor, it was an all-night espresso and dessert place, but downstairs, behind a wall of bottles, there was an after-hours VIP room with fancy leather chairs and couches and Persian car-pets on the floor, soft music playing. Beautiful, scantily clad women served drinks. The cigars were housed in a large humidor room made of cedar wood. We each chose a Romeo and Juliet, found a comfortable place to sit, and lit up. I enjoy a good cigar now and then, and it's hard to beat a Romeo and Juliet. Belladonna ordered Rémy, Louie the XIII cognac for both of us. When the cognac came, we touched glasses; "to the night," she said, and we drank. I never tasted such fine cognac. It was silky-smooth and fiery at the same time as it slowly went down. The cigar and the cognac gave me a pleasant buzz. I felt guilty for feeling so good. She leaned over and purred like a kitten into my neck, ever so gently kissed my lower lip. She moved closer. I put my arm around her. Some couple.

"I'm wondering why you aren't taken," I said.

"Most all the people I meet at the club are flaky in one way or another, and I'm not about to get mixed up with any of the musicians that are always hitting on me. . . . I did have a man—a very good man—but he was killed. He was one of the pilots on the Concorde that went down at the Paris airport . . . you remember?"

"Yes, a while back."

"Well, he was one of the two pilots."

"I'm sorry. Were you married?"

"No. But he stayed with me when he was in New York, and I stayed at his place outside of Paris a couple of months a year. That's the last time I had a serious relationship."

"Was he, if you don't mind my asking, a blood drinker?"

"No. I loved him very much."

"Seems you still do."

"I do, yes. Because someone dies, you don't stop loving them. I never had the chance to say good-bye. What a waste of a beautiful man. You know, Frank De Nardo, life on this planet can really suck."

"I know all about it," I said, thinking about my murdered wife, the ghastly things people do to each other, and we silently toasted, finished our first round, and ordered another.

"And you," she said. "Why aren't you taken?"

I wanted to tell her about Barbara's murder, how she had been killed for her bike in Central Park—a bike I had just given her for her birthday—how her loss changed me as a man, made me bitter and kept me from making a commitment, getting involved, pursuing a relationship. But I just looked at her and said nothing. Understanding my silence, she put her head on my shoulder.

"I've been hungry for you all day, De Nardo. Let's go, okay?" she said.

"We're out of here," I said, paid the check, and we left and without another word went straight back to her loft. In the elevator, she came to me and we began making love right there. By the time we reached her floor, she was naked as a jay-bird. I picked her up and carried her inside.

PART TWO

CHAPTER TEN

My cell phone suddenly woke me up. It was Bobby Marino.

"Frank," he said, "there's no way we can use the boat today. There's a ten-foot swell, and it looks like it's going to be this way for a few more days. We've got a huge storm front hitting us from Canada. I'm sorry, pal."

We made plans to talk later in the day; I thanked him for the call and hung up. I was afraid the weather would be a problem. Belladonna, to my right, slowly sat up in her coffin— a sobering sight no matter how many times I saw it. "Are you going fishing?" she asked.

"Why would you ask that?"

"I heard you talking about a boat."

"No, I'm not. Well, I guess in a sense I am, but not conventional fishing," I said, and no more. I did not want her to know what I was thinking about the river behind Dracol's property.

She said, "Please be so very careful in every-

157

thing you do. This is a serious business that you've gotten involved with here. I know you've walked some mean streets, but this is *different*."

"I know. Thanks for the advice," I said, looking at the second Band-Aid on my hand, her crystal glass still holding the remnants of my blood, which I'd freely given her. It was as if she'd put a spell on me, and as I thought about it, looked at her altar, she might very well have put a spell on me, I realized . . . if I believed in such things, which I don't. Least, I didn't.

"Would you like some tea or some of me?" she asked, stepping out of the coffin.

"I'd very much like some of both, but I've got to get uptown. I wanted to call you back yesterday and didn't have your number."

"I'll give you my card," she said, and I watched her walk across the room with her curves and white skin, and it was like seeing a perfect statue in a museum come to life and step off its pedestal. Her card was all red and said *Belladonna*, with a cell phone number and the insignia of a bat. "I have no land phone, just the cell, but I've got it with me most all the time," she said.

"I'll call you later," I said, hugged her, and was soon back in the elevator, remembering what we had done in it, though not feeling any kind of guilt anymore about being involved with her that way. It had been a very long time, far longer than I like to admit, since I had felt such passion for a woman. Most all my time has been taken up with my work, with other people's problems. Pretty much everyone that comes to me has a life-and-death situation, and it's an easy thing to get all caught up in it, your personal needs and desires becoming secondary. In the back of my mind somewhere, I had always imagined that I would find the right woman and have her next to me in my dream house near the ocean, surrounded by palm trees, beautiful sunsets, glorious mornings with colorful birds singing. But I never imagined she'd have pointed teeth and flesh as white as fresh snow. I laughed out loud at the thought of introducing Belladonna to my uncle Sal, my mother—my somewhat old-fashioned Italian family. How their eyes would open wide at the sight of her pointed teeth.

When I got outside, an ice-cold wind woke me right up. It was still snowing. It had gotten colder and everything had turned to ice, was hard and brittle, and I nearly slipped as I made my way to my SUV. Driving uptown was difficult. As I reached Eighth Street and Tenth Avenue, the idea that had brought this to a head came to me. I picked up my phone and called Bobby back.

"Bob, I've got a pressing situation here. I can't wait for the weather to get better. I was wondering if maybe I could lower the Fish Cam into the water from the cliffs. It's pretty much a straight drop, and there's nothing in the way," I explained.

"Sure. I've got plenty of line and can add an extension if necessary. The camera is built to get banged around."

"Can I borrow it?"

"Absolutely, but Frank, I can't get away today."

"No problem. I'll come get it now, if that's all right?"

"Okay, buddy, I'm waiting on you," he said. "I'll be at the loft."

I stopped at a deli, bought an egg sandwich and coffee, and drove over to Bob's place, in a hurry to get the Fish Cam in the water. I had this kind of itchy-hinky feeling at the nape of my neck that usually meant I was onto something.

I parked, went up one flight of stairs to Bobby's loft, and opened the door. He was talking on the phone. Bobby is a tall, muscular man with a serious face. He seems to be scowling all the time, but he is a real sweet guy with a heart of gold, a loyal, dedicated friend. He used to have a thick mop of black hair, which is now all salt and pepper. He hung up the phone. We hugged hello.

"How are you, Frank? What's new?"

"Same old same old."

"Seeing anyone?"

"Not . . . really."

"What's that mean?"

"I recently met someone—someone very . . . *different*."

"Great, bring her over for dinner. Rose and the kids would love to see you."

"I don't think so."

"Why not?"

"Let's just say she's, ahhh, how do I put this . . . she's unorthodox."

"Not for nothing, she's got to be unorthodox if

she's interested in you," he said. "Frank, when are you going to settle down? You don't want to get old by yourself, do you, pal?"

"That's exactly what my mother's saying all the time. I'm already old," I said, feeling my arthritis acting up, my right hand stiffening. His phone rang. He picked it up, pointing to a large blue plastic box near the door. The Fish Cam, a small monitor and a lot of line, was in it. The wind blew so hard, it rattled the large windows of the shop. Bobby hung up and showed me how to work the camera. It was actually quite simple, designed so a child could operate it.

"I'm sure," he said, "you are going to need light if you are putting it into the Hudson. The camera has a fluorescent lightbulb. Just push this and you'll have a hundred and fifty watts pointing dead ahead."

"How far, more or less, will I be able to see?"

"If it isn't too murky a good twenty, thirty feet. The battery is brand new. You should be able to operate it for two hours with no problems."

I thanked him again, hugged him, and made tentative plans to come to his place for a home-cooked meal. Bobby's wife, Rosemary, is an excellent cook, and eating at Bobby's is always a treat. I soon left and started uptown. There were a few things I needed before I could go back to Westchester and properly do the job. When I arrived home, I found a note from Louise telling me she had to go to the dentist. I took two aspirin for my arthritis, a hot shower, dressed all in black wool, and put on thick waterproof boots. I packed a sawed-off shotgun in a leather bag with a second 9mm auto and soon left the house and drove over to the West Side Highway.

As I slowly made my way north, it began to snow so hard I could barely make out the river. I didn't see the George Washington Bridge until I was directly under it. The weather reports were saying we were being hit with the worst blizzard since 1969, and I believed them. I thought of turning back but decided to drive on. When I reached Hastings-on-Hudson, I went straight to the road that led down to the cliffs behind Dracol's place, hoping I could overcome the weather and get the job done. I decided to walk instead of drive to the cliffs. The last thing I wanted to do was get stuck in the snow in this desolate place. The winds furiously whipped about the trees and bushes.

I shut the engine and stepped out of the car. The weather was so bad, the winds so strong, the river so rough, I knew I'd not be able to use the camera properly, even be able to see the monitor, but still I made my way down to the cliffs, struggling against the winds. I could barely see my hand in front of my face, it was snowing that hard. I was angry that I'd driven all the way out for nothing and reluctantly returned to the car. As I struggled back, I sensed something moving on my left, turned, but didn't see anything. I slid into my SUV and carefully drove off. When I reached the parkway, I called Bobby and told him I couldn't use the equipment because of the blizzard and would have to hold on to it for a few days.

"No problemo," he said. "I've got two of them. Bring it back when you're finished. Try and make it this weekend—and bring your friend, too." I told him I'd see him soon. When I arrived home, Louise told me Captain Roe had phoned and I called him right back.

"Frank," he said, "the mother of the Smith girl we found in the river was here a little while ago. She came up from New Orleans to see if we found out anything new. She's a really sweet woman, and I thought it might be helpful if you spoke to her, heard what she had to say. She's staying in the Best Western Hotel right over here on Broadway."

"I'll call her now."

"Frank, it was this woman who first linked Carole Smith to Dracol."

"Yeah, I remember. I'll contact her right away," I said, thanked him, made myself some tea, and called the hotel. She wasn't in. I left a message. Again I tried Marco Vacaresco, and this time he answered and I told him how my phone line had been down; that I'd not been able to call him right back.

"The woman," I explained, "who I was hired to find was a writer. She was doing a story on Dracol. We know she went to Romania, to Bucharest. Could she maybe have found some kind of proof about the things Dracol did there?"

"Most certainly. She might've come across something in the municipal records, but so much of all that was destroyed during the bad years of Nicolae Ceauşescu, another Romanian monster. But, really, it is no secret here in Romania what Santos Dracol is, you see."

"I'm curious—were Ceauşescu and Dracol friends?"

"Most definitely. Rivers of blood flowed because of Ceauşescu. This is one of the worst men in the history of the world, and he was a good friend of Dracol, you see. Two monsters . . . I tell you this true. You know, Ceauşescu was a sexual degenerate of the worst kind—both he and his wife, Elaina. We found a lot of pornography involving children and animals in the secret chambers of Ceauşescu palaces. He was fond of forcing whole families to have sex in front of a camera—then murdering them. I saw the films myself. For money, it was he who allowed Dracol to live in Romania with impunity, you see."

The other line rang. The machine picked up. It was Carole Smith's mother. I told Vacaresco I had to take another call. We made plans for me to phone him tomorrow. I picked up the second line. "Hello, Mrs. Smith," I said.

"Ah, so you are there."

"I was waiting for your call."

"Captain Roe told me that you are trying to put 'the fiend' where he belongs. I'd very much like to meet with you. I want you to know what really happened—what I know."

"I'd like that. Are you at the hotel now?"

"I am."

"I can meet you in the lobby in, say, fifteen minutes."

"I'd like that very much."

"I'm on my way," I said, and hung up. I tried to reach Belladonna, but she didn't answer her phone. I left a message for her to call, put on my coat and hat, and started toward Broadway, walking quickly, my mind playing over the things Vacaresco had told me.

I was nearly to Columbus Avenue when I spotted him, a pale gloomy-faced man wearing all black. He stepped out of a black Mercedes with tinted windows and started walking behind me. There was something about him, his white face, his body language, that caught and held my attention. He looked, I was thinking, like one of the men I'd seen in Dracol's house. I took a right on Columbus, and so did he. I made my way to Eighty-eighth and went west, and he did, too. On Broadway I began heading uptown, with him some fifty steps behind me. I was tempted to confront him but kept walking. Though, as I thought about it, I realized it would be a bad idea to let him see me meeting with Georgia Smith. I turned right on Eighty-ninth, entered a doorman building that was the width of the full block, and walked from one end to the other and exited on ninetieth. Then I doubled back to Broadway and saw him still waiting for me at Eighty-eighth Street.

I returned to Amsterdam Avenue, moved uptown to Ninety-third, hung a left, and started back to Broadway. It wasn't snowing as hard now, but the wind was relentless and people were slipping and falling all over the place. The frigid temperature and chilled winds had turned everything to glistening sheets of unfriendly ice. The Best Western Hotel is a moderately priced place at Ninety-fourth Street. I found her sitting in the lobby. She stood and moved toward me the moment I walked in the door.

"Mr. De Nardo?" she hopefully asked.

"Hello, Mrs. Smith," I said, taking off my glove and shaking her hand.

"It's so very nice of you to come out in the terrible weather. I never saw snow like this in my life."

"Worst storm we've had in a long time. How long will you be staying?"

"I have to leave tomorrow."

"There's a quiet place nearby where we can talk, just up Broadway."

"Okay, fine, let's go," she said, and we went outside and headed for the Key West Diner at Ninety-fifth. I took her arm and helped her walk on the slippery sidewalk. The wind blew my hat off, and I had to run half a block to catch it. The diner was nearly empty. We found a quiet table in the back. I sat down facing the entrance and ordered coffee for both of us. That's all she wanted. Greek music came from speakers near the ceiling.

"I first have to tell you," she said, "I have no

money to pay you. I need you to understand that."

"Don't concern yourself. I've already been retained by Anne Fitzgerald's father."

"But I want Dracol to pay for murdering my daughter. I know he killed her; I'm absolutely positive," she said with passionate certainty.

"He will. I'll make sure," I said, wanting to tell her that I'd been to the morgue, that I'd seen her daughter's corpse, how I had made a promise that I would find her killer—but I said nothing of this. She was a tall, thin woman with short gray hair. She might have once been beautiful, but now her face was lined and bitter and there were swollen circles under her light brown eyes. Her hands trembled. It seemed like she had some kind of nervous disorder. One of her lower front teeth was missing. She looked like she'd been through a hell of a lot in life, and most all of it was written on her face.

"I don't know where to begin," she said. "There's just so much to tell."

"I've got time," I told her. "This place is an all-night diner."

"You're very kind. I have some photographs of Carole I'd first like you to see," she said, taking a worn envelope out of her purse and opening it up. She handed me a photograph. I could barely take it, her hand was shaking so much.

"This is Carole when she was six," she said. I put on my glasses. For me it was always a difficult thing to see the photograph of a murder victim as a child. The adorable little girl I was looking at now was a far cry from what I'd seen in drawer number 201 at the morgue. In the photograph it was Christmas morning and Carole was in front of a lopsided Christmas tree, proudly holding a doll bigger than she was. She had a huge smile on her face and stick-straight blond hair glistening like polished gold in the flash of the camera.

"She was a beautiful child . . . so very well-behaved and polite; never cried as a little girl. She was always like this grown-up person in a little girl's body. In this one she was ten," she said, now handing me a color photograph. "I took it on Halloween." Here Carole was dressed as a scarecrow, a sparkling smile lighting up her face, the quintessential all-American teenager, though if you looked closely there was an unmistakable sadness in her eyes, about her face.

"She was very beautiful," I said.

"And this one was taken when she was seventeen," she said, and handed me a black-and-white photograph. It didn't look like the same girl. Something had dramatically changed her. There were dark circles under her eyes. She was pale, now had an angry razor slit where her beautiful smile had been.

"What happened to her," I asked, thinking she surely had become strung out on drugs; but it was far worse than that.

She took a long, deep breath. Her lower lip began to quiver.

"I want to first tell you that I'm sick—I've got Alzheimer's. I don't have too much time left before I won't be able to travel and . . . and remember things. I vowed that I would do all I could to make sure he doesn't get away with murdering my daughter like that . . . taking her blood, her life—discarding her in the river like an old shoe. This is the fourth time I've come to New York and the first time I feel there's any hope. And that hope is you, Mr. De Nardo."

"I'll do all I can," I said. "Please call me Frank."

"There's something about you," she said, "an intensity in your face—your eyes, that tells me you are the man that can do this. Whatever needs to be done."

"He'll have no peace with me around," I told her. Her right hand was trembling so hard now, she couldn't pick up the coffee cup.

"Let me begin at the beginning, if you don't mind."

"Please."

"I had very strict, religious parents, and I guess in the end it all stems from that. I had to be home right after school. I wasn't allowed to play with other children. I had to read the Bible for two hours every day, and if I didn't my father took a belt to me. He was a Baptist minister, and I swear I don't think I ever saw him laugh. All he ever did was talk about sin and temptation; how the Devil was always there, waiting to do you harm, to tempt you with sin, to get control of your soul. I could never figure out why the Devil would be so

169

interested in me, a little girl, but according to my father he was always there and he filled my head with images of hell and damnation if you sinned. I had nightmares all the time because of him. My mother was also a religious zealot, and like him she was stern and strict, and I often wondered how the heck the two of them ever managed to fall in love and have children. Every form of sex, to them, was a mortal sin.

"In my midteens I became very rebellious and started getting beatings pretty near every day from both my parents. My dress was too short, my sweater too tight, my hair too suggestive. One time my mother found a tube of lipstick—it was hidden in my bag—and oh my God, it was as though I committed a terrible sin, killed someone, and I got such a bad beating I couldn't go to school for two days. For weeks I had to cover the welts she put all over my back and legs. I wasn't allowed to leave the house 'cept to go to school.

"When I was fifteen I began making plans to run away, and on my sixteenth birthday I packed some clothes and left and never looked back. That's when I met Carole's father. He worked as a cabdriver in New Orleans. He saw me walking on the road with my suitcase, pulled over and offered me a ride, and the next thing I knew I was in his bed with him having sex.

"He was very handsome, smooth like butter, much older than me, but I kind of liked that—I mean that he, a grown-up, would be interested in me that way—with lust and desire. And I let him have me every which way he wanted, as much as he wanted. I guess it was all about my rebelling against my parents, all the punishment they had given me for nothing. I had no idea how wrong what he was doing really was. I was flattered by his attention, by his open carnal desire for me. What I should have done, I realize now, was go to the police and report him as a pervert, but what I did do was move in with him and let him . . . this is all very hard for me . . . I mean, to talk about it honestly, but I let him make a virtual sex slave out of me. I'm too embarrassed to tell you what he made me do . . . what I willingly did."

She stopped talking and stared at her coffee like I wasn't there, her hands trembling. I waited for her to come back from wherever she went. I had a feeling I knew where this was going. I felt a cold chill and looked toward the front of the restaurant to see him walk in the door, the pale-faced dude who had followed me. He took a seat at the counter and stared at me with a slight smirk on his face. I could just make out the points of his teeth. She said, "And before I knew it, I was pregnant. I didn't want to have a child—God, I was a child myself, but he wouldn't let me get an abortion and I gave birth to Carole that spring, on May 2. I had no idea what a mistake I was making. All my life I had been sheltered. I didn't have a clue about what the real world was like. The malice in people's hearts. My parents wouldn't even let me watch television. Anyway, I got a job as an accountant working for a bank four nights a week and he stayed home with Carole, and life wasn't all that bad for us. John turned out to be a loving, attentive father. I was pleasantly surprised. He could never get enough of Carole. It got so that he even took her in the cab with him when he went to work. Most all his customers just loved Carole there in the front seat and he'd always get better tips when she went along. She was such a beautiful, friendly child, people just took to her.

"Back then, if I had any complaints about John it was that he was oversexed. I mean, really oversexed. He wanted to have sex every hour on the hour. He used to come home on weekdays all the time just so he could have sex with me. I could never walk around the house naked, because he'd be on me like some kind of animal in heat. I thought as he got older it would lessen, but it didn't, just the opposite, and God forbid if I turned him down—he'd get violent, he'd break things, but he never hit Carole or me. In all the years I was with John, he never laid a hand on me, except during sex. I mean, he . . . he sometimes would tie me up and paddle me, but that was more, you know, consensual," she said, blushing red like a ripe strawberry.

"I didn't find out until after he died," she said, "that he was doing the same thing to my daughter, that he had started having sex with Carole when she was just a little girl. I didn't have a clue. He had somehow brainwashed her not to tell me, not to tell anyone, and she didn't. He convinced her that he was doing it, lusting after her that way, doing those things to her, because he loved her so much, and that if she ever told what he was doing he would be sent away to jail and she'd never see him again. . . .

"This is so hard for me, Mr. De Nardo . . . I hate to burden you with all my dirty laundry."

"You aren't burdening me at all. Please continue," I said in as soft a voice as I could muster, looking directly into her eyes, very aware of the pale-faced creep up front.

His open presence was, I knew, a threat. I don't take threats well.

"Well, so what happened was, I was at work and Carole called, all hysterical, saying that John had fallen on the floor and wasn't moving. She said she thought he had a heart attack and had already called for an ambulance. I left work right away, and when I got home I saw them . . . I saw them bringing John out in one of those black body bags, dead as a doorstop—and Carole was just hysterical. My God, I'll never forget how distraught she was. She was white like salt, went into shock and had to be sedated. She was thirteen years old.

"John died of a massive heart attack, but it wasn't until several months later that I found out what actually happened. My God . . . I don't know how I could have been so blind to it all. I believe that the Alzheimer's is punishment for what I let happen. I'm only forty-five, and soon I won't even know my own name. Hell of a thing." She stopped, began crying. I took her trembling hand and held it.

"Please, continue," I said, trying to draw her back, the wind howling outside, shaking the large glass panes of the front windows. I stared at him, and he stared right back.

"Carole," she said, "was never the same again. The child went out of her. Overnight she changed; she was all the time crying. I could sense that there was something more, some something under the surface.

"I see it now. I can see it all so clearly. I swear my heart rolls over like a poisoned animal at the sight of it. Even now, so many years later, I can see it all it like it was only yesterday. . . .

"So what happened was I went into her room one night and she was undressing, getting ready for bed, and she right away covered herself up. She had never been like that; it had always been difficult to keep clothes on her. But I did see her naked body for a moment, just a split second— and right off I saw what she was trying to hide. At first, though, it didn't register. Maybe I just couldn't conceive of it, but I knew she was pregnant and I demanded she let me see her. She absolutely refused, and we went at it and finally she showed me her body, and she *was* pregnant.

"I just went crazy. I slapped her and pulled her hair and hit her with my shoe. She had only just started menstruating. I couldn't understand how she could let someone make her pregnant, and I insisted that she tell me who it was. She wouldn't.

We fought all night long. Near dawn she finally broke down and told me . . . she told me how my husband had been having sex with her for years. This just devastated me. I had to sit down. I felt like I'd been hit by a truck. I looked her in the eyes and I knew she was telling the truth—the hurt, the pain was all there plain as day. I begged her to tell me why she never said something; that I would've stopped it; that I would've made him leave the house. She told me she didn't want to lose her father—that she loved him. That he would be sent to Stark Prison if anyone found out. He told her that. He even showed her photographs of the prison. He totally brainwashed her. I took her in my arms, and we both cried all over each other. Then she gently pushed me back and says, 'Momma . . . Momma, the night Daddy died he was doing it to me. He was on top of me, fast going in and out of me. He suddenly started gasping and he held his chest and he fell on me—right on top of me. I'm so sorry, Momma, I'm so sorry—I didn't mean to kill him.'

"For the first time I realized why she'd changed so much, why she was crying all the time, and I took her in my arms and held her close, so close, and I told her that it wasn't her fault, that none of it was her fault.

"So that same night, I realized, the night my husband died while having sex with my daughter, he got her pregnant. She didn't want the baby. She wanted to have an abortion, but she was too far into the pregnancy, and a few months later she gave birth to a baby girl. We named her Charlotte. We were planning to give the child to Catholic Charity and let them put her in a foster home, but we changed our minds and Charlotte came home with us from the hospital. The police had learned about it from the hospital, and Carole had to tell them how my husband had gotten her pregnant. Humiliating, it was so humiliating. They looked at me, the police, like I was a monster; like it all happened because *I* let it happen, because I wasn't a good mother. They made me feel worse than I already felt, and man that wasn't easy. If . . . if it wasn't for Carole, and little Charlotte, I would have lost it. I felt so guilty, I wanted to die. I wanted to be punished. And I was. I went to bars at night and let men take advantage of me, abuse me in all ways. I needed to be punished and degraded, and Lord knows I was. But thank the Lord I saw how wrong what I was doing was . . . that my daughter needed a grounded, loving mother—not a whore screwing three men at a time in an alley somewhere. You understand what I'm saying—what I became?"

"I understand," I said.

"So overnight I changed—totally. I did all and anything I could for my daughter and my granddaughter, and we fell into a comfortable rhythm, and as more time went by we began to leave it all in the past as though it had never really been. Carole and I became very close, best friends as well as mother and daughter. I worked two jobs and my parents helped us out. In his old age my father changed, and he was just nuts about Carole and Charlotte. Hmmm, funniest thing how different he became. I told him what happened. I had to. He was just great about it—amazing—not judgmental, didn't have a mean word to say. Go figure.

"So when Charlotte was five years old, we moved to New Orleans. Carole was in her first year of college. All through this she had continued with school. She wanted to be an attorney. Actually, she got very good grades and made the dean's list. Life didn't seem that bad now. I could see a silver lining in all that had happened. . . . That is, until Charles Boone came into our lives. Do you know who Charles Boone is, Mr. De Nardo?" The name immediately rang a bell. I knew who he was. "Is he on death row now in New Orleans?" I asked, dreading the answer.

"That's him."

"Yes . . . I know who he is," I said, getting a sickening feeling in my gut because Charles Boone was one of the most prolific serial killers in America; he murdered children in six different states.

"Well, Mr. De Nardo, the last child Charles Boone butchered was our Charlotte."

My God, I wanted to say, but I just kept looking into her sad brown eyes and kept my mouth shut.

She continued: "It happened on the Fourth of July. We went down to the beach to watch the fireworks, the three of us. It was very crowded. Perfect weather. Somehow Charlotte got separated from us for a few moments and she was just suddenly gone. I swear I didn't take my eyes off that child for more than five seconds, and she up and disappeared. Right away we told the police, but they treated it like just another lost little girl and didn't take it none too serious. Carole and me stayed all night and day down by the beach looking for her, calling out her name, both of us hysterical. Some friends and neighbors came and helped us.

"And later . . . later that day, near dusk, they found Charlotte. A fisherman found her body floating in one of the canals. He raped my granddaughter, tore her insides all up, and dumped her into the Intercoastal."

"I'm so very sorry," I said, feeling tears rolling down my face, thinking, *Life sucks.*

"Thank you," she said. "Boone was captured a week later. He was trying to take another child, but the girl's father and uncles caught him and pret' near beat him to death. They knew about Charlotte. Everyone did. It was all people were talking about all over New Orleans. And they found the fishing knife he had used on Charlotte. Her dried blood was still on it. We went to his trial every day; heard the testimony of the experts and saw all the photographs of Charlotte the way he had left her. . . . It was in the courtroom where we learned in detail exactly what he had done to my little sweet angel before he killed her.

"The day he was sentenced to die we were there, Carole and me and my mother and father. And when he was being led away, Carole went for him. She seemed to fly through the air, and she got to him before they could stop her and she scratched at his eyes like a wild animal. It took all of six deputies to get her off him. She managed to damage one of his eyes badly—pret' near tore it right out of his sick fucking head."

I remembered all this because I had seen it on Court TV, though I had no idea the woman I saw in the morgue was the outraged mother who had attacked Charles Boone in a packed New Orleans courtroom. Court TV had shown it over and over again for days. They later made it part of a trailer the station uses to advertise itself.

She tried to take a drink of her coffee. Her hand was shaking so much now, she couldn't pick up the cup. I went and got her a straw from the Greek waiter. She took a long drink with the straw, sat back, and stared at me. She said, "After that Carole changed, as you might imagine. This last photo was taken about a year after the trial. She began wearing all black, drinking heavily, and started hanging out with this real weird crowd: all these kind of heavy-metal types with their faces pierced and orange hair and all the rest. I had no control over her now. If I said one thing, she'd go crazy. She took to blaming me for everything. All she did was smoke pot and listen to heavy metal music—Ozzy Osborne, Marilyn Manson—and blamed me for *everything*. Truth is, she had every right. And this is when Santos Dracol came into the picture.

"As you might know, Dracol has a club in the

Quarter. I knew all about Dracol. He's quite famous in New Orleans—like a big celebrity. I used to see him strut around at night with his cape and white face like he was the king of France or something. He always had all these hangers-on with him . . . groupies, all of them pale and sickly-looking. The club is very popular. Every night there is a line a block long of people waiting to get in. From the very beginning, Dracol gave me the creeps. There was something about him, in his eyes, that was downright evil, and I went ballistic when I heard that Carole was working at the club; that she was hanging out with him, going to his mansion late at night. I confronted her. I begged her to get away from him. I said we could go away, move to another state—to New Orleans, even California, anywhere she wanted. But she wasn't going anywhere. In fact, she took all her things and moved out of the house . . . moved into his place, I found out later."

"I'm curious. Is his mansion near the water?"

"Sure is. Pontchartrain River is just out back."

"Please, continue," I said.

"I didn't see much of my daughter anymore. The few times I did see her, she looked like a ghost, skinny as a rail, pierced all over, even her breasts and vagina. I went to the police, but they pret' near told me to get lost. Carole was an adult now, and she was with him, with them, on her own free will. Mr. De Nardo," she said, "Dracol is a vampire. I mean, a real vampire, not just someone masquerading as one."

"Why do you say that?"

"Why . . . I have a good friend, and her daughter Lucy told my friend that she witnessed Dracol drink blood from a girl until she died, and that he can change form—that she saw him climb up a wall like a giant insect. Twice I confronted him, got in his face as he was strutting through the Quarter. He doesn't walk, he struts—and I begged him to make Carole come home, but he just looked through me like I was invisible and walked around me as if I smelled or something. It was then, when I looked into his eyes, when I was close up to him I mean, that I saw the pure evil. It's in his eyes, clear as a bell." She finished her coffee. I asked for more for the both of us.

"And the next thing I know," she continued, "they're showing Carole's photograph on the news. One of my neighbors saw it and called me, and I put on CNN and sure enough there she was. I swear when I saw it and heard what happened—I mean, that her bloodless body had been found in the Hudson River—it knocked me right down to the floor . . . literally. Passed out cold."

She began sobbing into her trembling, cupped hands. I waited, remembering the day the police came to my house to tell me my wife had been murdered; how I cried into my cupped hands.

With great effort she collected herself, said, "I had to come up to New York to identify her body. Some New York detectives met me at the bus terminal and drove me to the morgue. They brought what was left of her up in this little elevator—and it was her. It was my little girl. My God, what a sight that was—to see her there like that just tore my heart out," she said in little more than a whisper, tears hurrying from her sad brown eyes. He got up and left. She continued: "I told the police what I told you, more or less, but nothing's happened. I understand Dracol has surrounded himself with a gaggle of lawyers and won't even talk to the police. Some country we live in, where a bloodthirsty murderer like him can just do what he wants with total impunity; it's disgraceful . . . criminal; it's a downright sin.

"I went to his club here, the one down near the water, and I told those goons at the door to tell him that I will not rest until he pays for what he did to my Carole. One time I even saw him going into the club, and I went over to him and spit right smack in his evil face. He doesn't scare me. In New Orleans, I walk in front of the road to his house with a sign that says *Santos Dracol Murdered Carole Smith*. I also walk in front of his club with my sign, and they laugh and point at me and call me names. They think I'm a crazy old lady. I've been arrested twice for disturbing the peace. You believe that? They say, the New Orleans police, that I have no proof that Dracol murdered Carole or anyone else—that the New York police haven't so much as charged him with a crime. Then I get a knock on my door, and it's a process server with a notice that Dracol is suing me for slander, and they gave him an order of protection against me that said I couldn't go within fifty feet of his person, business or home, but I went anyway—and sure enough, they arrested me. A judge sentenced me to sixty days in the county jail. I just finished doing the sixty days. That's how I lost my tooth here. I got into a fight with an ugly butch-lesbian that I saw taking advantage of this sweet teenage girl, a runaway, and the lesbian up and punched me in the mouth and told me to mind my own. I had to get five stitches . . . and she knocked out this here tooth . . .

"I'm sorry to burden you with all this, Mr. De Nardo. Please understand I'm not trying to make you feel sorry for me or anything like that. I just want you to know the whole truth." With difficulty, she drank more of her coffee. My heart went out to her. I didn't quite feel like the same person anymore after hearing her story.

"So," she said, "I take the bus up to New York to let him know that I'm not stopping; that he can't scare me off with the law or with anything else.

"Maybe, I've been thinking, God sent you to put this thing right. Lord knows I've prayed endlessly for help, for the forces of good to help me against this evil, black-hearted creature from hell."

"Have you been down to the club recently, the one here in New York?"

"Yes. I was there just last night. I told the two cretins at the door to say hello to Dracol and, if he wants to find me, I'm staying at the Best Western."

"You told him where you are staying?"

"Yes—he doesn't scare me, and I want him to know it."

"You have to promise me something."

"Depends what," she told me. I admired her resolve, strength of will.

"If you want me to help, you have to promise to stop confronting him. That will only lead to no good. I know what I'm talking about. I'm a professional. This is what I do for a living. We're going to need you to tell your story in court one day in front of a jury—and I don't want anything to happen to you."

"I got to thinking he'd never see the inside of a courtroom. You know, he's got these vampire clubs all around the world. Down in New Orleans, he's like some kind of superstar. All these pseudo-vampires come from all over, dress up, and go there and act stupid. Man, they must be real bored with their lives to turn to such crap. But he . . . he's a real vampire; I've talked to people whose blood he drank."

"Yes, I've heard," I told her, humoring her. "So you promise me you'll leave him alone and let me do my thing?"

"I do," she said, "for now," and I went and sat next to her and gave her a long, hard hug, my heart aching at what this poor woman had been through.

"We'll get him," I told her, drew back, and looked her in the eyes. "You have my solemn word on the grave of my wife: I won't rest until we've done him in."

"Thank you," she said, and cried on my shoulder, her tears warm and wet on my cheek. "It will be okay," I said, and convinced her to go back to New Orleans that night. She and I soon left the restaurant and returned to her hotel. She checked out, and I took her by cab down to the Port Authority on Forty-second Street. A bus was leaving for New Orleans at 1:33 A.M. Outside the bus she gave me a news story in the *Daily News* about Carole's body being found. I quickly read it, tried to give it back to her, but she told me to keep it. This is what it said:

Crime Blotter:
The body of a naked female was discovered just south of the George Washington Bridge early Tuesday morning. Fisherman Enrique Alvarez was in the process of reeling in a bass when he spotted the corpse. "My God," he said. "At first I thought it was some kind of dead fish or something, but then I saw that it was, you know, a naked lady. I don't fish there anymore—no way," he said. According to police, the body had been in the water for several weeks and, the police say, there was no blood at all in it. Police ask that anyone with information call the NYPD homicide hot line at 888-476-9900 . . .

I folded it up, stuck it into my jacket pocket, helped her board the bus, and found her a seat. She wrapped her trembling arms around me. I made her promise me again that she would not confront Dracol. She took her seat. I slowly left the bus and walked to her window, not wanting to leave her alone. We stared at each other, much silently passing between us. The engine started up with a roar. We both put our hands on the glass, in line with each other. Tears flowed from her eyes. She mouthed the words *thank you;* the bus slowly pulled out. I waved until it was out of sight.

I consider myself a hard guy. I've been in law enforcement for a quarter of a century, have a master's degree in criminology from John Jay College. I've seen pretty much every inhumanity and cruelty people are capable of. But the story Georgia Smith had just told me weighted me down and depressed me, and harsh black-and-white images of Carole in the morgue ran through my head whether I wanted them to or not. I hailed a cab on Eighth Avenue and had it drop me on Central Park West. I slowly walked on to my block, hoping the creep who had come into the restaurant was there. I wanted to throw him a good beating, stick my gun in his face, send Dracol a message—a challenge—but neither he nor the car I saw him get out of was there. The block was all quiet and still as it can only be after a heavy snowfall. The wind had died down and the snow had just about stopped, I suddenly realized. I hadn't even noticed, my mind was so distracted by the agony in Georgia Smith's eyes and face as she talked. I thought of little Charlotte in the hands of Charles Boone—a genuine sadistic monster. I went inside. There was a message from Harold on my machine that Amy hadn't come to work, that her roommate was concerned. There was also a message from Belladonna:

"Frank," she said in little more than a whisper, "I overheard something . . . I found out what happened to the writer you're looking for. You must be very careful. You're in danger. Please call as soon as you can, I have to speak to you. I'll keep my cell phone with me."

I phoned her right back. After fifteen rings, I got a recording that said she was out of range. I kept trying her and kept getting the recording. Wondering what she had found out, I sat at my desk and looked at the photographs of Carole I'd taken at the morgue, feeling a closeness with her I hadn't known before. She was no longer just a body with no blood in it pulled from the Hudson River up near the George Washington Bridge. She now had a history, a concerned mother . . . a tragic life—a murdered child. I silently cursed her father for what he had done to her, again tried Belladonna, nothing. Now more than ever, I was convinced that Santos Dracol was using the Hudson River to get rid of bodies.

Again I tried Belladonna, and again reached the recording. She was not the kind of woman to leave such a message unless it was deadly serious. I listened to the message several times over, and the more I listened to it the more convinced I became that she was in danger. I already had all kinds of guilt about getting intimately involved with her so quickly, and I knew if she was having problems it was definitely because of me. I paced back and fourth, decided to go find her and hear what she had found out. As I was putting on my coat, the phone rang. It was Marco Vacaresco. I picked up.

"Hello, De Nardo," he said. "I call to tell you how you must protect yourself from Dracol. We have a priest here in Bucharest, Father Joseph, a very old man—even older than me; I am a teenager next to him. I told him about you and your struggle with Dracol. He has done battle with these creatures several times. He made me promise I would call you and tell you what you must do if you plan to fight Dracol. . . . You must first put the garlic on the door and all the windows, and also you must get yourself silver bullets. They are the only bullets that can harm him. I know this may sound crazy, but you must do this," he said with serious sincerity.

I thanked him for the call, for his concern, and soon hung up. I was not about to go get silver bullets. Forget it. I left and drove straight down to Belladonna's place, parked at the same fire hydrant, rang her bell, and called her on my cell phone for ten minutes. I made my way over to the club. There was a line of limousines in front of the place, a crowd waiting to get in. I double-parked across the street and walked up to the pointed-toothed bouncers at the door. It was the same two

I'd seen at the bar on Green Street. They didn't want to let me in. They said there was a private party, that I needed an invitation.

"I'm a friend of Belladonna. I need to talk with her just for a minute," I said.

"She's not here," the taller of the two said, all grim-faced. "She didn't come to work." He walked away from me. I went after him. "I need to go in and make sure for myself," I told him.

"Private party," he said. "Don't you under-fuckin'-stand English? Are you stupid?" he said.

I was in no mood to be spoken to like that, and I stepped over the fancy velvet rope, opened the door, and let myself in. They both came after me. The one who asked me if I was stupid grabbed me by the shoulder and roughly turned me around and tried to slap me. I ducked and hit him with a right hand directly on the chin and a sharp left hook as he was going down. The other goon started throwing high kicks, grunting like Bruce Lee. One of the kicks caught me in the right side and knocked the wind out of me. I waited for the right moment and coldcocked him with a left, and he went down and stayed there, out cold.

I now kicked him in the side and continued downstairs, looked everywhere for Belladonna, even in the ladies' room and the VIP room downstairs, but couldn't find her. I knocked on Dracol's office door. The door was opened by Oliver, the giant black dude with the snakelike dreadlocks. He didn't like me banging on the door. I told him I needed to talk with Belladonna, that it was an emergency. He, too, said she wasn't there, that she had phoned and said a relative was sick and she had to go to San Francisco. The two bouncers I knocked out came hurrying down the stairs. The one who asked me if I was stupid lunged for me. I stepped back and drew my piece in two movements.

"If anyone," I said in a calm voice, "lays a hand on me, I'm going to get upset." I had no patience for any of this anymore; far as I was concerned, I was in a war and they were a clear and present danger.

"Okay," Dreadlocks said, "chill, man."

"I want to talk with Santos."

"He's not here."

"Aren't you his personal bodyguard?"

"He doesn't need a bodyguard," he said. "As I think you'll soon find out."

"Tell him I'd like to talk with him," I said, and left.

One of the first things I learned about being a professional investigator was not to get mad, to keep your personal feelings to yourself, to stay objective. But I was allowing myself to get angry, I knew—not good. I sat in my car for a few minutes calming myself, reminding myself to stay cold-eyed, distant.

This story about a sick relative in San Francisco was bullshit. I took a couple of deep breaths, watching all these pale overserious people dressed in black lined up at the velvet rope. I slipped the SUV into gear and drove back to Belladonna's place. For twenty minutes I stood in front of her building, calling her, ringing her bell—no response. Then I rang the bells of her four neighbors. No one answered.

Before I began working homicides, I was in the Safe and Robbery Division of the NYPD. It was there I learned how to pick locks—in fact, I became very good at it. I went back to the car, grabbed the lock-pick set I keep in the glove compartment, and opened the Medico on the front door in a minute flat. The elevator key had a special Fichet lock and couldn't be picked by Houdini himself. Instead, I went over to the rear stairwell door, managed to pick it, and quietly went up the three flights of stairs to Belladonna's door. I knocked, not a sound. I put my ear to the floor—complete silence. I got down on my knees and sniffed the air coming from the crack under the door. The smell of her strange candle came from it, and with it everything we'd done returned to me in a kinetic rush of exotic images and sensations.

Reluctantly, I went back downstairs and left a note for her sticking out of her mailbox, which was marked *Belladonna*. I walked up and down both sides of the block but didn't see anything unusual, went back into my car and called my answering machine—no messages. I waited a while longer and slowly returned to my place, sat at my desk and thought about Belladonna, wondered where she was, what she had found out, feeling all guilty about getting involved with her; and I thought, too, about John Fitzgerald's sad face—the love in his eyes when he spoke about Anne; I thought about Carole Smith's childhood—her daughter Charlotte in Boone's hands; and I thought about the things Vacaresco had told me.

Rather than sit there feeling guilty and anxious, I decided to go for a run in the park, got dressed, warmed up, and went outside. It was still dark, but a sad dawn was slowly reddening the sky on the east side of the park. There was little wind, and I was hopeful I'd be able to go back to the cliffs and use the camera.

Central Park was all white and quiet—serene. I walked on paths already made by other die-hard runners to the track that circles the reservoir and began to run. The air was cold and fresh and good to breathe. As I ran along, I kept seeing, in my mind's eye, a forest of bodies at the bottom of the river. I finished my first lap and began a second, wondering where Belladonna was. On the uptown side of the reservoir, just above my head, a mob of noisy crows was battling with a huge red-tailed hawk.

When I finished my second lap, I left the track, feeling somewhat better, my head cleared—intent upon finding hard evidence that would nail Dracol to the wall. As I walked back to my place, I tried Belladonna on my cell phone. I didn't even get the recording this time—odd. I arrived home and checked my answering machine: no messages.

I showered and dressed and went back to Belladonna's place and rang the bell some more. No answer. I let myself in. My note was still sticking out of her mailbox. I rang the bells of her neighbors and asked the two I now found home if they had seen or heard anything unusual. They each said they hadn't. As I was leaving the building, however, I ran into a tall, skinny fellow with thick glasses and a tiny, white Chihuahua yapping like crazy on a long leash. I introduced myself, showed him my ID, and told him I was looking for Belladonna.

"I know her," he said. "I live in the apartment just below her. She's quiet like a mouse. I saw her leave the building last night with two men and a tall, pale woman. They all looked . . . well, kind of serious and gloomy. And they were all wearing black, like maybe they were going to a funeral; that's what I thought, you know, that someone had died. Has something happened to her?"

"No, I just need to find her. Did she look stressed at all?"

"Not particularly. I very rarely saw her. I think she worked at night, kept to herself. A beautiful woman, though, really lovely. She reminds me of Vivian Leigh. Hector liked her."

"Hector?"

"My dog," he said, picking up little Hector so I could pet him. Hector was shaking so much, it looked like he was going to pass out any moment. I tried to pet him; he tried to bite me. I gave Belladonna's neighbor my card and asked him to call if he saw or heard Belladonna, anything "unusual." He promised he would. I went back to my wheels and slowly drove uptown. The snow came down harder and harder still, but there was no wind and I was planning to go up to Westchester and see if I could use the Fish Cam. I hung a left and drove to West Street so I could see the Hudson River as I made my way uptown. It was much calmer now. I would definitely be able to use the camera.

When I arrived at my place, Louise was at her desk. She said John Fitzgerald had phoned. I called him back and told him there was nothing new to report. I thought about discussing his police record with him now, but I wanted to do it in person and we made plans to have lunch the following day. I was in a hurry to get up to Westchester. I turned on the weather station and they predicted snow but no hurricane-force winds. Sitting there, I remembered Marco Vacaresco telling me that I *must* get silver bullets. . . .

When I first heard him say that, I thought it was kind of absurd, actually ridiculous, but the more I thought about it the more convinced I became that I should maybe get my hands on some silver bullets. I took a long, deep breath and walked back and fourth, thinking this thing out, remembering what Carole's mom and Vacaresco had said about Dracol having preternatural powers, something I really didn't believe was possible—but, over the years, I reminded myself, if I had learned anything about good detective work, it was to keep an open mind to all possibilities.

Against my better judgment, I reluctantly picked up the phone and called a gunsmith friend of mine. His name is Jack Gorba. He works at Continental Arms on Madison Avenue. It was from Jack, over the years, that I'd gotten all my guns and special ammunition. Jack was old when I met him, and that was twenty-five years ago. But I hung up before Jack answered the phone. I wasn't about to get silver bullets. I didn't believe in preternatural vampires and wasn't going to run around Manhattan in a snowstorm trying to get silver bullets—forget it. I wasn't going to buy this line of bullshit Dracol was selling. Far as I was concerned, he was nothing more than a sexual sadist—a serial killer playing the part of a vampire.

I tried Belladonna again. Her phone just rang and rang. I had a quick sandwich and coffee, thought about phoning Captain Roe and asking him to come with me up to Westchester, but decided against it. All I was planning to do was to sneak, peek, and retreat—not confront anyone. If, in fact, I did discover bodies, I would call the police.

I soon grabbed my gun bag and left the house, got into my SUV, drove to a gas station on West Ninety-sixth Street, and had them put ribbed chains on my car tires. The last thing I wanted to do was get caught in the snow. I finally got on the

West Side Highway and headed north, a feeling of unease slowly welling up inside of me . . . wondering if maybe I should have gotten some silver bullets.

It was snowing lightly, but there was no wind and the river was calm. It was so cold that large, jagged chunks of ice had formed in the water. The traffic was surprisingly light. I tried to call Captain Roe to tell him what I was doing, but I couldn't get a line. I parked as far away from Dracol's house as possible, grabbed the camera and my gun bag, and made my way to the cliffs, then north along them to the area just behind Dracol's place. There was no wind now, and just a few lonely snowflakes forlornly fell from the darkening sky. I found a huge gray boulder. It blocked anyone from the house seeing me. I put my things down here and, without wasting any time, I walked to the cliffs—there was ice everywhere— and carefully lowered the football-shaped camera into the water.

Once the camera was a few feet down, I turned on the light and was amazed at how well I could see on the little video monitor. A huge, gold-eyed bass curiously swam by. When the camera reached the bottom, which was flat and sandy, the water surprisingly clean, I pulled it back up a few feet and began to walk along the cliffs, careful about where I stepped, careful not to get too close to the edge. I kept looking toward the house, making sure no one was coming.

I hadn't gone fifteen paces before I found the first body, and I swear I nearly fell over, I was so stunned and horrified—even though I was pretty certain I'd find something. It was a naked female, far into severe decomposition, and it was obvious that crabs and fish had fed on her flesh, eaten her eyes out. . . . "*My God*," I said out loud, knowing I now had Santos Dracol cold, that he was going down. I continued walking, and the little screen revealed more and more bodies, silently moving back and forth with the frigid winter currents just as I had imagined—children, too. They were each chained to some kind of weight, which I could not see because sand covered them. Most of the bodies were in a horizontal position, buoyed by gases in their stomachs, as if they were trying to reach the surface—just horrifying to see, a nightmare come true; I felt cold chills run up and down my back. I cursed Dracol.

I turned and walked back to the boulder, nauseous—angry beyond words. With my trembling right hand I shut off the monitor and light, quickly pulled the camera out of the water, put it back in its case, and turned to leave, in a hurry to go alert the authorities and come back with an army of cops to arrest Dracol and everyone else in that cursed house, my mind racing frantically all over the place. By now it was nearly dark, though it was easy to find the way I'd come by using a small penlight. After twenty steps or so, I looked back at the house to make sure no one was coming; all seemed clear, but when I turned toward my car and began walking, I saw someone standing in my footprints. I dropped everything and drew my Beretta, moved my light up to see who it was—and I was facing Oliver, Dracol's bodyguard, standing there like some kind of unmovable tank.

"I've got no beef with you, Oliver. Be smart. Let me pass."

"That ain't happening," he said.

I raised my piece. "I'm walking the fuck out of here, Oliver, and if you try to stop me, you're dead. Now, get out of my way!"

He stayed put. I noticed movement on my left and right. I was surrounded. Then I saw Dracol walking toward me, a nasty slit where his mouth had been.

"You think," he said, "you are *so* clever, De Nardo," hateful venom dripping from every syllable.

"Just doing my job," I said, realizing that there were shadowy forms all about me. The first one to go would be Dracol. If I was going, I'd take as many of them with me as possible.

Maybe, I was thinking, *if I kill him first the others will take off and leave me alone.* He was about eight feet away from me now. I focused on the place I would put my bullet: right between his black eyes. In one quick movement, I went low and brought my gun up, intent on killing him, but I didn't even raise my weapon when one of them threw something and hit me on the side of the head. I went down. They were suddenly all on top of me, stomping me, punching me, kicking me. Dracol grabbed me and lifted me up. He was incredibly strong. Oliver the giant hit me on the side of the head. I saw spinning, colorful stars, then everything went black, quiet . . . still.

CHAPTER ELEVEN

Hearing a voice coming from far away, I slowly regained consciousness. A woman was talking to me, I realized, but I didn't understand what she was saying, or even the language being spoken. Everything hurt. My neck burned. I turned to the direction of the voice and slowly opened my eyes.

She was standing over me, looking down at me with concern arching and lining her face. She had long black hair, a white face—it was Belladonna, I realized.

"He took a lot of blood from you," she said.

My neck burned terribly. I slowly reached for it.

"Leave it be. It's where he bit you."

Bit me?

I was desperate to ask her if I was now a vampire, but I couldn't talk. She knelt down. "Do you understand what I said?" she asked.

I managed to nod that I did.

"You've been unconscious for a long time.

Here," she said, "drink this," and she put a bottle of water to my lips. I drank greedily. I was so thirsty. After a time I slowly sat up, realizing for the first time that my right hand was chained to a metal ring that was bolted to a rough stone wall. I was in some kind of dungeon. The only light was that of two thick black candles, which caused sneaky shadows to skulk along the gray stone walls.

"I got your message. I looked all over. I couldn't find you," I said in a voice that didn't sound like mine.

"I heard him talking on his cell phone. They were going to come to your place to kill you. One of his people was following you. He wanted you dead. They came to my place and made me go with them. I didn't want to, but they forced me," she said. "They wanted to use me to get to you, but I wouldn't—"

"He's been weighting down his victims and dumping them in the Hudson right behind the house," I said. "He was doing that, disposing of bodies in a lake under a castle in Romania. There's a well in the basement that's above a bottomless underground lake—"

"How did you find that out?"

"The retired police inspector in Romania I told you about. His name is Marco Vacaresco. We've got to get out of here . . . he's got to be stopped."

"Tell me about it, but how? The walls are solid stone. The door is reinforced steel."

"I don't know, but we will. I'm not going to let

this scumbag drink from us until he's tired of our taste and dumps us in the river. That ain't happening," I said, sitting up, pissed off, angry at myself for allowing these cretins to get the drop on me.

I remembered my derringer, hopefully reached into my pants for it, but they'd taken the gun. I reached down to see if they'd found my knife, and they hadn't.

"This is how," I told her, slowly drawing the thin, razor-sharp blade out of its soft sheath. "It's a particular type of blade—very thin, so if you get frisked it's hard to find."

"Clever."

"Who has the keys to these locks?"

"I have no idea."

"If we try to escape, it's best if we do it when he's not around," I said, remembering his incredible strength. "You have any idea when and where he sleeps?"

"He's told me many times that he sleeps when the sun is up . . . in a coffin filled with dirt from the cemetery where his family is buried."

"You're kidding."

"Nope."

"Are you okay physically? Can you run—can you fight?"

"To get out of this, you bet I can run and fight."

"I'm so glad to see you," I said.

"And I you," she said, and we hugged each other tightly.

I said, "I'm sorry I got you into this."

"Nothing to be sorry about—I got myself into it."

"Have you seen Anne Fitzgerald—heard anything about her?"

"I did. He told me she's in New Orleans; that she willingly went there to interview him and some of his people and he found out that she was surreptitiously recording him and taking photographs and he went ballistic. He's keeping her prisoner in one of the places he has down there. He talked about making her write a book based on his life."

"A book on his life?"

"That's what he said, yes."

I heard footsteps. A key slide into the lock. The heavy door opened. It was Cassandra, the woman who had brought me the tea. She had left the key in the door lock. There was, I noticed, a key ring attached to it and small gold keys, which I was sure were the keys to open the locks on our chains, hung from it. She glared at me. I glared right back.

"You're going to pay dearly for all ze trouble you've caused us. I want you to zink about zat, while you still can zink," she said.

I thought about throwing my knife at her but decided against it.

"Thanks for the advice," I said.

She gave me a large malicious smile filled with pointed canine teeth.

"Why don't you go haunt a house somewhere?" I said, hoping she'd come close enough for me to get my hands on her. I'd cut her throat in a second.

"How did you know about ze river?" she demanded.

"I'm not telling you anything—go fuck yourself," I said. She glared at me but didn't come any closer. She kind of hissed at me, closed the door, and turned the lock. I listened carefully to the sound of the tumblers, her footsteps as they faded away. "Hate to meet her in a dark alley," I said, hearing the boiler kick on and remembering the oil delivery when Cassandra had come out of the house and invited me inside for tea. The room seemed to spin. I had to lie down. Belladonna asked me how I discovered the bodies, and I told her what Vacaresco had said about the underground lake tipped me off, and about Carole Smith—how her broken ankle and the chain marks on her leg got me to thinking that she had been weighed down and dumped in the river. I quickly ran down for her the story Carole's mother had told me.

"De Nardo, I want you to understand," she said, "I had no idea he was doing any of this—I swear. I feel terrible. We've got to stop him."

"We will. I promise we will," I said.

I grabbed my knife and, using the serrated edge, moved it back and forth on the clasp of the lock. I was sure I could make an incision in the clasp and might be able to pull it apart and get free.

"What are you doing?" she asked, her brow

creasing. I saw her pointed teeth. They really gave me the creeps now.

"You think you can cut that?" she asked.

"No, but I might be able to make a cut wide enough to force it open. We are getting out of here," I said.

Or die trying, I thought.

"I believe you."

I heard the boiler shut off. It was definitely to the left somewhere, and not too far. A plan involving the boiler began taking shape in the back of my head.

"This coffin he sleeps in, you say he told you it was in the basement."

"Actually, he said below ground—as though that had some kind of significance, that it was below ground."

"How many stairs did you come down when they brought you here?"

"Maybe a dozen."

"I felt his strength. It was like being handled by some kind of ape."

"I know—he's *very* strong."

She became quiet, and I patiently worked the serrated edge of the knife back and forth and little by little began to make an incision in the clasp. It was not that good a lock, and I became more and more convinced that I could open it.

"Please, can I help?" she asked.

"You can help by thinking positively. I want you to envision us running out the front door."

"Easy. That's all I've been doing since I've been

here. What about the dogs? There's two Doberman pinschers guarding the grounds."

"I saw them. They are going to have to be dealt with, too."

"How?"

"I don't know yet," I said, dreading the thought of tangling with those dogs with a knife in my weakened condition. More people began moving about upstairs. As much as I wanted to open the lock, I was tired and my eyes began closing whether I liked it or not; my vision blurred. There was a high-pitched buzzing in my ears, and before I knew it I was out cold.

When I woke up, the place where Dracol bit me burned. My head throbbed, my bones ached. Belladonna was sleeping soundly next to me, her breathing soft and rhythmic. She had a beautifully sculptured face, high cheekbones, full lips. I took a long, deep breath—angry at myself for allowing them to get the drop on me like that; it was the biggest fuckup I'd ever made. With a roar, the boiler kicked on. I began to doze. Someone stopped outside the door. I heard the key go in the lock and the door slowly opened. Santos Dracol strolled into the room. Belladonna bolted up with a start. He smiled at her. Those teeth of his never looked as menacing as they did now; they were like two small ivory daggers.

He said, "I must admit I admire your tenacity, De Nardo. I've never come across anyone quite like you. Very persistent. How did you know about the bodies in the water?"

"My secret," I told him. He didn't like that. His black shark eyes narrowed on me.

"That camera—very clever; I take my hat off to you."

"If it was so clever, I wouldn't be here."

"I want to know how you knew," he demanded. I didn't answer him. "How did you know!?" he hissed.

I remained quiet.

He walked toward me, grabbed me by the neck, effortlessly picked me up and brought me to him. I tried to resist him, but he had some kind of supernatural strength. He savagely bit into my neck and began drawing my blood. I tried to fight him off, but it was no use. Not believing this was actually happening, I reached for my knife.

"Stop! You'll kill him!" I heard Belladonna scream, and he literally threw me across the room—amazing strength.

Psychopaths, I knew, could be endowed with superhuman strength, remembering Darnell Williams—how incredibly strong he was—and if I was sure of anything at this point, it was that Santos Dracol was a raging, full-fledged psychopath and a bona fide blood freak.

"I so very much enjoy the blood of a warrior like you, De Nardo," he told me. "Who knew you were coming here?"

"No one," I lied.

"We shall see. Unfortunately, I must leave now. I cannot attend to you the way I want to just yet. But Cassandra will soon come visit you. She can

be very convincing; she has ways of getting people to talk," he said, turned away, and slammed
the door shut.

Not believing what he'd just done, how he
drank my blood, I was so weak I could barely
pick up my head. She wiped blood from my neck.

"I'm sorry," she whispered, tears filling her
eyes. "It's my fault. Of all people, I should have
known; forgive me." She took my hand. I again
began to lose consciousness, suddenly seeing
things from my childhood. Working in my uncle
Sal's garden, going on the rides at Coney Island,
hearing the roar of the Cyclone roller coaster
with all the girls screaming . . .

"Don't die! Don't die!" she begged, slapping
me hard, bringing me back. "Please don't die."

"We have to move fast. I can't take much more
of that," I said, and drifted off somewhere I'd
never been before:

I saw this soft-white light at the end of a long
tunnel. The tunnel smelled strongly of sulfur. I
heard a high-pitched, hyena-like cackle . . . the
howling of wolves. When I reached the end of the
tunnel, I stepped into the funeral home where my
wife had been laid out after her murder. My family and her family were all there. Everyone was
crying. It was the saddest day of my life. I looked
at my uncle Sal. With his eyes he silently told me
the punks responsible would suffer, and they did.
My dream began to fade, to mist over . . .

When I came to, Belladonna was sleeping right
next to me. I immediately went back to work on

the lock clasp, moving my knife back and forth on it. Knowing for sure that both our lives hinged on our getting free, I cut for nearly an hour and was making good progress. She woke up.

"How you making out?" she asked.

"I'm getting there," I said. Now about halfway through the clasp, I stood and, using my weight, began to pull on the chain, putting more and more pressure on the clasp.

Belladonna took hold of my waist and we both pulled, and kept pulling. Little by little the clasp began to bend and, finally, snapped, and I was suddenly free. She had a big smile on her face. "You are unbelievable—just unbelievable! Amazing. I didn't think you could really do it, but you did. Bravo!"

I was still weak, but the prospect of escaping, getting out of his control, energized me and drove me to get up and walk about the room. I became dizzy, had to sit down, but I forced myself to stand and move about. I didn't know when the door would be opened again, but we had to be ready. We would only have one shot, and I was intent upon making it work. I was not about to become another victim of Dracol. End up in the Hudson River as fish food. *Forget it*. I would escape or die trying. I carefully paced off the distance from the wall to the door and from the end of the chain to the door.

"This is the plan," I said. "When Cassandra comes back, immediately start talking to her, distract her; stand here, as close to her as possible.

I'm going to hide just behind the open door. By the time she realizes what's up, I'll have her."

"What if she screams? What if she's with someone?"

"I'm not going to give her the chance to scream. I'm going to steal her breath away. If someone's with her, we'll deal with it."

"De Nardo, she's a nasty nasty piece of work—and she's got really long nails."

"I'm going to show you what nasty is. What I want you to do is stand as close to her as possible at the end of the chain to block her line of sight behind you, and whatever you do, don't look at me. Make sure you look her in the eyes, engage her eyes. Got it?"

"Got it. I understand."

"Let's rehearse it a couple of times," I said, and made her stand exactly where I wanted her as I positioned myself against the wall to the immediate right of the door.

"When we get outside, I want to go left, to the boiler room."

"Why?" she asked, but before I could answer her, we heard approaching footsteps.

"Show time," I said. We hugged again. "Move close to her. Engage her eyes."

"I'm there," she whispered. "We are out of here!"

"We are out of here!"

The key went into the lock, the tumblers turned, and the door began to slowly open . . .

"I'm-in-terrible-pain," Belladonna said in a

rush of words. "It's my period; can you please get me something for the pain! Please." At that moment, I saw the back of Cassandra's head. She was carrying a stun gun. I quickly moved forward, slammed my left hand over her mouth, and told her to be quiet, to stay still, but she fought me, tried to shock me with the stun gun. Belladonna jumped on her. She shocked Belladonna and knocked her right down. She tried to sink her canines into my hand as she brought the stun gun to my arm. I hit her like she was a man and knocked her out cold. I looked at Belladonna. She was even whiter than she had been, not an easy thing.

"Good," she said.

"Come on," I said, picked up the stun gun, took her hand, and went into the foyer.

"Stay here," I whispered. We could hear people moving about upstairs, the beams in the wooden floor creaking. I hurried to the left and found the boiler room. It suddenly started up. I grabbed the copper feed line that ran from the pump into the fire chamber and, with three strong pulls, I snapped it. In a strong, steady stream oil began to squirt out all over the floor. I wedged the door open with a brick and aimed the broken line in the direction of the foyer; soon there was a thick, black finger of foul-smelling oil sinuously moving across the stone floor, like a snake with bad intentions.

Now I went looking for Dracol's coffin and found it in an all-black room at the end of the hall.

It was lighted by a lone black candle in a fancy golden candelabra. The coffin was red with the insignia of a pearl-inlaid dragon adorning it. It was closed, and I wasn't about to open it to see if he was inside, though I noticed a clear plastic tube running from a large black oxygen tank in the corner of the room into the side of the coffin. Foreboding portraits of Vlad Tepes and Radu the Handsome hung on the walls.

Sick fuck, I was thinking. I quickly took the candle, turned, and hurried back toward Belladonna. By now the oil had reached the end of the hall and began to flow inside the black room where Dracol's coffin was.

"I found the coffin," I whispered, hustled her over to the bottom of the steps, then carefully brought the flame of the candle to the puddle of oil. Immediately, the oil caught on fire. Hungry flames leaped to the ceiling. Adrenaline kicked in and I didn't feel weak or tired anymore; this, I knew, was a fight to the death. There would not be another chance. I grabbed her hand and together we bolted up the stairs. A smoke detector somewhere in the house went off. We reached the top of the stairs and heard people hurrying about. From where we were, I could see the front door. We were, I realized, in the back of the house, just off a kitchen.

"Are you ready?" I whispered.

"*Absolutely*," she said, and we hurried toward the front door, hadn't gone ten feet when a woman I'd never seen before attacked us, screaming like a banshee. She jumped on my back and clawed at my face. I shocked her with the stun gun, she screamed. Belladonna grabbed her by the hair. I punched her out.

They now came from every direction, men and women, clawing, punching, kicking. We furiously fought them. The stun gun was torn from my hand. One of them ripped off Belladonna's caftan and left her naked, beat her to the ground. They piled on top of me and got me down, too, kicked and pummeled me. Oliver the giant showed up and again hit me in the head—I saw stars, heard the sound of rushing water. Belladonna screamed for dear life. From the floor I was able to see my shoulder bag sitting on a black rattan table in the living room. Praying my guns were still in it, I fought them off me with the knife, made one last furious effort to get to my bag, got up and ran like a madman for the bag, opened it, and there was my Beretta—*hallelujah*. I pulled it out, and without a second's hesitation, began shooting people, Oliver first, going for the head and the chest—kill shots. I fired six times and dropped six of them. The last two turned and ran; one jumped out of a window to get away.

In a hurry, I opened the front door and we bolted toward the entrance gate, falling as we went. It was snowing heavily. Badly beaten, we were both a bloody mess. I heard the dogs before I saw them. They came running from the right side of the house, barking and slipping in the snow, intent upon tearing us apart. A haunting scream, the likes of which I never heard, came from the house. "What was that?" I asked.

"That was him," she said. We reached the front gate and moved through it just before the dogs could get us, then ran east as fast as we could, falling on sheets of ice as we went. I looked back at the house, and giant tongues of orange flames filled the windows as thick black smoke poured out the front door. On the other side of the fence, the two dogs ran along with us, baring their teeth, growling, barking. A siren began to wail somewhere in the distance. A fire truck with spinning red lights filled with wide-eyed firemen turned onto the block. Belladonna, completely naked, was oddly calm, covered in blood. I too, I realized, was a bloody mess.

"What happened?" one of the firemen demanded as he jumped out of the cab, his eyes not leaving Belladonna's incredible body. Before I could answer him, though, I passed out cold. Some tough guy.

PART THREE

THE SAINT LOUIS CEMETERY

CHAPTER TWELVE

When I woke up, I was in the emergency room of the Hastings General Hospital. A doctor with carrot-red hair and freckles was stitching wounds in my arm closed. When he saw me open my eyes, he said, "Welcome back. Had a pretty rough time, I hear."

"You could say that. Where is she?" I asked, trying to sit up.

"Being treated just next door—"

"She okay?"

"She's fine. She has a lot of bruises and scratches that Dr. Joseph is tending to, but no broken bones. I'm Dr. Kennedy. It's all just amazing . . . criminals like this here in Westchester—absolutely mind-boggling. I still can't believe it—none of us can."

"She told you?"

"Yes—mind-boggling. There's an army of reporters outside. I never saw anything like this in

Hastings, and I've lived here all my life. I understand the police are finding bodies of their victims in the river behind the house."

"Thank God," I said, lay back down, and said a silent prayer of thanks.

"Your blood pressure is low, but we'll get it back up. I've medicated your IV." I touched my neck. He told me he had carefully cleaned and bandaged the wounds.

"So he bit you there, drew blood?"

"Yes."

"In this day and age. I'm numb . . . it's so scary; my mother lives just down the road from them. She's staying with us now."

Wearing a hospital gown, Belladonna slowly walked in. Her jet-black hair was combed back tight against her scalp. She had bandages everywhere. When she saw me, she hurried over and put her arms around me. I held her tight, stroked her head. Her hair was soft like silk.

"You did it; I didn't think you could, but you did," she said.

"We did it together. Did you tell the police everything?"

"Yes, a half-dozen detectives interviewed me. At first they were really hostile; they thought I was one of them, but I explained everything and they became more friendly and listened to what I had to say. They sent a police boat to search the water behind the house and found bodies."

"They find Anne Fitzgerald?"

"Not that I know of. I'm pretty sure she is in New Orleans."

"Did they find Dracol?"

"No . . . not yet."

Burly, serious-faced detectives filled the door, the ones Belladonna had spoke to earlier, and they wanted to talk with me now. Dr. Kennedy told them that I needed rest, but I said it was okay. They asked Belladonna to step out of the room. I gave the detectives a brief rundown of what had happened. One of them was a captain named John Dauria, a tall thin man with a thick head of wavy blond hair. He said, "So far we've got six bodies up, and there's more down there— a few children, too. We had no idea any of this was going on. We feel like a bunch of stiffs. Right under our noses, and we didn't have a fuckin' clue."

"He was good at what he did," I said. "Is the house destroyed?"

"Pretty much. Just some of the foundation's left, and it's still burning."

"I'd like to check it out. Will you guys take me?"

"Any time you want," Dauria said. "Soon as you are up to it. I want to shake your hand, Frank. It's a pleasure to meet a guy like you," he said. They all, in turn, shook my hand. I told them I couldn't have done it without Belladonna's help. Captain Dauria asked me how I knew about the bodies in the river, and I explained what Vacaresco had told me and how I used the Fish

Cam. They also questioned me about Belladonna. They were very uncomfortable with her because of her pointed teeth, but I explained how she only worked at the club, had been kidnapped, that she'd been very helpful. Dr. Kennedy returned and asked them to leave. The captain gave me his card and, again, they all shook my hand and left. Belladonna came back and sat next to the bed, took my hand.

"I owe you my life," she said. "I'm sure he would have killed me. I feel so bad about all those people he murdered. De Nardo, I had no idea, I swear I had no idea. You believe me? Tell me you believe me—I need to hear that."

"Of course I believe you," I said, and before I knew it I had drifted off somewhere.

CHAPTER THIRTEEN

When I woke up, I was in a hospital room on a high floor. The sun was up now and the sky was blue and clear and friendly. The phone rang. Belladonna answered it, said, "He can't be disturbed," and hung up.

She saw that I was awake. "Good morning," she said.

"What time is it? How long have I been sleeping?"

"Nearly eleven. You slept the whole night. How're you feeling?"

"All right. You've been here all the while?"

"Yes. I'm not going anywhere until I know you are okay."

"Who was on the phone?"

"Another reporter. They are driving everyone at the hospital nuts. And your mother left two messages that you should phone her."

"You spoke to her?"

"No, she called the administration office. Also,

a Captain Ken Roe phoned twice, said he was a friend."

"A very good friend."

"He's coming up to see you."

"He's a great guy; he was my boss when I was with the NYPD."

"Here, you've got to eat," she said. "They brought you some lunch," and before I knew it she was feeding me watery chicken soup.

"I'm going to get rid of these teeth," she said. "I don't want them anymore. I used to think of them as a kind of badge of defiance, that I was different, mysterious, of the night, unconventional. Maybe even a little dangerous. But all that's changed now."

"I'm glad to hear that," I said.

"When we get back to New York, I'm going straight to the dentist and have him put bonding over them."

"I'm pleased."

"Policemen from everywhere have been stopping by to talk with you. It's all over the news."

"I'm not surprised."

I sat up. I was still being fed intravenously.

"They've brought up eleven bodies and there's still a few down there. Even the FBI has gotten involved."

"I want to get out of here. I'm feeling fine. I've got things to do."

"You need rest."

"I need to see if they found his body; I want to see the coffin. And I want to find Anne Fitzgerald."

"They've been showing what's left of the house on the news. There's no way he could have survived that. The oil made it like an inferno. That was such a clever idea."

"I want to make certain we got him," I said. "See his bones." I finished the soup. Dr. Kennedy came back in and checked my blood pressure, said it was much better, 110 over 80, and that I could leave the hospital, but that I should take it easy. He prescribed special iron tablets for me, antibiotics, and removed the IV feed from my arm. When I stood up, I was wobbly. My clothes were in the closet. They were a mess but would serve the purpose. As I was pulling them on, Captain Roe knocked on the door.

"Hello, pal," I said. "You didn't have to come up. I'm just leaving now. But it's good to see you."

"I wanted to see if you needed anything. I heard what happened. It's all over the news. . . . Close call, Frank."

"Very close—too close. Ken, I'd like you to meet Belladonna," I said.

They shook hands. "It's a pleasure to meet you, Belladonna," he said.

"Pleasure's mine," she said.

He saw her teeth, and his smile went away fast.

"She was helping me," I said, "and he kidnapped her. She's on our side."

"Glad to hear that," he said.

"Your friend here saved my life. Quite a guy," she said.

"The best. So you're okay?"

"I'm fine."

"That's so good to hear. If you need anything, here's my card; don't hesitate to call."

"Okay, thank you, Captain. I appreciate that."

I signed some release papers, called my mother, and told her I was okay. She was angry with me for not phoning sooner, said she was worried sick. That I had to stop doing these "types of things" and "settle down once and for all." I told her I had to go, that I'd call her back, and we went downstairs. There really was a mob of reporters outside. My SUV had been brought over by the Westchester detectives, Belladonna explained.

I said, "Before we go back to the city, I want to check out the house."

"You sure you are up to it?" she asked.

"I'm definitely up to it," I said, knowing that if Dracol hadn't been killed this was far from over.

"I'd like to see it, too," the captain said. A couple of Westchester cops escorted us outside. Reporters and cameramen surrounded us. I was nearly knocked down twice. What they really wanted were shots of Belladonna. The cops had to push them back. We piled into my SUV and followed the police back to Dracol's house, along scenic winter-white streets as pretty as Christmas postcards. The block on which Dracol lived was cordoned off on both ends. I was able to pull my car up to the front gate. Police, fire department, and FBI vehicles were parked all over the place.

The house was gone. All that remained of it were some smoldering, charred beams. It looked like a bomb had blown the place to pieces. Fine with me.

"Such a nice block, a nice neighborhood," Captain Roe said. "You'd *never* expect something like this."

"That's exactly why he chose it," Belladonna said.

We got out of the car. When the detectives, agents, and cops heard I was there, they all came over to say hello. The distinct smell of burnt flesh hung in the air. The bodies of the ones I had shot were lined up in black plastic body bags to the left of the horseshoe-shaped drive. Captain Dauria showed us around what was left. We walked to the back of the place and could see the Coast Guard and police launches still searching the river. The water was much calmer now. A half-dozen news helicopters circled overhead as if they were expectant vultures waiting for their chance at something dead. Now the skies were a clear winter blue, free of clouds. The low winter sun glistened off the river brilliantly.

We made our way back to the house. I wanted to see Dracol's coffin, and with some difficulty we made it down the stone steps to the basement. It reeked of burnt flesh. Most of the room where we had been kept was gone, though the chains that had held us were still there. I explained how I cut the clasp on the lock, overpowered Cassandra—whose body was not there—and broke the oil line and the rest of it. What was left of Dracol's coffin was exactly where it had been, but it was open now—gaping ominously. I slowly walked up to it, hoping that his rings were in the coffin, some charred bones; it was empty; just dirt. Captain Dauria said he had been there when they first located the coffin and they didn't find any body or rings.

We went back upstairs and silently returned to the driveway. I had seen enough. We soon got back into my SUV, returned to the hospital so Captain Roe could get his car, and headed back to the city. Two police cars escorted us to the Henry Hudson Parkway. Belladonna offered to drive, but I said I could handle it. I knew we'd been very lucky and gave quiet thanks to whatever powers are in charge of such things. I suggested she stay at my place until we knew it was safe for her to go back home. She agreed, but did so reluctantly.

"I don't," she said, "want to put you out at all. I've been a burden on you already."

"You won't be putting me out and you haven't been any kind of burden. I got myself into what happened, not you."

"I should have known. He was doing all that right under my nose, and I was blind to it. He used me."

"You aren't to blame."

"Are you planning to look for Anne still?"

"That's what I was hired to do, and I'm going to do it."

"Hmm," she said, nothing more.

When we passed under the George Washington Bridge, I felt compelled to pull over, knowing this was the place where Carole Smith had first been found, thinking about her sad life, what her father had done to her, how her little girl had been murdered by Charles Boone, harsh black-and-white images of Carole in the morgue coming to me. We both sat silently looking at the now-calm water. I took a long, deep breath, found my cell phone in the glove compartment where I'd left it, and called Bobby Marino to tell him how I had lost the camera, that I'd buy him another one. He said he heard all about what happened and told me that he had seen me walk out of Hastings General Hospital with Belladonna on the news.

"What a monster—Jesus! You should have told me," he said. "I would've been happy to go along, bro. The brunette you were with—that the woman you told me about?"

"That's her."

"Really beautiful. Looks like the actress Catherine Zeta-Jones."

"That's what I thought. Bobby, I'm sorry, but the camera was lost in the fire. I'll buy you another one."

"Don't worry about it. Lost to a good cause. It helped, right?"

"Absolutely. If you don't let me buy you another one, I'm never talking to you again."

"Okay, if you put it that way. Why don't you come over Sunday for a nice meal? Bring your friend. The kids and Rose would love to see you."

"I'll try."

"Come on, Frank, don't be a stiff."

"I'll let you know, buddy."

"All right. We hope to see you soon," he said.

I then called Captain Roe on his cell.

"Kenny," I said, "I'm thinking Dracol got away and that he's going to come around looking for revenge. Belladonna's going to be staying with me for a couple of days. If you don't mind, can you maybe post a couple of guys at my place? I'd appreciate it."

"No problem. Good idea. Be there ASAP," he said.

"Thanks, pal—you are the best," I said, knowing Dracol had dedicated followers. I was not about to underestimate him or his people again.

My uncle Sal called to tell me how much my mother had worried—that I should "find something else to do." I told him I was seriously thinking of retiring. He told me about a friend of my cousin Linda and that I should come out to the house to meet her.

"She's a real nice Italian girl," he said. "It's time you settle down. You don't want to get old by yourself, do you?" In no mood to hear this, I promised I would come to Brooklyn to meet my cousin's friend. My uncle then told me about a "vampire" who had plagued Sicily, killed scores of people; that "his friends" had found out where it slept and went and destroyed it during the day. He asked me if Dracol was still alive. I told him I thought he was. He offered to send "some people" to keep an eye on me. I thanked him and told him that wasn't necessary. Again, he made me promise to come to the house for Sunday dinner and we hung up, my head filled with what my uncle had told me . . . the bizarre spectacle of the Sicilian Mafia killing a vampire.

I called John Fitzgerald and briefly ran down to him what had happened, told him that I heard Anne went to New Orleans. He became silent, asked me if I was still willing to look for her there after all that had happened.

"Definitely. More so than ever," I said. He thanked me several times, told me he wanted to double my fee. I said that wasn't necessary, that I'd call him back on a land phone.

"She definitely wasn't in the water behind his house?" he asked.

"No, for sure not," I said, hung up, and got off the West Side Highway at Ninety-sixth Street, headed straight for a supermarket on Broadway, and bought some staples. In a hardware shop at Ninety-fifth, I purchased a motion detector with floodlamps for the backyard. I double-parked in front of my place to drop off my things. Louise came out and gave me a long hug, telling me how worried sick she'd been. I introduced her to Belladonna. So I wouldn't have to walk back, Louise took the SUV over to the garage for me.

As I entered my place, there was a smile on my face. Louise had a fire going in the fireplace—home sweet home. Belladonna said she'd like to take a shower. I showed her where everything was, gave her one of my bathrobes, said, "You make yourself completely at home. *Mi casa es tu casa.*" She smiled and thanked me. Her pointed teeth really gave me the creeps now. She seemed to sense that and told me she wanted to see her dentist "right away." I thought that a grand idea and told her so, put on CNN, and they were showing what was left of Dracol's house from a helicopter shot, the river calm and peaceful now, as if it was pleased to be rid of Dracol's victims and the terrible secret of their murders.

The sensation of Dracol drawing my blood, stealing my life force, returned with a rush. I had to sit down. Most all my life I had prepared myself to deal with anything I came up against, but this—this was something completely different. I shut off the TV and called Marco Vacaresco in Bucharest. He picked up on the first ring. He, too, said he saw what had happened on both CNN and the BBC.

"I see you, Frank De Nardo, walk out of the hospital. You destroyed them. You destroyed the house. It was you who set it on fire, no? Congratulations. And the bodies in the river just nearby—*you* found this out, didn't you?"

"Yes, I did, thanks to you. What you told me about the underground lake got me to thinking about the river, and one thing led to another."

"Ah, yes, of course—bravo, my friend. This makes me very so glad. He is dead, yes? Destroyed in the house. Fire would kill him, like I tell you."

"No, I think he got away," I said.

There was an awkward silence. "That is not good," he said. "You must be prepared—vampires are vindictive creatures. Did you find his coffin?"

"I did. It was in the basement, but it was empty. No bones—none of his rings when we went back."

"We are not, you understand, talking here about a creature from this world. He is a monster sent by the Devil himself. Be prepared, my friend, and whatever you do, you mustn't be afraid. Fear will make you vulnerable. Vampires are cowards. If he thinks you can hurt him or that he can be hurt trying to get at you, he will most likely move on; like all vampires, he enjoys having power over life and death."

"Thank you for all your good advice. I'd be lost without you," I said, still not buying into this preternatural vampire thing. Dracol was, I was sure, nothing more than a serial killer—an extreme psychopath, a sexual deviate and sadist masquerading as a vampire. But he was, I reminded myself, incredibly strong, which I was still attributing to his being a bona fide psychopath, and perhaps on drugs. . . .

"Don't thank me—in this we are brothers. You are my new very good friend, Frank De Nardo. It is my pleasure. If I was there, I would fight by your side. It is you we have to thank. You rousted him from his lair. Now the whole world is looking for him. Knows what he is. He can no longer kill with impunity, thanks to you. We will get him. Good will triumph over evil. In the end, it always does. Just you be careful."

"I hope we can meet one day, Marco."

"I would like that very much, my new so very good friend. When you come to Bucharest, you will be treated like a hero, I tell you, a hero."

I thanked him again and soon hung up, not feeling like I had won anything, but at least, as he had said, Dracol could not move about anymore with impunity, without looking over his shoulder. The world now knew him for the murdering fiend he really was.

The doorbell rang. I checked my security monitor and there were four stone-faced NYPD detectives Captain Roe had sent over. I went outside and said hello to them, thanked them for coming, and answered a few of their questions. I knew three of them, and for sure felt better having them outside, in a black van with tinted windows, all experienced hard-boiled New York City detectives with steely eyes and nerves to match. Belladonna came out of the bathroom. I gave her a pair of jeans and a work shirt to put on. We made plans to go to her place so she could pick up some clothes and personal things.

She helped me install the motion detector in the backyard. Louise returned and I gave her a brief rundown of what had happened, what I saw.

She didn't like Belladonna, and it was all over her face. I explained to Louise how Belladonna had helped me, that she didn't know what Dracol was really up to. I also told her that she shouldn't come to work for the next few days, until I was sure it was safe. She didn't like that either, but she agreed and soon left.

Belladonna and I sat on the couch in front of the fireplace. I put my arm around her and quietly stared at the flames, thinking about Dracol, the hateful gleam in his eyes, his teeth, how he picked me up as if I were a thing to eat—a sparerib or a chicken leg. Belladonna dozed off. I quietly got up, went and took two extra-strength aspirins, slipped the Beretta into my pants at the nape of my back, put my Walther PPK in the front room under a book and my Glock on the night table next to my bed. I also loaded my shotgun with Magnum rounds. The phone rang. I let the machine pick it up. I was in no mood to talk with anyone. It was a deep-voiced man with a slow southern accent. He said, "Name's Sam Henderson. I run the PD down here in New Orleans. I'm looking for a Mr. Frank De Nardo."

I picked up the phone. "You got him," I said.

"Hey, Frank, it's a pleasure. I've been watchin' on TV all about what happened up there. It's enough to make a person sick. I'm sure you know Dracol's got one of those freaky-deaky clubs down here, over in the Quarter. Lines of people there every night waiting to get in, all these pale vampire types. This whole vampire thing's a real big deal down here because of all the Rice books and movies. Far as I'm concerned, it's totally outta control. Satanic. Wouldn't you say? Got these nonstop vampire tours of all the cemeteries and old plantations; you'd think people could find somethin' better to do with their time and money.

"Dracol was like a big celebrity down here, strutting around like the king of France or something, you know. Anyway, I'm callin', Frank, 'cause he's got himself an old plantation right near Lake Pontchartrain and I'm thinking we should maybe check out the lake. Seems to me if he was doing that up there in the Hudson River and all, it stands to reason he'd been doing the same damn thing or even worse down here—wouldn't you say?"

"I'd be surprised if he wasn't."

"Right, exactly my thoughts. He's got all these women who adore him and follow him around like wide-eyed lovesick puppies, and I'd wager he's been doing all kinds of freaky things with them—drinkin' their blood and killing them too, and God only knows what kinds of perversions he made them do. I shudder at the thought. Was he killed in the fire?"

"We think he got away."

"Bummer. So why I'm callin' is his backyard is right up against the lake and there's one of those docks so you can walk out a hundred steps or so onto the water."

"The water deep?"

"Yeah, in some parts pretty deep, but I heard about this underwater camera you used. Is that true?"

"It's called a Fish Cam. You have an aquarium down there?"

"We've got a world-class aquarium to be proud of."

"Well, they will definitely have one or know where you can get it. They've got a fluorescent light if the water is too deep for natural light to reach the bottom."

"Okay, that's a help. So you think it's a worthwhile thing to do?"

"For sure. I was going to call you guys."

"The thing of it is, I hear he's got a couple places down here, but no one knows where exactly, 'cept, a course, the place I'm talkin' about."

"What about his club?"

"There was a fire at the club the other night and it's already out of business. Somebody spread some gas after it closed and put a match to it. Personally, I think it's an Evangelist group we have down here, but there's no proof a that."

"First good news I had all day."

"I popped a bottle of champagne when I heard. So I'm going to get on this thing right away; I'll keep you posted. We're having a warrant for the house drawn up because of your good work. You ever get down this way, you look me up. I'll take you for one of the best meals you ever had, I can guarantee you that. De Nardo—that's Italian, right?"

"It's Italian."

"Well, we got some of the finest Italian restaurants in all the world right here in New Orleans."

"I might just take you up on that, thank you," I said.

"Be my pleasure," he said, and we soon hung up and I sat there for a long time mulling over what I'd just heard. I was about to call Fred Reynolds, but the phone rang and it was Georgia Smith calling from New Orleans.

"Hello, Georgia, how are you?" I said.

"Oh, Mr. De Nardo, I just had to call and say thank you. I knew you could do it. The moment I saw you, I knew. It was in your eyes. Thank you so very much. God will bless you. They are saying on the news that fifteen bodies were found. Is that true?"

"Twelve so far."

"My Lord. Soon as I heard, I went to church and gave thanks and lit a candle for you. The Lord is on your side, Mr. De Nardo. If this isn't proof of that, nothing is."

"I can use all the help I can get."

"But he got away . . . didn't he?" she said, as if perhaps she knew something I didn't.

"It appears that way," I said.

"So it's true," she said.

"What's that?"

"Most all the folks down here know about my campaign against Dracol—you heard the club burnt down?"

"Yes."

"So as I was leaving church tonight, my friend Ella Rose St. Angelo stopped me. Remember I told you about her daughter Lucy—the little run-around—that she works for Santos Dracol. My friend Ella Rose heard her telling someone on the phone that *he's* here—"

"Dracol?" I said, feeling the blood leave my face, my stomach tightening.

"Yes. That's why I'm callin'. She told me Lucy said she saw him at a house he has over in the Quarter, down near the river."

"You tell the New Orleans police what you just told me?"

"In fact I did. I spoke to Sam Henderson himself. And he sent some of his best detectives to go talk to Lucy. I understand she denied everything; told the detectives her mother is senile and doesn't know what the heck she's talkin' about. Trouble is, Ella Rose *is* slightly out of touch, but I believe her. She surely knows the difference between something real and something imagined.

"Lucy is a vampire, sleeps in a coffin, has the pointed teeth and white skin—the whole enchilada. Ella Rose told me she drinks blood, too. Since she was a little girl, I always knew she would turn out bad, but I never imagined anything like this, you know. Fact is, she and Carole were friends for a while. She was a very bad influence on my daughter. She introduced Carole to Dracol."

"Have you spoken to Lucy?"

"Oh, no. She won't talk to me. She hates me.

She calls me names when she sees me and she spits at me. I'm going to go stake out the house. If he's here, I'll find out—"

"I don't think you should do that."

"That *thing* doesn't scare me. I've got a .45 pistol, and I'll put a slug into him before you can say how do you do."

"Georgia, please, don't confront him if—"

"Mr. De Nardo, I've got one mission in life, and that's sending this bastard back to hell."

"I know that, but if you see him just go tell Sam Henderson. Your letting the police know where he is, is help enough. There's no sense in your going and getting yourself hurt. We are going to need you as a witness, remember. I know you know how dangerous he is. Georgia, promise me that you'll go tell Sam Henderson and call me if you see him."

"I promise," she reluctantly said.

"I'll be here all night. Remember, don't confront him. Don't let him know you are there. That's the object—sneak, peek and retreat. Okay? Remember our talk."

"All right, okay, I've got it," she said. We soon hung up, and I sat there mulling this over, a bad feeling spreading inside. I got up and went back into the living room. Belladonna was awake.

"What's happening?" she asked.

"Georgia Smith called. A friend of hers has a daughter who works for Santos, and this friend overheard the daughter telling someone that Santos is there, in New Orleans."

"I was afraid of that. Did she tell the police this?"

"She did, and they went and questioned the daughter and she clammed up." We fell silent. The wood in the fire crackled and popped. Hot embers bounced off the screen.

I said, "I'm thinking if he's really alive, it's just a matter of time before he comes looking for revenge—you agree?"

"Yes. . . . There's no way he's going to leave this alone. You destroyed his life; he's a wanted man all over the world now because of you . . . because of us. I am as deep in this as you. He won't rest until we are dead . . . or worse."

"Worse?"

"Yes, worse."

"Well, I'm not about to just sit around and wait for something to happen."

"Somehow that doesn't surprise me. If you are planning to go down there, you've got to take me with you. I can help in many ways. I know New Orleans really well. I know where he has houses, who works for him, the whole scene down there."

"I usually work alone," I said.

"Well, you can't this time. I can make all the difference. I'm in just as much danger as you, maybe more. I have the right. Don't shut me out. I can help in numerous ways, and you know it."

"I'll think about it."

"There's nothing to think about—it would be stupid to shut me out. Have you been to New Orleans?"

"Not for a while."

"Well, I used to live there. I managed the New Orleans club. There's a whole vamp subculture going on down there—all these vamp shops and tours because of vamp writers and Dracol."

"Sam Henderson was telling me."

I knew she was right but was hesitant about bringing her; if something happened to her, I'd be responsible.

"You can't shut me out," she said. "I have the right. I'm in this with you to the wall!"

"You do have the right, but I don't want to see anything happen to you—"

"Don't worry about me. Let's concern ourselves with one thing—stopping him. Getting him. Let's work as a team, okay?"

"Okay," I said, but was still not sure.

I put my feet up on the coffee table. She nestled her head against my shoulder.

"I'm sorry I got you involved in all this," I said.

"Don't say that. I'm glad you did. I had no idea what a monster he really was. I always thought of him as just a really shrewd, slightly kinky vamp. I swear I had no idea. You believe that, don't you?"

I didn't answer.

"Please, De Nardo, I need to know you realize that. If I knew what he was truly into, I would have gone to the police—I swear on the soul of my grandmother."

"I believe you," I said.

"You exposed him; you stopped him. Don't apologize to me, okay?"

"Okay," I said, and soon dozed off and dreamed about New Orleans, saw in my dreams Anne Fitzgerald as a vampire stalking people in New Orleans.

CHAPTER FOURTEEN

The phone woke me up. I heard Georgia Smith leaving a message. I hurried into the office. It was three A.M. I picked up. "I'm here," I said.

"Mr. De Nardo, I'm so sorry to be calling this late, but I saw him!"

"Where—are you sure it was him?"

"Sure as rain, I spoke to him. He hurt me. I'm in a hospital right now."

"What happened?"

"I was standing in the doorway of number one hundred seventy-three, on Sixth Street, and I . . . I kind of sensed someone approaching me from the opposite direction of his house. So I'm looking down the street and I hear a noise above me, and my God, I see him up on the roof, glaring down at me. Then, like some kind of giant insect, he came crawling down the building, his eyes popping out of his head. I had my gun all ready, but the sight of him coming down the side of the building like that unhinged me like nothing in

245

my life, and before I could take a bead on him, he took my pistol out of my hand. I tried to scratch him with my nails, but he picked me up and held me, snarling and baring his teeth. I told him he didn't scare me and spit right smack in his face. With that he threw me through the air. I was lucky and landed in a thick bunch of bushes, but still I broke my arm, and I'm all scratched up. I'm in St. Mary's Hospital right now. They just finished taking the X-rays, and I'm waiting for the doctor to put a cast on my arm.

"So I'm lying there not believing what happened, and he running real quick down the street toward me. I swear, the sight of him coming at me like that made my heart come up to my throat. . . .

"He told me that I should tell you that he's waiting for you, that he is in New Orleans waiting for you. He called you the Mafia detective. 'Tell the Mafia detective I'm here,' he said. Are you in the Mafia, Mr. De Nardo?"

"Of course not. What else did he say?"

"That's it. He walked away calm as could be. I picked myself up and struggled to the hospital and here I am."

"Have you reported this to the police yet?"

"I first told a uniform cop on guard at the hospital what happened, and he called the detectives and they came right over with the sirens going and all. I wanted to call you first, but they made me tell them what happened, and I did.

"I'm sure he would have killed me if he didn't want to use me to give you his message. He had such *hatred* in his eyes. Whatever you do, Mr. De Nardo, don't come here, he'll surely kill you—maybe even something worse: He'll make you one of them. You can't protect yourself from such a thing; he's not of this world . . . my God—oh my God."

"You just concern yourself with getting treatment and staying safe. I'll call you later to see how you are, and whatever you do, don't go looking to confront him."

"I'm not. I'll be home," she said, in obvious pain.

"Okay, we'll talk later," I said, and slowly hung up, sat there thinking about what I had just heard, knowing now for sure that he had not only survived but was taunting me, daring me to come and find him. I looked up, and Belladonna was standing in the doorway.

"When are we leaving?" she said.

"*We* are going under one condition," I said.

"Depends?" she said.

"I call the shots."

"Hey, you are the professional, of course."

"Okay," I said. We kissed, soon went to bed, held each other, and like that fell asleep.

When I woke up, I found Belladonna at my desk, on the phone, trying to make an appointment with her dentist. Angry, she hung up. "He's on vacation," she said. "I really want to get rid of these, and I want to start wearing colorful clothes, and going out during the day, and I'm never going to drink blood again. That's all over."

"I've got a good dentist right over here on Eighty-sixth Street—Dr. Massi."

"If he'll see me, I'll go this morning."

"You don't have to do this for me—"

"I'm doing it for myself. I can't look in the mirror anymore," she said, and I called Dr. Massi, said it was an emergency, and he said he could see her in one hour. We had a light breakfast, washed up, and walked over to Dr. Massi's, three heavily armed detectives shadowing us. Dr. Massi got a kick out of Belladonna's teeth, said to cover them with bonding would be easy, and took her in the office. She asked me to stay with her, and I held her hand as he covered her fangs with bonding compound, using a purple light to harden the compound, cracking jokes about vampires. He finished in less than a half hour, and you couldn't tell she ever had pointed canines, and she looked completely different without the fangs, softer, prettier—more wholesome. He gave her a handheld mirror so she could see for herself. "Amazing," she said. "Thank you. They look perfect," and they did.

Back at my place, Louise had arrived and was manning the phones. This was going to be her last day before she went south to visit her family—her parents and three sisters. It seemed every news outlet in the world wanted to interview Belladonna and me. Producers from all over were calling and even ringing my bell. As has always been my policy over the years, I don't do interviews. The last thing I wanted was my face all over national television. My thing has always been about stealth and secrecy, and a P.I. who is a publicity hound—as many are these days—flies in the face of both our tradition and common sense. Belladonna went to take a shower.

I keep a professional Everlast heavy bag bolted to a beam in the basement, and I went downstairs now, slipped on my old boxing gloves, and went to work on the bag, hitting it with lefts and rights and different combinations, thinking this thing out, taking my frustration and anger out on the bag, my neck beginning to burn where Dracol had bitten into me. I would never forget that—how effortlessly he picked me up, drank my blood.

I knew that once we went to New Orleans we'd be in Dracol's territory—maybe even walking into a carefully laid trap. This time, however, I was going to pick the time and place to fight him, and I would be properly prepared.

After fifteen minutes of punching the heavy bag, flushing this thing out, I went back upstairs and had Louise reserve a car for me from Hertz on West Seventy-seventh Street. I couldn't fly down to New Orleans because of the weapons I planned to take, and I wasn't about to drive down in my SUV. I went and opened the hidden panel in my closet, the place where I keep my weapons.

If, I knew, I was going to come out of this alive, I had to be cunning and ruthless in the extreme. Truth is, I didn't like taking Belladonna, but I knew she could be a big help in many ways.

Jack Gorba, a gunsmith friend of mine, had designed and built for me a unique apparatus that straps to the inside of a forearm; he calls it a Gorba Slide. It holds in place a three-shot nine-millimeter derringer, which hooks onto a spring-cocked lever. The derringer stays at the upper end of the Slide, near the elbow, until you are ready to use it. You can trip the spring by bending your wrist just so, and the derringer shoots forward and is suddenly in your hand, ready to be fired. I loaded three rounds into the derringer and put it and the Gorba Slide into a leather carrying case. I also put in the case two cigarette-pack-sized plastic explosive charges, a sawed-off shotgun, three more pistols, and a silencer for my Beretta. This was a war I was absolutely intent upon winning.

I thought about calling New Orleans chief of police Sam Henderson but decided against it. He inevitably would tell his detectives, and they in turn would tell people, and it would be just a matter of time before everyone in New Orleans knew I was coming. The element of surprise had to stay mine. I was also tempted to telephone Georgia Smith and tell her I was on the way, but I decided against that, too. I packed some clothes and toiletries, tape and rope, several sets of handcuffs and my lock-pick set, and was soon ready to go. But before we could leave, I called Captain Roe and asked if I could come by the precinct. He said he'd be there most of the day unless an emergency came up.

Belladonna came out of the bathroom. Her hair was slicked back. She had a big smile on her beautiful face. I was really glad she'd gotten rid of the fangs—and I took her in my arms and gave her a long, passionate kiss. Her face flushed.

"If something happens to you in New Orleans, I couldn't look myself in the mirror—you have to promise to do all that I say," I said.

"Of course; I promise. You are the boss. I just want to help, and I can. You know that."

"I do. We are leaving today—in a little while, okay? You ready?"

"I'm ready."

"You know how to use a handgun?"

"Yes. Well, I used to own one."

I handed her a 9mm Walther, a sleek, light-weight, very accurate automatic.

"When are we going?"

"In a little while. I want to keep the element of surprise ours. You need anything—clothes and stuff?"

"I can get everything I need down there. Let's go; let's do it. I'm ready."

And we soon left for New Orleans. The detectives who had been assigned to guard us gave us a lift down to Hertz to pick up my rental car, a souped-up black Taurus. I went from there straight to the Twenty-fourth Precinct to see Captain Roe, left her in the car double-parked out front, and found him at the coffee machine. He made me a cup, and we sat down at his desk and

I told him about Georgia Smith's call; that I was going to New Orleans to find Dracol. I didn't mention Belladonna.

"When?" he asked, frowning as he sipped his coffee, his light blue eyes narrowing on me.

"I'm leaving right now, driving down."

"I know you didn't come here to hear me try to talk you out of this, but, Frank, this could be a one-way trip. Let the New Orleans cops handle him. Sam Henderson is an experienced man and he knows his p's and q's; there's no reason to put yourself in harm's way like this—"

"Ken, I have to go. I just wanted you to know what I was up to; that I could call on you if I do need help."

"Until you are back, I'll sleep with my cell phone. Don't hesitate to call—no matter what time, you hear?"

"Thanks, pal."

"You been to New Orleans before?"

"Yeah, on the Stevenson kidnapping case."

"Yes, I remember. Where will you be staying?"

"Not sure yet. But I'll always have the cell with me."

"Okay. Godspeed," he said. We hugged, and I was soon heading south on the I-95. As I drove, Belladonna and I discussed the best way to find Dracol. She said she knew Lucy St. Angelo, that she was a trusted confidante of Dracol; that if we followed her, she'd lead us to him sooner or later. We discussed what we'd do when we did find him—the best way to bring him down. She talked about putting a stake through his heart, cutting his head off, and stuff like that. I still didn't believe he had any kind of preternatural powers, but Belladonna wasn't so sure anymore. "Remember," she said, "how strong he was—how he picked you up. I saw it, you saw it."

"You have a point," I said, and she did, I knew.

"Let's proceed," she said, "with the assumption that he is preternatural—never underestimate your enemy."

She was right and I had to agree with her, but I still wasn't buying the fact that he had any kind of supernatural powers. Far as I was concerned, he was nothing more than a homicidal maniac playing a vampire; for him, every day was Halloween. She looked at her teeth in the mirror behind the visor.

"I'm really glad they are gone," she said, smiling.

"So am I."

I called my uncle Sal to tell him where I was going and what I was doing. He told me, which I already knew, that he had some "good friends," in New Orleans and I shouldn't hesitate to phone them if I needed some extra help, and he gave me two cell phone numbers. I thanked him, hung up, and explained to Belladonna who my uncle was and what he did. She became quiet and contemplative. After a time, she said: "Maybe we could use the help of people like that."

"If we need them, they are there."

"Just like that?"

"Yeah, just like that . . . it's a blood tie."

"Interesting. Were you ever in the Mafia?"

"No," I said. "I went in the other direction."

"What other direction?"

"Law enforcement."

CHAPTER FIFTEEN

Using false ID I keep handy for such purposes, we checked into the Peter's Inn on St. Charles Street in the Art District. At this point, I didn't want any record of our being in New Orleans because I had no idea how this would turn out. The Peter's Inn was a small, out-of-the-way place where we could come and go without having to pass the front desk. After unloading my gear, I called Georgia Smith on my cell phone and told her I was in my office—and I was able to get from her Lucy St. Angelo's most current address. She told me that she had not seen or heard from Dracol, that the police were checking out his plantation near the lake. We freshened up, went and found the building where St. Angelo lived. It was on Dauphine, just off Duamine, a quiet one-way street, perfect for what I had in mind. From there I took Belladonna to a shopping mall, she bought some clothes and toiletries, and we went back to the hotel. I armed myself, strapped on the Gorba

Slide, put a 9mm auto in my pants, gave Belladonna the Walther. We had something to eat and drove back to the house.

It was a balmy seventy degrees, but there was much wind, and angry clouds hurried across the sky like ghosts on their way to no good. There was a nearly full moon, but the clouds hid it on and off. There was a storm brewing, about to strike New Orleans. One of the most beautiful cities in the country with its old world Deco charm and quaint, colorful buildings. It was kind of ironic, I was thinking, how Dracol and others like him gravitated to New Orleans, which clearly also had a sinister underbelly, which you could sense when you walked down its narrow streets, which creatures of the night apparently found appealing. Belladonna told me from the very beginning, New Orleans was a magnet for people involved in the occult, in the black arts, necromania, voodoo, and various magical mumbo jumbo brought over from Africa with the many slaves put to work on New Orleans's sprawling plantations. She told me, too, that preternatural vampires had truly lived in New Orleans in the seventeenth and eighteenth centuries; that Anne Rice and other popular writers had gotten their ideas for books and movies and plays from the stories of these vampires' bloody exploits.

We headed back to Dauphine. The wind built up and blew with a vengeance, palm trees bending and bowing. I parked under a thick oak tree, and we sat there waiting, the wind blowing might-ily, as Belladonna regaled me with the bloody exploits of a famous French vampire who haunted New Orleans in the 1700s, who had, she said, a particular penchant for the blood of children.

"He was," she said, "related to the infamous Hungarian Countess Erzsébet Báthory, who murdered over six hundred girls, who drank and bathed in their blood."

"Interesting," I said.

Lucy St. Angelo lived in a pastel-blue three-story town house with planters and flowers in all of its windows. From where we were, we had an unobstructed view of number 19. It was already near midnight, and few people were out. We stayed there until dawn and didn't get so much as a glimpse of St. Angelo. We finally went back to the hotel, had breakfast, and I phoned my office and retrieved my messages. We lay down and quickly fell asleep, the sound of the wind constant. If I didn't get some sleep, I'd be no good for anything.

I had sex-infused dreams about the vampire Belladonna had told me about, Count Charles Radcliff. When I woke up, I didn't feel rested. The storm had grown. We had some breakfast, left the hotel, and I drove to the Flower District where St. Angelo lived and carefully studied the area, then drove along the Mississippi River looking for a secluded place I could use to force her to tell us what we needed to know, if it came to that, when and if we found her. Powerful winds blew. The sky was the color of iron. Lightning bolts suddenly danced madly.

We then did a tour of New Orleans, and Belladonna showed me where the club had been—all boarded up now—and Dracol's place on Lake Pontchartrain. It was a secluded chateau surrounded by a tall, white stucco wall covered with thick vines. There were police vehicles parked all over, and we could see police on the pier out back and police helicopters buzzing overhead. She showed me two other houses he owned and we got out of the car and carefully checked them out, but neither of them looked like anyone had been there in a long time; spiderwebs and dust covered the entrances, doors, windows. We returned to the hotel, suited up and went back to Dauphine, and again staked out Lucy St. Angelo's place. Belladonna said Lucy was a creature of the night, that she slept during the day and came out only after dark. It began raining lightly. Solitary drops dotted the windshield.

We were there little more than two hours when I saw movement in the rearview mirror—a tall, thin woman wearing all black with long dark hair came hurrying along the street. "That's her, that's her," Belladonna said in little more than a whisper. She stopped in front of number 19, took keys out of her purse, and went inside. Lights in the second-floor apartment soon went on. After twenty minutes or so, the lights went off. I knew there was no way we could properly interrogate St. Angelo in her apartment, and I explained to Belladonna that I wanted to get her somewhere secluded, near the river. She didn't question me at all. I waited a while more, pulled the car up and parked in front of number 19, told her I'd be right back. Using my lock picks, I easily opened the front door, quietly went upstairs on the balls of my feet. She had one good Medico lock, which I opened in two minutes, and I quickly went inside. A single black candle burned on a table. In its flickering light, I was able to see her soundly sleeping in an open coffin trimmed in purple velvet. I took out my Beretta and moved to the coffin, suddenly slammed my hand over her mouth at the same time I put my gun to her head, pressing it up against her temple. Her eyes burst open.

"I've been sent by the Pope himself," I whispered in her ear. "We know all about you. This gun has a silencer on it. If you so much as make a peep, I'll blow your brains all over your nice coffin—understand?"

She nodded that she understood.

"Okay, Lucy, listen very carefully. We don't want to hurt you. What we want is to find Santos Dracol. I know you know where he is, and I want you to tell me—it's that simple, understand?" Again she nodded that she understood, rapidly blinking her eyes. I slowly removed my hand from her mouth.

"You asshole," she said, and tried to bite me, clawed at my face, surprising me. I slugged her on the point of her chin and knocked her out cold, taped her mouth shut, bound her hands, wrapped her in a blanket, picked her up, and quickly went down the stairs with her on my shoulder like a dirty bag of laundry, put her in the trunk. Belladonna was all wide-eyed. I slowly drove to Esplanade Avenue and made my way east along the river, took a right onto a dirt road that serpentined to a cove off the river. The wind had died down somewhat, but lightning bolts ripped and tore the sky apart. It was high tide now and the surface of the water in the cove was calm—perfect for what I had in mind. The suddenly brilliant moon showed itself and laid a jagged lunar highway the color of sweet cream on the Mississippi. I pulled up close to the water and stopped. She started kicking the inside of the trunk. I told Belladonna to stay in the car, that I didn't want St. Angelo to see her. I got out of the car, picked her up, laid her on the ground, unwrapped her, and took the tape off her mouth.

"How dare you! You will suffer for this—you have no idea who you are fucking with, you asshole!"

"Listen," I stopped her, "I'm in no mood for this. Either you tell me what I need to know or life is going to take a serious turn for the worse for you—"

"Fuck yourself!" she said.

Ballsy woman. I quickly taped her mouth shut and tied the rope tightly around both her ankles, picked her up, and without another word dropped her in the water headfirst. I let the upper part of her body stay submerged for a few seconds as she flopped about. I wasn't enjoying this, but I had to do what needed to be done. I pulled her out of the water and laid her on the ground. She looked at me with serious hatred in her eyes.

"You going to tell me where he is?" I asked. She nodded in the affirmative. I pulled the duct tape off her mouth. "I don't know where he sleeps," she garbled as she spit out water, her eyes bulging with fear. "He doesn't trust anyone after what happened in New York. I know who you are now; you're the one who caused all the problems."

"You got that wrong, lady—he's the one who caused the problems."

"He's lived in New Orleans for many years. He's got houses, places to stay, crypts in different cemeteries all over the city. I don't know where he is. That's the truth, mister. Please let me go, leave me alone. I've never done anything to you."

"Is he here?"

"Yes . . . he's here."

"When and where did you last see him?"

"Yesterday. He called me on my cell phone and told me to meet him at a house near the lake."

"The writer, Anne Fitzgerald—is she here, have you seen her?"

"Yes, she's here."

"Where?"

"In a house near the St. Louis cemetery."

"Where in the house?"

"In the basement."

"Is he there?"

"I don't know. I swear I don't know," she said,

and I didn't know if I should believe her or not. I went and told Belladonna what she had said.

"I know exactly where the house is. It's a large old mansion. There was a big party there on Halloween night a couple of years ago that I went to."

"So we'll check it out."

"Sure . . . but he might be there. Remember that. We can't just go barging in."

"We won't," I said.

I taped St. Angelo's mouth shut again, put her back in the trunk—she was heavier wet—and we headed out to this house near the St. Louis cemetery. Belladonna said that an elderly French woman who was a devotee of Dracol owned the place, and that the famous voodoo queen, Marie Laveau, was entombed in the St. Louis cemetery. Belladonna said Marie Laveau "hated" Dracol. Some people even say he had her poisoned, but that's only a rumor. The more I think about it, though, he could very well be there. De Nardo, we must be very careful from here on in. It's nighttime—he's definitely up and about."

"We'll be careful," I said, having a feeling that all this would soon come to a head. My stomach tightened at the thought of confronting Dracol here on his turf again, remembering his amazing strength, how he picked me up.

The cemetery and house were on the north side of town in a quiet, residential area with old, stately mansions lined up behind ivory-covered walls and tall fences. By now it was near midnight and the streets were empty. The St. Louis cemetery was small and intimate. The dead were kept in white mausoleums, which glistened brilliantly when the moon showed itself. Belladonna said the ground in New Orleans was too wet to properly bury bodies. There was a tall, pointed metal fence surrounding the cemetery. As we slowly drove past it, we could see candles flickering ominously in tall, colored-glass cylinders, red and blue and green, seeming to float in the dark throughout the cemetery. If any cemetery was haunted, it was surely this one.

The house, once the center of a large sugar plantation, stood alone and aloof. It was a large mansion with tall, once-gracious pillars out front. The back faced the cemetery. There were no lights on in any of the windows. Thick ropes of moss hung from the many trees on the grounds, causing snakelike shadows in the pale, indifferent light of the moon. The place gave me the creeps. I parked down the block and turned to Belladonna, glad she was there, I must admit.

"You stay here. I'm going to—"

"Hold on, stop right there. I'm going with you—I didn't come all the way down here to sit in a car while you put it on the line. We are in this together, De Nardo. I can shoot, and four eyes are better than two. And I know the house—I know the grounds. I'm going with you," she said.

I knew there was no changing her mind, and, in truth, she was right.

"Okay, you'll watch my back."

"Yes, exactly," she said. "You can count on me," she said, and I believed her.

I thought now about calling my uncle's friends and moving forward with their help, but decided against it. I had plenty of firepower, and I wasn't even sure Dracol was here. I opened the leather duffel bag with my guns, loaded my shotgun, connected a plastic explosive to a timer, and we walked along the shadow-strewn sidewalk to the house. She said, "It might be better if we first went into the cemetery, made our way round the back of the house, then checked it out."

"Can you climb the fence?"

"Are you kidding? I was a tomboy," she said.

We made it to the cemetery, carefully went over the fence, and walked east. We could see well in the light of the moon when it appeared, as we quietly made our way along narrow lanes between the mausoleums. We came upon some kind of ceremony in front of one of the mausoleums. As clouds covered the moon, it suddenly became dark, was hard to see. A group of people, all naked, were praying around the prostrate form of a woman on the ground. There was some kind of dead animal on her stomach, spooky there in the cemetery in the light of the moon. We ignored them, they us, and we made our way to the back of the mansion, climbed the fence, and approached the house from the rear. Here we could see lights on in a few of the ground-floor windows. There was a pond off to the left. Belladonna pointed to a door at the top of three steps and told me it led to the kitchen, which was between a formal dining room and a large living room with a double-hung ceiling. We hid behind a bush and watched the place, saw no movement inside whatsoever. Lightning struck, thunder boomed like large cannons. A dog barked somewhere off in the distance. Some kind of fish leaped out of the pond, making a splash. I wanted to get the lay of the land, let my eyes properly adjust to the dark before we moved.

"We've got to get inside. I'm going to see if I can open the kitchen door. You stay behind me and keep quiet, okay?"

"Okay."

"First thing I want to do is check the basement, see if Anne is really there. If she is, I want to get her away. That's what we are here for."

"Let's go, I'm ready," she said.

"You sure you know how to shoot?"

"I'm a good shot, don't you worry."

"Could you do it if it came to that?"

"You mean shoot him?"

"Yes."

"Fucking A," she said. "After what he's done, be my pleasure," she added.

"Okay, good, let's go," I said, and we quickly made our way to the back of the house, went up the stairs. The lock was an inexpensive Segal and I got it open in no time. "You ready?" I whispered.

"Absolutely," she said with resolve, and I opened the door and in we went. The kitchen was large copper pots and pans hung from racks attached to the ceiling. All was quiet. Not a sound. We found the door that led to the basement and slowly made our way down the wooden steps. I used my penlight so we could see. An odd smell hung in the air. The steps squeaked under our weight. Spooky.

Downstairs, we found a storage room filled with jars and drying herbs, a wine cellar, another small room with an empty coffin in it, and a thick wooden door bolted shut. The distinct rotten, rancid smell of death hung in the air. I carefully pulled the bolt and opened the door, pointing my Beretta. A woman, sound asleep, was lying on a small bed against the far wall. Chains were bolted to the stone walls. On the left there was a writing desk, a gooseneck lamp, a pile of yellow legal pads, and some quill pens. I motioned for Belladonna to keep lookout, made my way to the bed, and was astonished to see Anne Fitzgerald. She was breathing. Fearing she might scream out if I woke her up, I gently put my hand on her mouth. Her eyes burst open, her body stiffened.

"Anne, your father sent me. I'm here to rescue you, do you understand?" I told her. She nodded that she understood. I slowly took my hand from her mouth.

"Thank God. How did you find me? Who are you?" she asked, her eyes moving to the door.

"It's a long story. Let's get out of here and I'll tell you everything."

"I'm with you," she said, and stood. She was

very pale and there were bite wounds on her neck, but she was good to go.

"Is Dracol here in the house?"

"I don't know, but he's definitely in New Orleans. I saw him last night." She was startled when she saw Belladonna in the hall with her white face, but I told her she was with me and we made it back to the stairs. I went up them first and we hurried to the rear kitchen door. All was quiet, still. I opened the door. We went down the three steps and back to the cemetery fence. Anne said she didn't know if she could climb the fence in her weakened condition, and we started to walk along the fence back to the street. As we made our way, I noticed something move inside the cemetery—a ghostly pale face. I helped Anne so she could walk faster. . . .

Up ahead, on our right as we went, there was movement on top of one of the mausoleums just near the fence, the quick rustling of silky fabric. I looked up—and Dracol was standing there glaring down at us. In one leap, he vaulted over the fence and landed squarely on his feet. Anne screamed; she was obviously deathly afraid of him, and she trembled like a leaf in strong wind. I raised my Beretta and took a calm bead on him.

A large, malicious, pointed-tooth smile slowly spread across his white face. With no fear whatsoever, he boldly walked toward us.

"I should have killed you when the opportunity first presented itself," he said. "I underestimated you. I was foolish. It's a mistake I shall not make again."

I was just about to shoot him, but he suddenly came at me with blinding speed. I fired and blew his left ear clean off, but before I could shoot again, he got my gun away. We fought furiously. His strength was awesome. I wasn't able to get the derringer that was up my sleeve. He tried to bite my hand. I saw Belladonna raise her gun, but he kicked it from her hand.

"You fool," he hissed. "You didn't learn anything." His hands were like an iron vise. He had superhuman, apelike strength. Belladonna attacked him, but he knocked her down. Anne screamed. I finally managed to straighten my arm and bend my wrist, and the derringer was suddenly in my hand. Before he could do anything more, I shot him right in the face.

Shocked, he bellowed and ran toward the pond, but tripped after twenty feet. I went after him. He was still very much alive, cursing me, glaring at me, blood gushing from the wound in his face. I took out a pair of handcuffs. If possible, I wanted to take him alive. As I bent to cuff him, though, he used his feet and tripped me, got me to the ground, and again began choking me as he tried to twist my head so he could snap my neck. I resisted him with every ounce of strength I had, but felt like I was a child fighting an adult. I began to pass out. I could feel the top of my spine twisting, the vertebrae cracking loudly. He smiled down at me, his blood dripping into my eyes. Just as I was losing consciousness, Belladonna suddenly appeared over me, and without hesitation she shot him. He let go of me. She shot again, missed. "I'm going to fucking kill you," she said, and fired again, missed. She pulled the trigger again, but the gun, I could see, jammed. He got up and began toward her. I grabbed my Beretta.

"Freeze," I said. He stopped and faced me. "Come on, scumbag—you think you can do that again, try it," I said. He put his hands up.

"Shoot him, Frank!" Belladonna screamed. "Kill him while you can!"

"Get down," I told him, knowing if I shot him now in cold blood, with his hands up—in front of two witnesses—I could very well be charged with murder.

"Get down!" I repeated. As he began to go down, he suddenly went low and dived into the pond. I shot at him, but I didn't know if I had hit him.

"Fuck," I said, mad at myself for letting him get away.

"Why didn't you shoot him?" Belladonna begged. "What's wrong with my gun?" I took it and cleared the jammed shell out of the breech, gave it back to her, and stood at the pond's edge, waiting for him to come up. "Cover the other side," I told Belladonna, and as she hurried to the far bank, the moon glistening brilliantly on the water, he came up and began to climb out of the water. That was it. No more Mr. Nice Guy. I aimed and fired; he again went low and began to serpentine toward a stand of trees. I kept firing. He seemed to anticipate the rounds and managed to elude my shots. Belladonna fired at him, too. He disappeared, as if he never was, into the trees. I ran over to the trees. No sign of him. I wanted to get Anne to safety.

Back at the car, I used my cell phone and called Sam Henderson, the head of the New Orleans Police Department, and soon the calm New Orleans night was shattered by the panicky sound of screaming sirens.

Chapter Sixteen

Anne had to be hospitalized. A police car took her to St. Luke's over on University Street. Dracol had taken a lot of blood from her over the many days he held her captive, and she needed to be given blood, vitamins, minerals, and antibiotics intravenously. The police searched the woods where Dracol had run. There was no sign of him. Bloodhounds were brought in. They lost his scent in the cemetery.

After making certain Anne was in good hands, being properly attended to, Belladonna and I went to the police station and gave signed statements about what had happened.

From the police station, I phoned John Fitzgerald and told him that we'd found Anne, that she was okay, now in St. Luke's Hospital, and briefly ran down for him what had occurred. He began crying, he was so happy, and said he was on the way, that he wanted to be by his daughter's side. For a while, I have to admit, I was thinking that

Fitzgerald had something to do with Anne's disappearance, and I felt guilty for that now. The press, of course, heard all about what had happened, and a noisy, unruly mob of reporters and news producers gathered outside the station house.

Chief Sam Henderson was a large, friendly man with a thick head of gray hair, combed back, and a large bulbous nose that held up silver-framed granny glasses. He wore a baggy three-piece suit and two-tone shoes. He couldn't have been more helpful, friendly, and hospitable, and he insisted on taking Belladonna and me to dinner after we'd given our statements. I told him that wasn't necessary, that we didn't want to impose, but he insisted, said we were "brave heroes" and that the city of New Orleans was indebted to us for exposing Dracol once and for all.

"Outside, you know," he said, "there is a whole gaggle of his groupies . . . a big crowd of them pale-faced freaks. You believe that? What this world has come to is totally beyond me. I mean, I like to think of myself as a progressive modern man open to both sides of any argument, but these people are friggin' sick and should all be kept in cages, don't you think?"

Both Belladonna and I agreed. I was really glad that she'd gotten rid of her fangs.

We soon fought our way through the press and Dracol's pale-faced groupies outside and went to a restaurant called Michella's Tuscan Inn. We had an incredible four-course meal as Sam told us sad stories about runaway girls who had gotten mixed up with Dracol and were never seen again.

There were not, as it turned out, any bodies in Lake Pontchartrain, but there were bodies in the pond near the house where Anne had been held. The water in the pond was fifty feet deep, and divers had discovered fourteen corpses—all women and girls, including the elderly French lady who owned the house. She had signed the deed over to Dracol; he killed her, weighed her down, and dumped her in the lake.

After we ate, Sam drove us back to our hotel. We were both exhausted, emotionally drained, but in the quiet privacy of our room, I took Belladonna in my arms, held her close, and we made love, intense and rough, soft and gentle all at the same time. She fell asleep. I lay there all angry at myself for not killing him when I could have, wondering if maybe it was time to find something else to do. I was too cautious. *You should have killed him and put a gun in his hand*, I kept saying to myself, but what was done was done, couldn't be changed. It was time to leave New Orleans and go back home.

CHAPTER SEVENTEEN

In the morning, we went back to St. Luke's Hospital. There were even more reporters there now. Both Belladonna and I made statements to the press and we went up to Anne's room on the fourth floor.

They had moved her to a private room at the end of the hall. Uniform policemen were guarding her. They both shook my and Belladonna's hand and let us enter the room.

Anne looked much better. She had color now. Her golden hair was pulled back into a tight ponytail. She was a genuinely beautiful woman with walnut-sized blue eyes, full lips, a perfectly oval-shaped face. The day was clear and brilliant, and sunshine streamed into the room. She was all smiles when she saw us, made us sit in chairs near her bed, and tell her everything that had happened; and, beginning with the day her father first came to me for help, I ran it all down for her. Her right eyebrow arched when I told her

Belladonna had worked for Dracol, that I met her at the New York club, but we both saw Belladonna shoot Dracol, and when she said she had no idea what Dracol was really into, she believed her. As did I.

Anne, in turn, told us what happened to her; she said: "Everything was going smoothly. I did two interviews with him and had no problems. He had to leave for New Orleans, and he invited me to come with him, but I didn't want to travel with him, though I did agree to come and continue interviewing him here. And he agreed to let me take photos of him in front of his mansion on Lake Pontchartrain and around New Orleans, which I thought would be good for the article, as well as a book I was planning to write.

"So what happened was, I wanted to document—be able to prove—everything he said and was surreptitiously taping him. He found the tape, went absolutely ballistic, and the next thing I knew he was on me, biting my neck. For sure he would have killed me, but he wanted me to write his life story. That's the only reason, I'm sure, he didn't kill me. That's what I was doing in that room, that dungeon, writing his memoir. He was making me write it with an old-fashioned quill in fresh blood. Fucking maniac."

She stopped, slowly shook her head from side to side.

"I was foolish. I should have never met him alone. Never trusted him. I knew he was dangerous, but I didn't know how dangerous, how completely psychotic he was. . . . Dumb of me."

"Why didn't you tell your father you came down here?"

"It was really just a spur-of-the-moment thing. Plus I didn't want to worry him. I told him about the article, about Dracol, and he would have only been worried. I was going to tell Alice Watkins, my agent, but he took me the night that I arrived. I was going to call her in the morning, but was never able to. . . .

"You . . . you two saved my life. I don't know how to say thank you, how can I ever thank you." She stopped and began to cry, angrily wiping at the tears.

"I'm sorry," she said. "I never thought I'd get out of there alive, see the light of day."

"There's no need to thank us. Just seeing you okay is thanks enough," I said.

"You . . . people like you—you make the world a better place," she said.

"That's nice of you to say," Belladonna said.

I said, "I found the tapes you had in your closet—"

"Really?"

"Yes, and the interview you did on the seventh suddenly ended. What happened?"

"What happened was the recorder just stopped working. I was really pissed. I'd gotten a lot from him that first night."

There was a soft knock on the door. I opened it

and John Fitzgerald stood there, a hesitant smile on his face; but when he saw Anne, his face broke into one large grin and he hurried to her and they hugged, and seeing them together like that made my heart roll over in my chest, suddenly made everything I do worthwhile.

I looked at Belladonna, and there were tears in her large black eyes and a smile on her face.

"Bravo, Frank De Nardo," she whispered.

"Let's leave them alone," I said, put my arm around her narrow waist. We quietly left the room and I gently closed the door.

CHAPTER EIGHTEEN

Now finding Santos Dracol was a police matter. What he had done, the fiend he truly was, was common knowledge, and not only the New Orleans police were looking for him but the FBI and Interpol as well. Far as I was concerned, this case was over and done. The job had been to find Anne, and we'd done that.

We left New Orleans later that same day, both of us tired, quiet, introspective. We didn't say much until we reached East Virginia, when Belladonna said: "You know, all my life, I realize now, I was lost. There was something missing inside me. Something necessary to be a whole person. I don't know how it happened exactly—if it was my childhood or I was just maybe born that way or what. But now, because of you, De Nardo, I feel *different*; I mean, really different—deep inside."

"How so?" I asked, pleased to be hearing this.

"I feel whole and complete. I feel . . . I think life is worth living. That in addition to life having a dark side—a terribly dark side—there's a bright side. I can't tell you how good it made me feel when I saw Mr. Fitzgerald take Anne in his arms and them crying and holding each other like that with the sunshine streaming into the room. I was so touched . . . so moved. I felt ten feet tall, you know?"

"Yes, yes, I do know," I said. "I know exactly what you mean."

She took my hand, gently kissed it, and became quiet again. After a time, she said, "I want to . . . please don't think I'm nuts, but I want to experience that again. I want to become a private investigator. I want to help people who have nowhere else to turn. I know . . . I really know what a dark, rotten world this could be, and I think I'd be good. Do you think I would? Please be honest; please tell me true."

"I think you'd be great, not good. I saw you in action—cool as a cucumber."

"Really?"

"Yes, really."

She smiled. "Could I maybe work with you? Would you like that? Would you—I hope I'm not being presumptuous here—but would you like a partner, an assistant, Frank De Nardo?"

This caught me off guard. I didn't know what to say. I always worked alone.

"I . . . I don't know. What I do is dangerous," I said, knowing we'd be a hell of a team, maybe unbeatable, but wary about doing something like that with her because I had feelings for her. Intense, heartfelt feelings, I realized.

"I'll think about it," I said.

"Promise?"

"I promise."

"Let's shake on it," she said, and I reached out and we shook hands. She put her head on my shoulder. I put my arm around her and we sped on toward New York, dusk coming on quickly now, giant lightning bolts dancing madly in darkening skies up ahead. It began to rain, and the rain appeared like tears hurrying across the windshield in many directions at once.

"You know," she said, "you are a hell of a man, Frank De Nardo."

"And you're a hell of a lady, Belladonna," I said. She reached over and kissed me.

CHAPTER NINETEEN

When we arrived in New York it was snowing again, though there was no wind and the large flakes fell languidly, appearing like millions of white-winged butterflies in the shaped light of streetlamps, meandering in the calm, chilled air. I parked in the garage. Belladonna and I made our way back to my place. I was pleased this case was over with, pleased that we managed to get Anne away from Dracol. But, I hate to admit, I had this hinky feeling in the back of my neck, a kind of buzzing inside my head, that this was not over yet.

I put my arm around Belladonna, she her arm around me, and we silently walked east, our steps crushing the soft-packed snow. When we reached Columbus Avenue, I said, "I don't like saying this, but I have a feeling this isn't over yet."

"Hmm . . . I feel the same way," she said. "I don't want to, but . . . but I do. He is not the type of man to turn the other cheek. He . . . he will want revenge. . . .

"I think, Frank, I think it might be a good idea if we . . . we get out of town for a while."

"I don't want to run. If there's a problem, I want to face it. It's best we picked the time and place to . . . to fight—not them," I said, surprised that I said *we*. When did *I* become a *we*?

"Guess you have a point, but it'd be nice to get away, don't you think? We could both use some R and R," she added. "After what we've been though—don't you think?"

I knew she was right. Truth is, I was bone tired, tired of the cold, tired of the wind, tired of my arthritis hurting, tired of the snow.

"When would you like to go?" I asked.

"So you want to leave for a while?"

"Sure. You are right. It'd be a good idea, and we can use it."

"Somewhere warm," she said. "Where there's . . . sun."

" 'Sun' . . . I thought you don't like the sun."

"I've changed," she said, smiling her lovely smile. I remembered her fangs and was glad they were gone. I stopped and kissed her long and hard, feeling myself get hard—wanting her.

"Okay . . . anywhere you want to go is fine with me," I said. We walked on in silence.

"How about Cuba?" she suggested. "I've always wanted to go there and we'd be . . . safe there. He's got no people there, I'm sure."

"Perfect. I, too, always wanted to go to Cuba, but we'd have to go through Mexico."

"This stupid embargo the government has is really ridiculous," she said.

"I agree."

"What do you think of Bush, by the way?" she asked. "We've never talked politics."

"I don't know if we should."

"Sure, why not? We can talk about anything, Frank De Nardo."

"I think Bush could barely walk and talk at the same time. I think he's a deceptive, slippery snake—and the dumbest president in history."

"Me too," she said. "This ridiculous war he led us into is the most immoral thing I've ever seen a president do. Anyone in politics ever do."

"For sure," I said, liking Belladonna even more. I wondered if she could cook. I thought about introducing her to my family, my mother and uncle Sal. "So Cuba it is," I said, "okay?"

"When do you want to go?"

"Hmm . . . how about tomorrow?" I said.

"Perfect," she said.

We reached my place. The super had shoveled my sidewalk and laid out salt. We went inside. I found a pile of stepped-on menus in the vestibule, picked them up, cursing the restaurants that allow this daily littering for the ten thousandth time. I opened my apartment door. The smell hit me immediately—like a sudden stop.

The unmistakable smell of death; of human death. I quickly drew my Beretta, cocked it.

"Stay in the hall," I told her, switching on the

lights, automatically moving into combat position; coiled tense and catlike.

"What's wrong?" she asked. "Talk to me."

"Don't you smell that?"

"Yes, I do now—what is it?"

"Just stay in the hall," I said, moving inside cautiously. I first noticed the blood, a large dried pool of it on the parquet floor in Louise's office.

The blood, a wide trail of it the color of wine, led into the living room—as if a bleeding body had been dragged. My stomach tightened, my mouth became dry.

Down low now, all tense, ready to shoot, I moved into the living room, the smell becoming stronger and stronger still. The first thing I saw was the head on the fireplace mantel—Louise's head.

Stunned, shocked, fiery rage filling me, my head spun, my world was suddenly upside down. "No, no!" I screamed.

"What's wrong?" Belladonna called.

"Stay there," I told her.

Then I saw her arms, one on the windowsill, another on the floor near the kitchen entrance. A set of handcuffs hung from the wrist. There was blood everywhere. I found what was left of Louise hanging on my pots and pans rack in the kitchen. . . .

"Louise, my God . . . Louise," I whispered, feeling myself getting small, shrinking from this rotten world . . . wondering how the hell they found her, who did it, knowing, though, that Santos Dracol was surely responsible for this.

After making certain no one was in the house, clearing it, I went to my deck, called Captain Roe, and told him what I'd found.

"Get out of there!" he said. "We'll be right over!"

"Frank, what's wrong, what is it?" Belladonna demanded again from the door. She had stayed put like I told her.

"It's Louise; they killed her," I called back. "Don't come in!" I said, now making my way back to the front door. It was then I spotted the note tacked to the wall to the left of the living room doorway. It said *Santos*.

CHAPTER TWENTY

Words could never express how distraught I was over Louise's murder and mutilation. I loved Louise. She was like a sister to me, closer even than a sister. She'd been my soul mate, my confidante, my helpmate, my companion in arms, my lover, my true friend—and now this despicable infamy. She'd not done anything. She was an innocent. I was despondent.

When Louise's remains were autopsied, I found out that she'd been tortured before they killed her; that broken bottles had been roughly forced inside her while she was still alive, handcuffed—that her tongue had been ripped out of her mouth, torn from its roots by a mighty force.

This is exactly why people in my line of work—regularly dealing with the diabolical of this world—shouldn't get close to anyone, man or beast. Having emotional ties makes you vulnerable and susceptible to pain, to heartache, hurt, a broken heart—tortured soul, as mine was now.

Belladonna was helpful. There in all ways for me. But as I looked at her, felt for her, appreciated her, I knew I had to rid myself of her. She made me vulnerable. She was a weak link in my armor. I so wanted her with me—her love, her caresses, her hugs and kisses and soft, sweet words. But I knew all those luxuries were not mine. My getting so involved with her from the beginning was a mistake, not professional—was boyish and stupid and would lead only to no good. The more I felt for her, the more I knew I had to stay away from her.

Now what I wanted was revenge. Pure and simple. Hate slowly began to replace my pain. I'd find him and make him suffer way beyond the pain he caused Louise, caused me. I would not rest until I found him. My life as it was had one purpose—finding and slowly destroying Santos Dracol.

We buried Louise in St. John Cemetery out on Long Island two days later. Her mother, two sisters, aunts and uncles, as well as my whole family, were there. I felt responsible—I was responsible—for what happened, and everyone knew it. I couldn't look any of Louise's people in the eye. Everyone also knew who Belladonna was, that she had worked with Dracol, and they gave her cold-curious-apprehensive icy stares, as if she was somehow responsible, not me. They needed someone to focus their hurt and anger upon, and Belladonna fit the bill well.

Normally, after a burial, the families would go somewhere to eat, to share stories of the deceased, to have coffee and sweets. But no such occasion happened after Louise's burial.

As Belladonna and I slowly made our way back to my car that gray cold terrible day, my uncle Sal motioned me over. I excused myself from Belladonna and slowly moved over to him, feeling weak and beat up, a shell of who I was.

My uncle knew Louise well. She had been to numerous family functions. He was particularly fond of her because he thought she was "stand-up," he said, as indeed she was. She had more balls than most men I met in my life.

"Nephew," he said, "I know what you plan to do—as you should. I'm not going to try and dissuade you of this, but think with your head here, not your emotions. Not your heart. You're very vulnerable right now. Let the anger abate . . . then do what you must do. Listen to me well—think of your mother, think of the people who love you, Francesco. . . .

"Nephew, if you're not cold and careful and calculating, it could be you we next bury!

"Franchesco, you are from the street—you know the evil that lives in men's hearts. How cunning men can be. Remember all the hard-earned lessons you came away with.

"I would be," he continued, "only too happy to help you send the scum back to the hell from which he comes, you understand? You're not in this alone."

"I understand," I said, hugged and kissed him, and we walked to my car arm and arm. The cemetery was all white, a macabre winter wonderland from which a forest of somber tombstones rose. Crows cawed from bare trees incessantly.

"Can you," he asked, "trust this Belladonna?"

"She's proven herself over and over again," I told him, remembering the shooting of Dracol, demanding I kill him. God, how I wished I had. Had I killed him, Louise would probably still be alive, I knew.

"Careful with her. A tigress can never lose its stripes."

I found out from Louise's sister that Louise didn't leave town straightaway because she had a toothache. She needed her new insurance card, which she'd left on her desk. When, apparently, she'd come back to the office to retrieve it, they grabbed her. I went and spoke to my tenants and neighbors and people on the block; no one saw anything out of line.

CHAPTER TWENTY-ONE

"What do you mean," Belladonna said, "you want to do this alone? How could you say that to me with a straight face after all we've been through? Don't shut me out, Frank. We are a team. You need me. I'm in this to the end," she said.

We were now in a restaurant I like on Amsterdam Avenue called Neptune's.

"Frank, I know what this is all about—you are worried about me; you think I make you vulnerable."

"Don't think you do—I know you do," I said.

"So that is it."

"That's it in a nutshell. Belladonna, I've always worked alone. I like it that way. Even when I was a cop, I worked alone."

"This is different—way different. The fact that we care for one another is an asset—don't you see that? Get over it, Frank. You are a man, a very tough, accomplished individual. Don't push me away, because we care for each other."

"I don't want to mix what I do—what must be done—with . . . well . . . my heart. What's left of it."

"I can help. I'll watch your back. Frank, he was killing you. I stopped him, okay—remember that?" she blatantly reminded me, looking at me with her large unblinking black eyes. "Because," she said, "we are lovers doesn't mean we can't do this together. . . ."

I ate the paella we were sharing. Though the food here was exceptional, it tasted bland and meaningless, and I was really just going through the motion of eating. I wasn't hungry. This was the first time I had sat down to eat, at Belladonna's urging, since we arrived back in New York. She poured me some white wine. I knocked off the glass. She poured me some more. "Use me. I want you to. I'm here for you ten thousand percent in all ways."

"I know that, I feel that—that's the problem. What if something happens to you? How the fuck could I look in a mirror? Tell me that."

"I'm the solution, Frank. Get over it. See beyond this mirror. Let's find this fucker and end this once and for all. You owe me that much at least, Frank. Remember what he's done to me; remember where you found me. I have every fucking right, man. I've earned it, Frank."

We both drank our wine, silently ate.

She made, I knew, perfect sense. Maybe she was right, I was thinking. She was, I knew, a very rare woman, and truth was I was reticent about closing the door in her face. Plus, as I thought about it, she was right—she had earned the right to be part of what was to come.

"You think he's still in New Orleans?" I asked.

"Hard to say. He's got places all over the world, literally. New Orleans right now is too hot for him, I think."

"I'm thinking he might've fled to Romania, somewhere in Europe."

"How do we find him?"

"That's the million-dollar question."

"I'm sure it's just a matter of time before he comes looking for you, for us—for me. He wanted to hurt you first—that's why he had that done to Louise. I think he'll let you live with that for a while—stew with it—then look to get his hands on you . . . and me. Remember, I shot him. There's no way he'll ever forget that. I'm in just as much danger as you, Frank. More. I'm sure he feels I betrayed him. He'll not rest until he makes me pay—makes me pay dearly," she said, her voice becoming small.

We again ate in silence.

"Drink more wine. I ordered another bottle."

"I think," she said, "Cassandra might be the answer."

"How do you mean?"

"She made it out of the house for sure, right?"

"Right."

"She's blindly dedicated to him. He trusts her more than anyone. She's always where he is. I know that for sure."

"How do we find her?"

"I have an idea," she said.

"What's that?"

"This," she said, taking out a little black leather phone book with her name in gold on it.

"I have her cell phone number. . . . Do you think that can help?"

"Absofuckinglutely," I said.

CHAPTER TWENTY-TWO

The New York Police Department has an intelligence division. It is located in an underground chamber at One Police Plaza downtown. The guy that runs the division, Captain John Roe, is my pal Ken Roe's older brother. I knew John well. He, like Ken, is a gregarious, outgoing Irishman, came up the ranks through hard work, perseverance, and wearing down shoe leather. Ken was kind enough to reach out to his brother; he agreed to help, and permission was sought and given from above.

The following afternoon, Belladonna and I left my house to go see John Roe. I was carrying a black leather case. In it I had an UZI and a Mac 10, each a machine gun, loaded with soft-head rounds that mushroom on impact. In each of my overcoat pockets I had chambered autos, cleaned and oiled and ready. Now, far as I was concerned, I was in a war to the death. A war I was not only intent upon winning, but a war I would fight without mercy, quarter or mercy—no reprieve for the enemy.

This, now, was personal. No longer a job.

John Roe is a tall, lanky man. He kind of resembles Jimmy Stewart. He has thick gray hair neatly parted and carefully combed to the left, intelligent blue eyes that—like his brother's—see through all the bullshit right to the core of whatever they come to rest on. He greeted me with a warm handshake and hug, said how sorry he was about Louise. Everyone in the NYPD knew what had happened to Louise. She'd been a cop; she was one of them. Everyone was only too happy to help. I introduced John to Belladonna. He led us to his office. He was a Yankee fan, and the walls were adorned with Yankee pennants and other memorabilia. A baseball on his desk, mounted in brass, was signed by Yogi Bera. I briefly explained the situation as it was to him.

"Is she still using the phone?" he asked. "Just having the number won't help at all. She has to answer the phone. If she does, we can pinpoint her in no time; I can tell you exactly where she is—to within several feet," he said with confidence.

Belladonna answered him, "We don't know. We thought it best we didn't call until we saw you."

"Okay, that's good. She might've known it was

you phoning and dumped the phone. Let's give it a try," he said, and now led us to a windowless room that was lined with white Formica desks on which were all kinds of computers. Men and women were busy at the computers, didn't look up. John sat down at one of the computers, booted it up, waited a few seconds, said, "Here goes," and dialed the number Belladonna gave him. We could hear the call go through. The phone rang and rang. No answer. No recording. I had been so very hopeful this was the answer, I felt my heart slowly sink in my chest. It'd been too good to be true. After about fifteen rings, John said, "Sorry, Frank, seems she's not picking up. We'll wait a bit more." The phone continued to ring for what seemed an eternity.

"Sorry, pal," John said, and was just about to hang up when the phone was answered.

"Hello," we heard. It was unmistakably Cassandra, her accent, her nasty voice. John quickly said, "Tony there—I need to speak to him? It's important!"

"No Tonys," she barked, hung up.

"We got her," he said, punched a few keys, worked the mouse, and suddenly a very detailed map appeared on the screen.

"The computer is talking to the satellites. Give it a minute," he said, and within fifteen seconds or so a map of Italy appeared on the screen. *Italy?* I thought. John used the mouse and the map of Italy faded to a red and yellow map of Rome.

John zoomed in on this map. "She's in Rome. Here," he said, pointing to a red dot on the screen that was blinking on the map, becoming larger and larger still.

"Of course," Belladonna said. "The catacombs. I completely forgot about them."

"Catacombs?" I asked.

"Yes, in Rome, under the streets, there are catacombs filled with the dead back all the way to ancient Rome. Santos *loved* this place. I heard him speak about it several times. Seems he managed to pay a caretaker and had some kind of hideaway there. He just loved the place. That photo of him at the club in front of the skulls—that's in the catacombs. It's on the club's site, too."

"Could this be that easy?" I asked John.

"Absolutely. She's there in Rome, for sure," he said. "She should not have answered that phone. That's an immediate pinpoint. You can take that to the bank, Frank."

"Karma," Belladonna said.

Karma, indeed, I thought. She didn't know the half of it.

"Looks like we are going to Rome, not Cuba," she said.

"One of my favorite places," I said, thinking this all seemed somehow too pat—perhaps a well-laid trap.

I thanked John Roe several times over. He kept saying he was "only too happy" to help. "Don't mention it," he said.

In the elevator on the way back upstairs to the

garage, I said, "Could this really be that easy? It seems just too easy."

"She fucked up," Belladonna said. "She might have forgotten I even had the number—who knows, you know? But, Frank, if she's there it's because Santos is there. That's a given."

If, I knew, we had to go to Italy and confront Dracol there, I was going to call upon my uncle and his people. You could only fight fire with fire, and the Sicilian Mafia could be the fire of hell itself. "He made a big mistake going to Italy," I said.

"Why . . . why do you say that?" she asked.

"You'll find out," I said.

"You in the Mafia? I've thought that all along."

"No, I'm not in the Mafia," I told her again.

Soon as we got outside, I called my uncle Sal. I reached him at the house. He told me I could come right over. I was hesitant about bringing Belladonna with me to Brooklyn but decided to take her. What the hell.

When we arrived at the house on Ocean Parkway, my uncle told me my mother and aunt had gone shopping, that there was a linen sale they had to go to. He was warm enough to Belladonna, but not as friendly as he might have been. He served her espresso with anisette and chocolate biscotti in the kitchen. My aunt Lu Lu made the biscotti. We left her there and went to his study. He put an unlit Cohiba in his mouth. "I'm cutting down these," he said, a thing he'd been saying for twenty years. I explained what happened. He smiled when he heard Dracol was in Italy—a subtle, wolflike grin. He reminded me of a smiling wolf. Indeed, that was his nickname in the underworld, because he had, as a youth, smiled while getting rid of enemies. My uncle, I knew, had been one of the key assassins in the war between the Bonnano and the Genovese factions of the New York Mafia. This was a true Smiling Wolf.

"When are you leaving?" he asked, his eyes smiling, too.

"Soon as possible. There's no telling how long he'll be there—if he's really there—and Belladonna says this woman who answered the phone is *always* with him."

"They fucked up," he said, echoing Belladonna's words.

"Yes, looks that way," I said.

"Okay, as you know, Nephew, we have very good friends there. I will start making calls. You need to find out what flight you'll be on; I'll arrange for you to be met when you step off the plane. Don't underestimate this man again. Come at him hard and sure. I'll tell our friends just who he is—about the young girls and women he killed; about what he did to Louise."

"Thank you, Uncle," I said.

"Nephew, this is something we will do gladly. A monster like this has no right to breathe the same air as we do."

"*I* personally want to do this," I said. "You understand, he must fucking suffer—"

"No problem, of course, Nephew. As it should be. Whatever you need they'll gladly provide, and make sure he does not get away."

I stood and gave him a long, hard hug. "Thank you, Uncle," I repeated.

"Don't thank me; that is what family is for. We are blood—your enemies are my enemies. . . . Frank, you sure this isn't some kind of setup?"

"Yes, positive."

"Okay," he said. "Whatever it is, you will be well protected."

The first plane to Rome was an Italia flight that left at 5:40 P.M. the next day. I made two reservations on it, called my uncle, and gave him the flight number—313.

Thirteen has always been my lucky number.

Chapter Twenty-three

I could not take any weapons on the plane, though I knew anything I needed would be provided by my uncle's "friends." I was still wary about having Belladonna with me, concerned about her safety, concerned about my feelings for her. This was the first time I'd gotten emotionally involved with a woman I met on a job. It was, I knew, not only against tradition and protocol, but flew in the face of reason and good sense. Still, she had, so far, been a great help. That was undeniable—she had saved my life.

I thought about Dracol's unusual strength, how fast he moved, how he leapt from the top of the mausoleum like some kind of large cat. If I didn't know better, it would seem he really did have some kind of "supernatural" abilities. I was tempted to ask Belladonna if, in fact, he could be endowed with some little-known, little-understood power, but decided against that. I wrote it up, in my mind, that he was nothing more than a raging psychopath and that was why he was so strong. Simple. Surely that was it. I personally knew, as I said, psychopaths to have superhuman power. Sitting there on the plane as it sped toward Europe, I remembered times when I was a uniformed cop and had to deal with "psychos," as we called them. I remembered four and five cops having to be called to subdue one man. Belladonna put her head on my shoulder. I put my arms around her. I wanted to tell her of my affection for her; how much I cared for her, but said nothing of this. She fell asleep. I kept seeing stark, horrible images of Louise, what they'd done to her, how they left her. I tried hard to push these images away. It wasn't possible. I began to cry. Hot tears hurried down my face. I silently cursed Dracol, heaven, and hell for allowing such a thing. All my life I had always tried to do the right thing, and now this. What, I wondered, had I done to deserve such a fate? I underestimated Dracol, I knew. That's what I did. That was the bottom line here, and I hated myself for it.

At some point, I thankfully dozed off and dreamed about the catacombs; how it was filled with the pale-faced ghosts of the dead who were all conspiring to protect Dracol, to harm me, to destroy Belladonna.

When we cleared customs in Rome it was 9:00 A.M. there. I slept only a few hours and was exhausted. The day was overcast. A light rain fell.

When we went outside, they were there waiting
for us—three grave-faced, stoic men wearing
wraparound dark sunglasses. Introductions were
made. They were polite, stiff, and formal, as if
greeting us at a wake. We all knew my reason for
being there—revenge, murder, the drawing of
blood—and there were no smiles, only solemn
handshakes. They were Nino, Giovanni, and Carlos. Giovanni and Carlos were brothers, dark-
haired and handsome. Nino was the oldest, fair
with a knife wound on his left cheek. They each
had strong, callused hands, broad shoulders,
were slow-moving and powerful, as are fearless
heavyweight prizefighters in their prime. They
had a black Mercedes SUV waiting at the curb. I'd
been expecting to stay at a hotel, the Excelsior on
Via Venato, but they informed me that a villa was
waiting for us. We sped to the villa. It was in the
Frascatti wine region just outside of Rome proper.
The villa was all gleaming white stucco with red
shutters, surrounded by red flowers on a
grapevine-covered hill affording a magnificent
view of the ancient city with its violent, kinky,
rough-and-tumble history. I laughed to myself as
I thought about the present-day S & M scene,
about the Club Blood and Harold's place; that
was all so ridiculously tame compared to what
the Romans were doing hundreds of years ago. I
had been to Rome several times and loved the
timeless city. It was where I honeymooned. Being
back here reminded me of my wife, of her murder

in Central Park. What a fucked-up world this can be, I was thinking, depressed and tired and pissed off.

At the villa, which was behind thick stucco walls adorned with shards of different-colored broken glass, we met Don Pietro Abruzi, a notorious Sicilian mafioso I knew. *Time* magazine had actually done a cover story on him a while back. He was a heavyset individual, about seventy, wore a worn black vest, had a thick head of bright silver hair combed straight back. He wore purple-tinted glasses. There was a huge diamond pinkie ring on his right hand. I'd never met him, but I knew well his reputation as a ruthless, very cunning man. We sat down at a beautiful tiled dining table—I, Belladonna, and Don Pietro. Pleasantries were exchanged. He asked about our trip, if it was a good one, how the weather in New York was. He loved, he said, New York, had a lot of relatives in Bensonhurst, Brooklyn. We were going to talk about murder now and he obviously didn't want to do that in front of Belladonna. This, of course, was perfectly understandable—indeed, to be expected. He arranged for an elderly woman, the cook, to show Belladonna around the grounds, the vineyards, and the fruit orchard. To my surprise, Belladonna spoke reasonably good Italian. Espresso was served with homemade anisette. Belladonna soon left with the cook. Don Pietro spoke English with a heavy accent. I first thanked him for his kind assistance and hospitality. He said:

"Francesco, there is no need to thank me. Your uncle is my dear friend. Close to me as a brother. We know one another since we were kids in Palermo. He told me everything—about this monster; what he did to your friend. If he is truly here, in Roma, we will make sure he never leaves. This would be our pleasure. I tell you this true. Such ones should not be allowed to walk among our women and children. The problem is the catacombs. They are numerous, and there are ones that still no one knows about. If he is hiding out in one of these, it will be very difficult to find him, but we will not stop looking."

I told him about the photograph of Dracol in front of the skulls, that it was supposedly taken in the catacombs. He asked to see it. There was a computer in the house, and I used it to show him the photo.

"He looks," he said with disdain, "like an evil son-ma-bitch. White like chalk."

We printed the photograph and would use it to show to people who, he said, knew much about the catacombs.

We soon sat down for an elaborate four-course lunch. The cook, Antonia—Belladonna's new friend—was amazing. She served up grilled artichoke hearts and sliced endive, pesto pasta, veal marsala, and a big bowl of salad, with peaches in a sweet marsala wine for dessert. Belladonna and Antonia hit it off. Antonia kept saying that she, Belladonna, was the most beautiful woman she'd ever seen. I agreed with her; she was the most beautiful woman I'd ever seen. After we ate, Don Pietro said there was something he wanted to show me and he led me to a small, windowless room at the back of the house. In it there were all kinds of guns in gun racks on three of the four walls. On the fourth wall were neatly lined wooden shelves filled with boxes of ammunition. He was obviously expecting war, was well prepared—intent upon winning. He showed me a cut-down Magnum shotgun.

"This," he said, "will do the job well," and he handed me the shells, twice the size of a normal shotgun shell, maybe five inches long and as thick as a Churchill cigar. He explained that it contained twenty marble-size steel balls all connected to one another by strong wire.

"Its purpose," he said, "is to cut and break up whatever it hits. The wire acts like a scalpel pulled by the strong velocity of the balls."

"Perfect," I said.

Now the question of Belladonna, her seeing what happens, came up. I explained to him how Belladonna had saved my life; how she had shot Dracol.

"You vouch for her?" he asked, dead serious.

"Yes, absolutely," I said, equally serious.

"You trust her?" he asked.

"With my life," I said.

"So be it," he said.

CHAPTER TWENTY-FOUR

After we slept for a few hours we left the house—
Belladonna, myself, and Don Pietro's three men.
Nino carried a large suitcase. In the suitcase were
four of the cut-down shotguns and other
weapons. We first went to the place in town
where Cassandra answered the cell phone. It was
in the center of Rome, on Via Nationale, just near
the Central Station. There were no catacombs here
at all. We next made our way all over the outskirts
of the city, interrogating different caretakers of
catacombs. Nino explained that the dead had
been forbidden to be buried in ancient Rome, and
thus the catacombs were created outside the city
limits proper. Some of them were huge, he said,
holding hundreds of thousands of dead; others
were small, meant for the rich and affluent. Some,
he said, were one and two stories below ground;
others were deep—six and seven stories down.
Now, he said, the catacombs were cared for by the
Catholic Church; the Vatican. This I found ironic.

For hours on end we interrogated different caretakers, all elderly men, showing Dracol's photo, and none of them knew anything, they said. It wasn't looking good. This went on for several days. We searched high and low. We even checked out catacombs that were supposed to be built under the Coliseum, but couldn't find them. There were, however, catacombs near the infamous Circus Maximus. We found the caretaker with much difficulty, but he knew nothing of Santos Dracol or any of his minions. Maybe, I was thinking, we had it all wrong, that it really was too good to be true. Belladonna, however, was still hopeful and upbeat. She kept saying she was sure he was here, that she could "sense" Dracol was "here somewhere."

Don Pietro's hospitality was boundless. He made sure we ate like kings every day, the best of everything. He put his people at our constant disposal. At one point I went to the church inside Vatican City, lit a candle for Louise, and prayed that we found Dracol, that what he was and what he represented was finally stopped—ended, for good. I had come to view the Church as a big playground for child molesters, a safe haven for obsessed pedophiles, and I had no use for the Church or the hypocrites who have hijacked it. Yet I believe in God, a higher power, and I now beseeched that higher power to help us locate Dracol. Belladonna refused to even enter the church because former Boston cardinal Bernard Law was put in charge of it—talk about sin. And sure enough, I saw Law walking near the altar with two altar boys. Go figure. Hell of a thing.

Near four A.M. on the fourth night, we arrived at a small, ancient building the color of dried mustard on Via Ostiensis, where lived still another care-taker for some nearby catacombs. Don Pietro's men—Nino, Giovanni, and Carlos—stepped from the car, as they had done many times by now, walked to the front door, and knocked. No one answered. They kept knocking. These guys were relentless, stubborn . . . like bulldogs. Fi-nally, the door slowly opened. A small old man stood there, angrily waving his hands. Nino spoke to him. He tried to close the door on them. This caught my attention. I sat up. They pushed their way into the house and the door closed with an audible bang.

"What was that about?" Belladonna said.

"We'll soon find out." After fifteen minutes or so, Carlos opened the door and waved us over. Curious, Belladonna and I stepped from the car and made our way inside. An owl hooted, as if on cue, from a nearby tree. Off in the distance, a large dog barked.

The old man was now sitting in a worn fabric chair. He was obviously petrified, bleeding from the left side of his mouth, his eyes wide and filled with terror. Carlos said, "We showed him the photo and he says he knows nothing, but we can see he does. We ask him nice four, five times. He says we must leave, he'll call the police if we don't. In the end, we make him talk. He knows where he is. He paid him money under the table, you know, to stay here in a special catacomb that had been prepared by a very wealthy Roman family. He says it has magical powers; he says it is the gate to hell; he says it is haunted."

"The gate to hell?" I said.

"That's what he says."

"Is he there now?" I asked, just the thought exciting me. "Does he know?"

"He doesn't know. He hasn't seen him in days. He has no idea when he goes and when he comes, he says. He is with others—both men and women. He says also there are two ways to get in and out of this place. What do you want to do, Don Francesco?" he asked. I looked at Belladonna. With her eyes she spoke to me.

Let's get the fucker, she silently said.

"We are five," I said. "Let's find him. Three of us go in one way, two the other, okay?"

"Good. This is our thought, too," Carlos said. He took out a set of handcuffs and cuffed the old man to a pipe.

"We must make sure he doesn't warn him," he explained. "Let's get ready."

We made our way back to the SUV. Nino opened the black suitcase and we silently armed ourselves. He gave me one of the cut-down shotguns, a Lupo, they called it, and a dozen of the large shells, which I filled my coat pockets with.

"I want a gun," Belladonna said. He looked to me, unsure what to do.

"Please," I said, "it's okay."

He gave her a 9mm Beretta. He also gave us flashlights that mounted onto the weapons.

"These guys come prepared," Belladonna said.

Carlos went back to the house and got the old man. He had wet his pants. I kind of felt bad for him. Then I thought about Louise and didn't feel bad anymore. He led us to a narrow flagstone path that serpentined through a cluster of tall, elegant cypress trees that swayed rhythmically in a strong breeze. The sky was clear. A waning moon the color of American cheese lighted the way. We came to a fountain. Elegant streams of water issued from the open mouths of lionesses into a white marble pool. The moonlight glistened on the goldfish-colored surface of the pool. Behind this, the caretaker showed us, was a steel door that led to one of the entrances. Clever. He opened the door with a large, old-fashioned key. These catacombs, he said, Carlos translating for my benefit, were deep—over a hundred steps down. Here Carlos, Belladonna, and I would enter, it was decided. The second entrance was a two-minute walk away. All was quiet and still. The wind hurried through the cypress trees, making a rustling silklike sound. My stomach became tense. Adrenaline made my senses more acute. I prayed he was here. I prayed this ended now once and for all—the way I planned. Carlos would communicate, if necessary, with Nino and Giovanni via cell phones. After getting the layout of the catacombs, just where Dracol might be,

Carlos brought the caretaker back to the house and again cuffed him to the pipe. We weren't going to bring him with us for fear he might somehow warn Dracol.

It was time; I warned them several times about Dracol's unusual strength and amazing speed. They listened gravely. Carlos said, "He will have no chance to do anything. *Fini.*"

With that we separated. We waited for Giovanni and Nino to get into position, opened the vaultlike door—it creaked loudly—and slowly went down a very steep set of stone steps, using flashlights to see. A strange, foreboding smell I'd never known came to us—the smell of ancient death, sulfur and incense of some kind. These steps turned into another set of steps. This happened three times. We finally reached the bottom and moved toward the vault the caretaker said he was in. The walls were filled with sarcophagis on which dates and strange names were expertly chiseled into the stone, which were about twenty-by-twenty-inch squares. Here the floor was natural rock. We walked forward. The smell became stronger. A rat hurried out of our way. Faintly, we could hear people talking. Then the sudden sound of gunshots—the cannonlike roar of the shotguns—shattered the silence. We froze. Carlos tried to reach the others. A door on our left, maybe fifteen feet away, suddenly burst open. Two men dressed in black hurried from it right toward us. Carlos shot them with the Lupo—

literally blowing them apart. Talk about killer instincts. Cassandra now suddenly appeared.

"Where is he?" I demanded.

"Fuck you," she said when she realized it was me. She turned back and began to run. Belladonna shot her dead.

Carlos looked at Belladonna with newfound respect. *"Mamma mia,"* he said.

Then, suddenly, Santos Dracol himself appeared, cursing us, cursing me. He seemed to fly toward us, possessed of some demonic force. Carlos was reloading his weapon. I had one thing to say now, and I said it with the shotgun—I aimed it and pulled the trigger as fast as I could. It roared and jerked in my hands like a wild animal. His right arm, at the shoulder, disappeared. A torrent of blood gushed from the stump. He screamed and came on with a vengeance. I shot him again—hitting him now square in the chest, below the line of his collarbones, creating a hole there the size of a soccer ball. He went right down, crumbled actually, twitching and shaking like a decapitated chicken.

I waited, ready to shoot again, cursing him. He finally became still, was dead, his canines visible. They seemed huge.

"Mamma mia," Carlos said. "What a thing."

"Mamma mia, indeed," I said.

"I know what must be done. Permit me," he said.

Carlos withdrew a kind of small, black-handled butcher cleaver from his belt. He knelt down, roughly grabbed Dracol's long hair, and proceeded to cut Dracol's head off with knowing efficiency.

Thinking all this was not necessary, slightly aghast, Belladonna and I looked at each other.

"You cannot," he explained, "leave the head on such a one as these. We have had experience with these *monstras* before in Sicily," he assured us.

Belladonna came to me. I put my arm around her. He finished his grisly task. As Nino and Giovanni made sure there weren't any more of them, we went back the way we'd come, Carlos casually carrying Dracol's head by its long hair—a surreal thing to see, particularly in this ages-old place of death.

"What do you plan to do with that?" I asked him as we reached the steep stairs and made our way back up.

"We will feed it to the fish," he said. "This is what must be done so it can never reunite with the body."

"Oh," I said.

"These guys are amazing," Belladonna said. "Who are they?"

"I'll tell you later," I said.

We reached the top of the stairs. Fresh air greeted us. As we went back outside, I had, I realized, a slight smile on my face. I didn't want to, but I did. The air felt wonderful, was sweet and filled with the clean, good-to-be-alive smell of fresh pine. I asked Carlos to hold up the head. He did. I stared into Dracol's lifeless eyes, could see the wounds we caused him. I spit into the unseeing open eyes and enjoyed doing it.

"Bravo," Carlos said.

We walked back to the black SUV. Carlos put the head in a leather sack. The others soon joined us. We somberly headed back to the villa.

Belladonna and I stayed in Rome for three full weeks. We played tourists, saw all the sites, the Coliseum, the Sistine Chapel, the Circus Maximus, the Piazza Narvona. We had wonderful meals, amazing wines. We made love several times a day. We kissed like teenagers in love who couldn't keep their hands off each other at the Trevi Fountain.

Slowly, it all became a thing of the past, a bad dream, a nightmare you forget after a while without really trying. But I knew I'd never forget what they'd done to Louise, the sight of her, the way they left her. That had changed my life, who I am. I would never be the same again, I knew.

Still, it was, for the first time in a very long time, good to be alive.

—Frank De Nardo

POSTSCRIPT

Amy, the woman who worked at the Bottoms Up Club, was found murdered by cod fishermen on a party boat near the Verrazano Bridge. She had been, an autopsy revealed, beaten to death.

DAVID LAWRENCE

CIRCLE
OF THE DEAD

The man died of a broken heart. Literally. But what broke his heart was a sharp object shoved hard between his ribs. When they found him he was sitting in a circle with three other corpses in a London apartment. That's when Detective Stella Mooney got the case. Suffering from brutal nightmares and a fondness for too much vodka, Stella's trying to hold it together long enough to find the answers to this bizarre puzzle. But the closer she comes to cracking the case, the more her personal life seems to fall apart. From the glamorous homes of the wealthy to the decidedly tougher parts of town, Stella has to follow the evidence—even when it seems to be leading her in circles.

ALAN RUSSELL
MULTIPLE WOUNDS

Holly Troy is a beautiful and talented sculptor whose only sanctuary is her art. She also lives with dissociative identity disorder, her personality split into many different and completely separate selves—including a frightened five-year-old girl. But now Holly's gallery owner has been found murdered, surrounded by Holly's sculptures. Holly doesn't know if she was a witness to the crime, or if she committed it. She doesn't know where she was that night. She doesn't even know *who* she was.